FUTURE
IMPERFECT

FUTURE IMPERFECT

K. RYER BREESE

Thomas Dunne Books · St. Martin's Griffin · New York · 📖

THOMAS DUNNE BOOKS.
An imprint of St. Martin's Press.

FUTURE IMPERFECT. Copyright © 2011 by K. Ryer Breese. All rights reserved. Printed in the United States of America. For information, address St. Martin's Press, 175 Fifth Avenue, New York, N.Y. 10010.

www.thomasdunnebooks.com
www.stmartins.com

Book design by Rich Arnold and Angela Goddard

Library of Congress Cataloging-in-Publication Data

Breese, K. Ryer.
    Future imperfect / K. Ryer Breese.—1st ed.
        p. cm.
    Summary: Seventeen-year-old Ade is addicted to the feeling he gets after knocking himself unconscious brings visions of the future, but when he meets Vauxhall, with whom he knows he will fall in love, he discovers that she also has an addiction and that together they may be able to do the impossible—change the future.
    ISBN 978-0-312-64151-1
    1. Clairvoyance—Fiction. 2. Self-destructive behavior—Fiction. 3. Interpersonal relations—Fiction. 4. High schools—Fiction. 5. Schools—Fiction. I. Title.
    PZ7.B74824Fut 2011
    [Fic]—dc22
                                                                                2010043622

First Edition: April 2011

10 9 8 7 6 5 4 3 2 1

For Russell Hoban

ACKNOWLEDGMENTS

Countless thanks to my agent, Jessica Regel, for her insight and enthusiasm, guidance and grace; an endless supply of gratitude to John Schoenfelder, a genius master of storytelling, and Russell Ackerman, a diviner in his own right; heapings of appreciation to Brendan Deneen for his superhuman editorial skills; and boundless love to Jess, EE, Mo, and Hedge, P-Dogg (Mutants!), Saba and Savta, and Grandpa and Grandma.

PROLOGUE

Jimi Ministry didn't have this many tattoos two weeks ago.

The ones on his wrists, it's obvious that they're pretty fresh.

Maybe it's the fact that they're still bright red, spanked raw and swollen, but looking at them I see my family. My distant family.

On his left wrist I think I see my great-grandmother Ethyl on my mother's side. And I've only ever seen her in pictures.

On the right wrist, that's got to be my dad's favorite uncle, the one who died in Korea. Was his name Benson?

It could be the fact that it's night and Jimi's underwater, but the images on his flesh are blurry. Like they're dancing just under the surface of the lake. And his knuckles have gone cold white from grabbing on to my arms so tight.

This is because I'm holding him down.

This is because I'm drowning him.

Jimi's face, it looks almost serene.

It's not like in the movies where people thrash around, kick the water into a froth, and their faces get all distorted with fear.

No, Jimi's practically calm and all this is happening very slowly. The night above us is cool and bursting with stars. On the beach behind me there's only the tiny lapping of waves. Like many dogs drinking water.

With my hands around Jimi's neck, squeezing the air out of him, I can't help but get nostalgic. The rage in me has reached such a fevered pitch my hair's on end. If you took my temperature right now I'm sure it'd look fatal.

But Jimi's finally under control.

He's fading so fast.

The love of my life, she's back there in the night. She's waiting, anxious.

Probably gripping the straps of her purse as tightly as I've got Jimi's throat.

On Jimi's thumb knuckle on his right hand there's a tattoo of a turtle. Most turtles look the same unless they're exotic. You know, like some Amazonian turtle. But this one, I'm pretty sure it's the same box turtle I had in fifth grade. His name was Metatron, after the archangel in the Hebrew scripture. My mom found him on one of her dashes through Pueblo. I'd know his shell pattern anywhere.

Right now is right now.

Every half-second clicks into place as deafening as thunder.

Right now is all that matters

And right now, Jimi's underwater and his face is relaxing into darkness.

The fury in me is so ferocious that I'm likely to split in half.

This is what the Metal Sisters assured me. What Grandpa Razor was so confident about. All the experts, all the professionals

I've talked to, this is exactly why they told me they didn't know. This was inevitable.

Call it fate.

Call it destiny.

Whatever you call it, it's murder.

ONE MONTH EARLIER

CHAPTER ONE

ONE

Mr. von Ravengate
Raven's Magikal Gifts, Aurora Mall
Aurora, CO

Thanks for the letter, Heinz.

Off the bat, I should mention I'm not religious. My mom's super into Jesus, but that really hasn't rubbed off on me. Not to say I'd dig Satanism either. Sorry, but that'd kill my mom. Stroke for sure. Good to know you find it meaningful though, and, hey, I am intrigued about the whole Atlantis psychic thing. But not so much the goat with a thousand eyes business.

Anyway, to answer a few of your questions:

1. No. I've never seen any strange vistas that resemble Yes album covers. I've never seen a Yes album cover. I just see the future and it looks pretty much like now.

2. No. No demons. Or Daemons. Or whatever.

3. Sure, there are Rules. Two major ones, really. Seeing the future's the easy part; the hard part's what comes after. It's breaking the Rules that's tough. These Rules, they're mine. Didn't take long for me to figure them out either.

Rule No. 1. The future can't be changed once it's been seen.

See, it's not like on television or in the movies. It's not racing against the clock to make sure that x *(the car, the tree, the cat, the ax, the bus, the moon) doesn't fall on* y *(the girl, the baby, the cat, the house, the church, the school). There's no shouting into the phone trying to convince the police of something. What I see, it always happens. Always.*

Rule No. 2. If you ignore Rule No. 1 and try to change the future, you'll end up only making a mess of things.

This is the sucky part. I've got all sorts of stories about things going really wrong when playing superhero. Once, I saw this guy die in a fire, just him wearing a suit of flames. Took me a long time to figure out who the dude was but when I did, I called him anonymously and warned him. Told him it would happen in like a week or so. The dude just totally freaked out, got off the phone, jumped in his car, and crashed into a semi. Burned to a crisp. Voilà. Twice I tried to change things directly. Both times ended badly. Really really badly.

4. Exactly. Directional. If I focus hard enough, kind of clear my mind and then push down hard, you know, like when you focus on something really close to your eyes, the way those hidden picture posters work, then I can see really far out. Like decades. If I don't, if I just let the hit happen and not try to focus in, then I see maybe weeks out. Days. Once, even hours. But I try to avoid doing that. Doesn't have the same, well, effect.

5. Yes.

6. *Like in comics? No. Once, I tried. You know, got a suit at a costume shop and tried to stop this dude from getting stabbed outside Rock Island. See answer #3 as to what happened.*

7. *Nope. Far as I know, I'm the only person who can do this. I've never seen anyone else, never met anyone else. Who knows though, right? Maybe there are some other freaks out there.*

Dude, sorry I can't be of any help regarding your "transitional journeys" and "black magic manifesto." And I can't focus in and see if your novel will get published and become a bestseller. Really, it doesn't work like that.

Heinz, why I've been writing to you is because I need some help. If you were to consult your "alchemical tomes" and "dark scrolls," ask a few minor devils or whatnot, do you think you could tell me how I can change the future once I've seen it? Can you tell me how I can break the rules?

Thanks, Heinz.
And love the cape.

Ade Patience

TWO

Last night at the All Souls Chapel I told my mom's Jesus friends I had a knockout summer.

"Knock. Out," I said all slow. "Know what I mean?"

Mom knew what I meant and gave me a thumbs-up.

Her pals, they just nodded and smiled.

In their eyes, I'm such a freaking good kid.

When summer break started I actually did keep things simple. For a while, anyway. Nothing too bold, nothing exceptionally daring. Not like what I'd done over winter break. There were the usual fights; mostly it was East football players and a couple run-ins with the bikers you always find outside the Piper Inn. And, yeah, I was black and bruised, bloodied even, but that's par for the course. Wasn't until mid-month that I decided to kick things up a notch. You know, experiment a bit.

Do stuff the All Souls Chapel ladies would find, well, *worrisome*.

There's this half-pipe at the Denver Skate Park that I'd had my eye on for like months. It's typical, concrete and tagged all over, maybe six feet at the top. I'd skated off it before and liked the way it bottomed out. Smooth. It was afternoon, hot day, and the sky was bright and blue and cloudless. They won't let you in without a deck or a helmet, so I brought both just for the show of it. Once I was at the top of the half-pipe I tossed my deck, let my helmet roll down to the bottom, and then I took a deep breath and dove.

Yeah, dove.

I didn't jump. I pulled a move like I was diving into a swim pool with my arms at my sides. Looked pretty impressive too. Up, arc, and then down. Took a lot of training, and I'm talking a lot, to get to the point that I can dive like that and not put my hands out in front of me to break the fall at the last second. My wrists, I've broken them maybe five times. But that day everything went perfect.

The sound my head made when it hit that concrete, it was priceless.

The concussion felt almost as good as being in love.

The skate park, it joins a long list of places I'm not allowed back at.

Ever.

Rest of May I wasn't quite as clever. A few car accidents, several bike crashes, and a fairly decent brawl in the Cherry Creek Mall.

Those concussions were good but not great.

In June I decided to push things even further.

I paid a guy five bucks to hit me in the back of the head with a two-by-four in the vacant lot behind the train station. I was hit by a car and went flying thirty-two feet on Hampden in front of the Whole Foods. Threw myself down one of those long staircases at the Performing Arts Complex. Even took a bike off the side of the Millennium Bridge.

After that it was hard going back to the usual.

The "accidents" just weren't delivering.

My best friend, Paige, she was not at all happy. I can't even count how many times she threatened to ditch me. How many times she called me the most selfish person she'd ever met after seeing me at the hospital. How many times she suggested I just go ahead and schedule the lobotomy the usual way. How many times she cried and hit me.

The All Souls Chapel ladies, they'd never understand this. My mom, she gets it because I'm her only kid and I'm giving her what she wants. My coma dad, if he was awake I'm sure he might have had a problem with it all. Guess we'll never know.

Anyway, early July is when I sort of reached a peak.

It had been a slow day, I'd made the rounds downtown, trying to jump in front of the mall buses, but they were all going too slow to do anything but knock me down. I entertained the thought of getting hit by a light-rail train but didn't want to get mangled. So I wound up at Monaco Lanes Bowling.

Good thing the Skins were there.

I'd seen these particular skinheads at the bowling alley before. There was the one with the Mohawk and the combat boots and the older, pudgy one with the really lame mustache. All told there were five including a girl and she was wearing tons of mascara and had a swastika tattoo on her neck.

The day had been such a bust I figured this would be fairly easy.

I walked in and got some shoes and a ball and then took a lane a few over from the skinhead gang. This was maybe at two in the afternoon and besides me and the punks the place was pretty much empty. A lone bowler at the end in a bowling jersey like he really took the sport seriously and the guy working the counter.

I threw a few gutter balls and got antsy.

I was thinking of what to yell over to these Skins, eager to get the show going, when one of them, the pudgster with the caterpillar on his lip, shouted over, "Why are you even trying? You suck."

This was my opening and I walked over to them, them all standing up, eyes narrowed, putting on their violent faces, and poked the pudgy dude in the chest. I said, "I might suck, but not as much as your mom does when I'm visiting her in the nursing home."

And voilà! The magic happened. The girl hit me with her bowling ball in the lower back. That kicked my breath out, and knocked me to the floor, and then the Mohawk dude just started stomping. Actually, all of them just started stomping. So predictable. I was out fast.

Unconscious for nearly two days.

Saw footage of the beat down on the news the evening I woke up in the hospital. Those skinheads sure were inventive after I was unconscious. One of them slid me hard down the lane and I hit the bowling pins something terrible. Got a strike for sure. This video, last time I checked it, had a million plus views online. Good to know I can provide some entertainment.

Last night, if my mom's Friends-in-Christ at the All Souls Chapel heard all this, they'd have freaked out. They'd have laughed, wondering if I was joking, and then, when they saw I was serious, gone all pale and walked away. I've seen that so many times.

I started my junior year at Mantlo High two weeks ago.

Summer's gone and I'm stuck chasing down concussions at school. Pretty much just guarantees me getting suspended a whole grip of times. But this year, it's going to be different. This year, it will be the best year of my life. The year where everything changes. I know because I've already seen it.

Fact is: I don't hit my head for the pain. This isn't some masochistic thing.

I have a gift. A power.

I am an oracle.

A soothsayer.

When my head gets rocked, when my skull cracks and my brain bounces, there is this tunnel of light that appears and in my mind I dive down into it. This tunnel, it doesn't lead to Heaven or some other universe, it leads to what comes next.

When I get a concussion I can see into the future.

THREE

So it makes sense that in about forty-five seconds I'm going to jump off the roof of my school.

It's about two stories up and I'm expecting a pretty major concussion.

For me, this roof is a stepping-stone. Just like today and tomorrow are only heartbeats in the way of what's coming.

What's next is all that matters.

Fact is: When I'm not in the future the world just seems so slowed down.

The right here, the right now, for me it's like an ancient civilization.

On the lawn right now, snacking on their lunches and guzzling sodas, making out and smoking, my fellow classmates are Romans and Greeks. They are soon to be fossils and ash sculptures from Vesuvius. Stuck in time the way trees are.

But me, I'm always moving forward.

How do I do it?

How does me getting my head bashed in send me spinning into the future?

Who knows?

I've been writing to experts, people like doctors and physicists and philosophers, but none of them can give me a straight answer as to why. Either they don't believe me or they feel sorry for me. Like, short bus sorry for me.

All but one guy and he's my shrink.

His name is Dr. Reginald Borgo and he knows that what I can

do is real. He's mentioned to me that he's seen others, people who can do some pretty spectacular shit, but I've yet to meet any of them. Borgo assures me they're out there. That it's just a matter of time. I should also mention that most medical professionals consider Borgo a quack. Figures, right?

Thirty-six seconds from jumping and my sneakers are already half off the roof.

I'm moving out of Denver.

I'm quickly moving out of my junior year at Mantlo High School.

I'm moving away from my coma father and my Jesus-obsessed mother.

But I'm going to get into all that soon enough.

Today, it's the roof and the ground and my eyes on the prize: When She and I are together and moving toward what comes next at lightning speed.

Who is She?

Only the most astonishing girl in the world. I've only ever seen Her once and it wasn't now. Like not in the present. I don't know Her name or where She's from. I saw Her in a vision in eighth grade, one of my very first visions, and I know that we'll be in love. As cheesy as it sounds, I know this girl's the one.

Us meeting will be classic.

Blockbuster.

Twenty-one seconds.

How it'll go down is like this: She will walk into the lunchroom with Jimi Ministry like they own the place and She'll get on top of a table. Jimi'll beat-box and She, standing there bright as a burning building, will sing. Yeah, She'll sing.

Her voice will be low and smoky and start almost like a whisper.

She'll sing, *"Your own personal Jesus . . . Someone to hear your prayers . . ."*

And then She'll move over to me. Me sitting there enraptured.

"Your own personal Jesus . . ."

And I won't feel myself stand but will see my perspective change as I rise up above the table and over my little lesbian friend Paige's sloping shoulders. It'll feel like I'm going to float to the ceiling, but I'll stop, caught up in that voice. She and I, we'll stand there, staring into each other, for what will seem like millennia. Clouds'll swirl, mountain ranges'll rise and crumble to dust, oceans'll swallow land and then retreat, leaving lakes and sinuous rivers, and dubbed on top of it all will be this girl's voice.

It'll be epically sick.

But I realize now there'll be a little wrinkle in our whirlwind romance. This is because Jimi Ministry is there with Her. He's an asshole. And the fact that he introduces Her, well, I didn't know it a year ago but I know now that it's not good. I can't put my finger on it, but things could get ugly. With Jimi, that would make sense.

Ten seconds.

Below me no one looks up.

Below me it's just the ground rushing.

I've spent two years of sleepless, clammy nights waiting for Her to arrive.

Six seconds.

Good thing I noticed the calendar in the vision. Right there on the wall just under the poster of the food pyramid. The date I've been counting down to for twenty-four months is August 10, 2010.

Three seconds.

Want to know the best part?

August 10, 2010, is tomorrow.

FOUR

It's an old joke, but it's true: Jumping off a roof is easy; it's the landing that's hard.

I need to land on the lawn.

Last time, the time that Nancy Springer saw me and puked, I missed the lawn by two feet and hit the bike rack. Took twenty-seven stitches to get my scalp back on.

Today, I'm feeling confident.

My aim is good.

There is a fury of wind.

The flapping of my clothes.

And then, well, forget the rolling, skip the falling on your side, the key to me making this a successful journey into my near future is by hitting my head at just the right angle and not busting up the globe of it too bad. From what I've read on the Internet, I'm guessing that giving the "dorsolateral prefrontal associative" area a decent wallop is what makes the magic happen.

Smack.

Crunch.

Going unconscious, it's like standing in an explosion.

Most times, like this time, I find myself in a tunnel. I go down the tunnel and the lights whiz by me and then, where it ends, the light parts and I dive into the darkness between.

It's dizziness and sleep and then only pure, beautiful, matte black.

And I open my eyes to the future.

Today, what I see is me ten years in the future. How I know it's the future is because things look plastic. Not twisted or distorted the way they do it up in the movies. No CGI, no carnival colors. Just plastic like you're in the suburbs. Plastic the way the waxed-up leaves are on the zebra bushes in the planters by the play space at the Cherry Creek Mall. My skin is shiny. My body feels so much more malleable.

And in this plastic future I seem happy.

Really happy.

I'm walking downtown, still Denver. This time I'm wearing a suit and it's very sunny and I can feel the first pinpricks of sweat popping up in the small of my back. I think about taking off my coat but don't because I'm turning the corner and now I'm on the shady side of another street. Downtown is busy. Cars pulling people places. Buses heaving back and forth on the mall. This must be spring because the sun is small and tight in the sky and the air smells like rain though there are no clouds anywhere. I walk into an office building and wave to someone, a woman with brown hair and thick-framed glasses sitting at a small desk, and then take an elevator to the fiftieth floor. When I get out, I stand at a bank of windows and admire the hustle and bustle of downtown, the mountains where there is snow.

In this vision I've got a backpack on but it's not heavy. No one mentions it.

I take a flight of stairs to fifty-one and walk through a maze of offices where people wave at me. Then I walk out onto a balcony. I'm sweating more, but it's not from the heat.

What I do next is I climb up onto the railing.

I stand there for a few seconds, swaying gently, my arms out-stretched, just balancing on this two-inch-wide tube of metal. I'm thinking I'm glad it's not a windy day.

And then I jump.

I fall face-first.

Arms at my side the way soldiers drop out of planes in the mov-ies. The wind's rushing up into my eyes and ears, grabbing at my hair and making my cheeks float open like the cheeks of astronauts do when they're in simulation machines.

The backpack, it's a parachute.

I don't pull the cord until I'm fifty seconds from hitting pave-ment; I time it on my wristwatch. And when I do pull the cord, and the chute explodes behind me, I'm smiling so wide that I can see the white of my teeth reflected into the dark windows of the office build-ings as I rush past them.

The way the chute's set up, my fall won't be totally broken.

I'm going to hit the ground and hit it hard.

My future: It's just me getting crazier and crazier.

I'm guessing I have the ultimate concussion from the fall. How crazy is it that I see myself in the future jumping off a roof just to see the future? I assume that I don't actually die. Maybe I do. Can you imagine the future I'll see in those few split seconds before my soul jets skyward? Must be like a thousand years in the future.

I don't see the landing.

Instead of being there and finding out, I'm here with someone calling my name and I rocket back through the tunnel, the lights spastic. When the tunnel vanishes is when I open my eyes.

My left eye, actually. The right one is swelled shut already.

Everything's blurry, but I'm on the ground at Mantlo High and there are people standing over me. I can see two of them shaking their heads.

Already they're shaking their heads.

Me, back in the present, I'm on my back lying on some tossed cigarettes and wilted grass just after lunch has ended and everyone else at my high school is getting ready to go back to class. All of them have to walk past me as they go to physics and gym and whatever it is that Mr. O'Connor feels like teaching today in American history. Right now, they just think I'm a few concussions away from full vegetable. A few knockouts from the way my dad is.

Someone, a girl, maybe Kristen LaFontaine, judging by the voice, says, "It's only Tuesday and he's already at it."

And someone else, someone gay, most likely Eric Hovda, says, "At least he waited until the second week of school. Don't even know why they keep letting him come back."

I just close my eyes and try and let the vision drift back in.

I wonder: What do I see next? Is She there too? Waiting for me in a getaway car?

What happens *after* I hit that pavement?

FIVE

I'm woozy walking into school.

I'm also bleeding from my head.

This long stretch of crimson just shattering the nice white of my shirt.

The way I'm walking, I look like a zombie.

I barely notice because my body's still jittery from the Buzz.

The Buzz is what happens when I break the laws of physics, what happens when I see into the future. It's getting a massive jolt of energy. Every nerve, every muscle fiber is jittery and on fire in the most beautiful way imaginable. It's the equivalent of smoking a blunt, of downing some beers, of popping X, and then kissing.

The Buzz is my high of choice.

This is the second time this week I've gotten high via concussion.

Right now, I'm trying to drink from the water fountain just outside Mr. Eveready's office, and "trying" is the key word here as really all I'm doing is dribbling blood all over the hallway and trying to focus on working the fountain. Of course a hall monitor, David "Suck Up" Lopez, notices me.

"Dude, seriously?" he asks. This is what he usually asks when he see me.

Then he just points down the hall.

"Before I need to call an ambulance," he says.

Second time this week I've been sent to see the school nurse, Mrs. Caronna.

As expected, she's totally not happy to see me.

Sitting here, the cotton balls getting heavy with blood, my skin is still vibrating. My head, whether it's from the concussion or the high, is heavy and light at the same time, the way a really big pillow can be super heavy and yet perfectly light. I nod off every few minutes, eyes just dim like a computer when it's not been touched for a while.

Caronna shakes me awake in her unloving way. "You think you can fly, Ade?"

I shake my head.

"Why did you jump off the roof?"

Again, I shake my head. "Hard to explain."

"Try me."

I shrug. "An experiment?"

The look on her face is pure disgust. Then she hands me her cell phone. "Dr. Borgo," she says, and her lips are all puckered.

I ask Mrs. Caronna for some privacy before I talk to my shrink and she gets up slowly, eyeballing me the whole while, before walking out and slamming the door.

"Hey, Doc," I say into the phone.

"Ade? Jesus, are you okay?"

"Yeah, of course. Just the usual. Doc, you're the only person in the entire medical world who believes me. Don't start doubting me now. That would kill—"

"I'm not doubting you, Ade."

"What are you saying then?"

"Can you at least take a few days off? Maybe a week? Nurse says you look like hell. Like you were hit with a baseball bat. Is that what happened? Again?"

"No. I jumped off the roof. Again."

Into the phone, my shrink groans. "Ade, the number of concussions you've had puts you at significant risk for developing Alzheimer's, Parkinson's. You're seventeen and already your head has been bruised and battered like you were a prizefighter. Please, Ade, please, take a week off."

"I have the strange feeling you've told me this before."

"Memory loss isn't something to joke about."

"Honestly, Doc. Promise I'll be good. Any chance you can pacify the blowhards? They keep threatening me with expulsion and, well, this time I think they—"

"I'll see what I can do, Ade. Have your mom wake you every two hours tonight, don't want you slipping off into a coma."

I can only imagine. "By the way, not sure if you remembered or not, but tomorrow's the big day."

"I've got it marked on my calendar right here. Been marked for over a year."

"Well, it's going down, Doc. My life changes tomorrow."

"If it happens, it sure will."

"Don't be such a doubter, Doc."

I lean forward, open the door, and wave for Mrs. Caronna to come back to the phone. She storms back in huffing and puffing. Sweating and shaking. Veins popping out of her forehead like worms struggling out of puddles. She grabs the receiver and puts her head to it. She grunts a few times. Nods twice. Says, "Okay, Dr. Borgo. We'll certainly take that into account. Yes. We do. Of course."

Then she hangs up and gives me this scary smile. "I don't mean this to be offensive," she says. "But one day I hope you break your neck."

SIX

Mom's great about waking me during Concussion Time.

She goes to bed early. Sets an alarm for every two hours and rocks me—hand on my shoulder since I sleep on my side—awake gently. Mom in her bathrobe with her big glasses on and her hair pulled back asks me, "Are you feeling sick?"

Just the fact that I wake up means that I'll be okay.

Plopping herself down on the end of my bed, with the Revelation Book under her arm, Mom says, "I'm making short ribs again. With the brown sugar the way you like it."

I say, "Yum. With mashed potatoes?"

"Garlic and Parmesan."

Mom opens the Revelation Book on her lap and licks the point of her pen and then looks at me, eyes wide, for me to bust out a new segment of my future history.

"I'm downtown. Maybe ten years from now. Feel great," I say.

Mom scribbles it down. Asks, "Were you wearing the black suit?"

I think back. Close my eyes. "Not sure."

Mom, back to writing, says, "Probably the black suit. If it's ten years, then, yeah. You said it was warm but not hot, so most likely early May or maybe, at the earliest, mid-April. Get a sense of the direction of the sun. I mean, how were the shadows? Longer?"

"Not sure, Mom."

Mom nods and keeps writing. Talking to herself out loud she says, "Fiftieth floor. Good sign." And, "Woman at the desk is named Louise. You met her during the interview, right?"

I just shrug, not sure.

I describe the rest. The jump. The chute. Mom says, "You're my little stuntman." And she pats me on the head like I'm five.

To make Mom happy, I add, "Also there was a cloud in the sky, looked just like a hand. I don't know if this means anything, but it was pointing east."

This, it makes Mom swoon.

See, my mom has my whole adult life mapped out.

Every vision I've had of myself somewhere in the future, she's written it down and traced it out the way explorers chart rivers. Since the visions are quick and nonlinear, she's painstakingly pieced together a basic narrative over the past three years. "Basic" is the key word. Lots of times she just fills in the blanks with guesses.

In her room, there's one wall completely filled, top to bottom, with index cards. At the top of each card, a date. Each one a day in the life of my future self. There are sketches of clothes, of buildings. She's got blueprints of rooms that I haven't been in yet. Rooms that no one's been in yet. Mom's written it all down, this time line of me, looking for one thing: Jesus.

She's looking for the Rapture.

The Second Coming.

The Antichrist.

All those good things.

I think it started at her church, someone mentioning how there will be signs and portents for the Second Coming. Only, the key to seeing them was you had to know where to look. You had to be open to receiving them. Mom latched on to that idea something fierce. The past seven years she's been looking everywhere for those signs, those portents, and found them in my visions. My visions, they're like her road map to Heaven. Mom's peek into the clockwork of God.

Fact is: The visions in the Revelation Book are real.

But the details that Mom writes down, mostly I just make those up to make her happy. I'll make up the tiny miracles. The little portents. Like how my seeing a mule with three legs was a sure sign peace would be coming to the Middle East in a matter of years. Maybe as soon as three. I lay it out so that the chrysanthemum I saw was a sign that Grandma was well and smiling from up in Heaven. I feel bad every time I lie, but keep on doing it because Mom is always ecstatic. And when she's ecstatic she's so nice to be around. I'm cool playing the little golden goose.

Tonight, sitting there writing away, Mom says, "It's been two years, right?"

"Yeah."

Mom, she smiles so hard it's like she's got the moon in her mouth.

"Tomorrow will be so beautiful. Will you tell it to me again?"

This is my mom, I oblige her.

And once again I describe how it'll happen, how the girl I've been dreaming about for twenty-four aching months will show up and sing to me, I hit all the beats, and for the first time this evening she looks up from her notebook and takes her glasses off. As I run through the story, she's grinning and nodding. When I finish she sighs and rubs my head the way she did when I was just old enough to ride a Big Wheel.

"The waiting is so hard," Mom says. She frowns as though she really knows.

"Yeah. It almost made me crazy."

"And what will you say to her?"

"I've told you how this works. You know how this works. I just wait."

Mom tells me she's very proud. She tells me that it's clear that Jesus has special things planned for me. She says, "You are a very fine blessing. So very strong."

Then she stands up and straightens out her nightgown and leaves. Closing the door slowly, she whispers, "By the way, I'm sure your dad is very proud of you."

"*Is* very proud?"

"Of course."

"Mom, Dad hasn't been anything but a vegetable for three years. I don't think he's proud of me. I don't think he's proud of anything. Dad's just a lump lying in a hospital bed, growing its hair and nails out."

The look on my mom's face, it's disappointment. It's deep down, very hurt. Her face still scrunched up with emotion, wedged there in the door, Mom says, "He's very, very proud of you." And then the door closes and I turn the light out.

Tomorrow, I say to myself. *Tomorrow it will happen and my life will begin.*

Tomorrow.

CHAPTER TWO

ONE

Dad—

You remember that time we went to the sand dunes?

You and Mom were still together and I was maybe six. My memories from the trip are pretty choppy, but I do remember us walking in that really shallow creek and climbing the dunes. I remember sleeping in a tent. But most of all I remember something that you told me. We were sitting at the campfire, Mom had gone to bed, and you were looking at the way the smoke was twisting up into the sky, up into the stars, and you said, "When you get older, you're going to want to escape sometime. Escape from what you made, from what you can't change. And the only way to really do it, to get away from this, from everything that's been done, is to lose yourself in repetition." And I asked you what you meant and you just shook your head and said, "You'll figure it out later."

I'm guessing you meant drugs. For you, I'm guessing it was tipping back the brews. Uncorking the wines. Sip and sip and sip and repeat. Right? That's what you meant, right? If so, I get the point. Only I'm not older and already I'm getting into the joys of repetition. Concussion, future, bliss, and repeat. Voilà. Should I be worried?

For a long time, when you moved away, I thought you were trying to escape from me. Mom, sure, but me too. But now because I'm older and, maybe just a bit wiser, I think it's because you're hiding. I have lost myself in repetition, Dad. And it's kind of saved me. Kind of captured me too.

I wish you'd stop lying in that bed faking. I wish you'd snap out of your coma, snap out of your nap. I wish you'd just call me and ask me what my deal is. I wish you'd just sit me down and say, "Ade, I've noticed all the gashes and bruises and hospital bills. I'm worried." Most dads, they'd slap me if they saw me the way I am.

But you're lost between the lines.

You escaped so far there's no way back.

Ade

TWO

Of course, I already know what I'm wearing.

I want to look good, but it's hard given the bruising and the cuts. It's hard given the fact that I've got one eye that's all bloody in the white of it. I dutifully slick my hair with pomade. I brush my teeth three times. I put a fresh stretch of gauze around my head.

First thing I do before school is go visit my dad. Mr. Coma.

What's funny, and I think this every time I visit him, which isn't that often, is that for my dad, the future is gone. He's all past now. Not even present. If I didn't know any better, I'd think God was playing some joke on me.

Me knocking myself unconscious all the time, this is how I'm supposed to look.

It's not pretty.

On television, in the movies, you see these people in comas all sleeping prettily like they're straight out of a fairly tale. They lie there, arms folded over their chests, their skin light and cool as a blanket of fresh snow.

These pop-culture coma people, they're bullshit.

Here's what it really looks like: my pop. He's actually in a Persistent Vegetative State, which I think is just another thirty-dollar doctor term for coma. What makes it interesting is that he's not exactly like furniture. He can kind of do things sometimes. Not on purpose but just because part of his brain, the reptile part down deep, is ticking off movements. He cries sometimes. Sometimes he sneezes. He coughs. He drools. He shits his pants this horrible liquidy stuff.

What's really spooky about Dad is when he reacts to things.

You can yell at him and sometimes he'll turn his head to look at you. Only his eyes won't be open and, as the doctors have had to explain to Mom and me a thousand times, he doesn't actually hear. Like not really really hear. He's just on autopilot. His body doing its reptile things.

This morning I walk in and let my dad know the scoop.

"Today, Dad, is the day I've been telling you about," I say as I sit in the chair across from him. This chair, it's a rolly office deal and it's been here for years. The leather is cracked and faded on it.

Dad doesn't move.

His chest goes up and down. There is some drool on his shirt. Eyes closed.

Recently I've been coming to see dad without mentioning it to my mom. I've just been talking to him, getting into everything going on in my life, kind of like he's recording it. And maybe he is. He's my own personal unconscious diary.

Sitting there across from him, I bring up my worries. "See, it's the Jimi thing that's the problem. Like I told you last time, something straight up wrong is going on. A year ago, I wasn't stressed. But now, I'm paying more attention. I just know he's going to be a problem. Just know it."

My dad, I think he farts.

The expression on his face is no expression at all.

I tell him again how Jimi's an enigma. I tell my dad that the rumors are Jimi lives in a trailer home, that his parents are drunks, that he smokes a pack of cloves a day, that he won the Colorado Teen Thespian of the Year Award two years running, that he sleeps only two hours a night and drinks coffee laced with some suspicious Mexican energy drink powder he bought online. To my coma dad I say, "And those are the rumors most everyone has heard. The ones easiest to prove. The others, the rumors people only whisper, are almost too outrageous to be true: That he deflowered both Nelle Wishman and Jodi Criswell at the same time last summer at a pool party. That he blackmailed Mr. Rosen after catching our married algebra teacher making out one of the lunch ladies. That sometimes he has bruises on his back from where his parents beat him."

My dad, for his part, just stares into the silence between us.

This gap of nothing, it's pretty much his whole life now.

"Anyway," I say, "guy with rumors like that has to be trouble."

I walk over to my dad's bedside and look closely at his eyelids. The balls of his eyes move slowly under the thin skin the way sullen fish do under ice. "But I know the future always works itself out. It's like karma. Can't change what's coming down the tracks."

I have flashbacks to the times I tried to change what I saw.

I see a car accident with my friend in the middle.

I see a church burning to the ground.

I see nothing good.

I pat my dad on the shoulder, tell him that I'll be back to update him on my situation in a few days. I tell him that he should not worry about me, that everything will end up just fine. "I've seen it already, Pops," I say. "Down to the last second."

And then, just as I turn to leave the room, I ask, "If there really is some meaning behind all this, some master plan, and you're like a metaphor or some sort of sign for me, then wake up right now and shout, 'Hallelujah!'"

My dad, he just farts in his sleep again.

THREE

Mantlo's your typical high school.

We have our jocks, our wavers, our geeks, our punk rockers, our acidheads, our preps, goths, hipsters, stoners, nerds, bohemians, furries, mods, Teddy boys, metalheads, bodybuilders, otaku, gamers, soulboys, artists, glam rockers, skinheads, hackers, anarchists, cosplayers, swing kids, bikers, grebos, scooters, psychobillies, gangsters, queers, freaks, outsiders, and dirties. Just all of them are limper. All of them are caricatures in reverse.

But not Jimi and I.

Fact is: It's only at Mantlo that we can get away with what we do.

The place is so boring, so white-bread and predictable, that we, the unpredictable element, bring a whole uneasy new vibe to the place. What's good about it is that our being so "badly behaved" lets everyone else go covert. All the kids on drugs, all the gay kids, all the gangsters, all of them rest easy knowing that no one is going to pick on them 'cause they've got us. Me with my ability, Jimi with his outrageousness, we're the magnets.

Just having us around keeps everything else on the downlow.

The other students, none of them seems to appreciate it. The staff does, though. At least for me. Even though Mrs. Caronna is getting sick of seeing me, I give her something to do, someone to treat, to make her job meaningful. Same with Eveready. Can't be an effective principal if you haven't got a troublemaker keeping you on your toes. Fact is: There're a whole slew of people whose jobs pretty much depend on me doing my damaged thing. I'm like an insurance policy.

And today, that policy is about to pay out.

Lunchtime.

Cafeteria is full and my heart is racing.

Paige, she takes her place beside me just like always and just like always she sings, all sarcastic, "This is the day your life will surely change." But today, she adds, "Rumor has it there's a new hottie at school. She and Jimi have been making the rounds."

I just point at the calendar beneath the food pyramid.

The date there is so bold it's painful.

Clockwork.

Jimi comes strutting into the cafeteria and Paige says, "And here we go."

I'm trying to control my pulse.

Jimi, swinging his arms like he's going to take flight in his leather coat and blood-ox Docs and eyeliner and mullet, he is just beaming. But already this moment is stale.

I know what comes next. I've known for so very long.

Love fever.

Epic bliss.

Me, right now I'm trying to figure out when I can hit my head again.

When I can see what happens after this.

After this, I'm drawing kind of a blank.

Jimi marches to the center of the lunchroom and then, like always, climbs up on an empty table and puts his hands to his mouth. He arches back, shouting up into the rafters. "Ladies and gentleman, boys and girls, gather 'round. Have I got a spectacle for you!"

And then there she is.

The girl from my vision comes in behind Jimi all business. The way she walks in, it's like one of those movies where the action blurs right before a musical number. And everyone notices right away she's beautiful. Wearing all gray with her hair short and curling at the ends, my future girl has this small, perfectly fragile face at odds with the fully realized body in tow. Those overwhelming green eyes.

Paige elbows me. "I think I just swallowed my gum."

I ignore her. This is my moment.

And Paige flicks me on the side of the head where a sprout of hair sticks out from the bandages that circle my forehead like a sweatband. "You so rock," she says.

What this is, it's exactly like watching someone film a movie. I've read the script a thousand times and now it's happening.

Only there are no cameras.

Only it's for real.

Jimi introduces her with a wild flourish, says, "This is Vauxhall!"

The name hits me like a hammer to the stomach and at the same time it's like being kissed, just so, on the ear. Of course, I realize that it's the best name ever. That all the names I came up with, all the ones I made ludicrous lists of, were totally off. Over the past six months alone I'd come up with Zoe, Seraphim, Giselle, and Ava, but seeing her now, none of those work.

Paige, her fingers cold on the back of my neck, says, "I'm already in love."

Vauxhall gets up on the table next to Jimi.

She's calm, standing there as though this whole thing has been rehearsed a thousand times. There is silence. The ones eating chew slowly, as quietly as possible.

Jimi steps off the table and starts beat-boxing.

Someone yells, "Faggot!"

And that's when Vauxhall extends her arms out wide and sings. Bright as a burning building, she sings and her voice is low and smoky and starts almost like a whisper. She sings, *"Your own personal Jesus . . . Someone to hear your prayers . . ."*

Paige looks at me. "Did you think it'd be this good?"

"Never."

Vauxhall lowers her arms and stares out. Her eyes pin us to our chairs. Pin us to the spot like the butterflies cottoned and pinned in Mr. Weber's room.

And what happens happens, exactly the way I saw it.

Down to the very glance.

She moves over to me. Me sitting there enraptured.

"Your own personal Jesus . . ."

And just like the million times I've seen it in my head, I feel like I'm floating and I feel like the two of us, me and Vauxhall, are the only ones there and all the forces of nature swirl around us as time grinds down to nothing. To only a heartbeat. A blink.

The most beautiful déjà vu. And then it's over.

Jimi stops. Vauxhall stops.

They step down from the table and the lunchroom is broken from its trance.

And the space where the music was, it's overwhelmed with noise: the scuttle and squeak of sneakers on tile, laughter and cursing, sighs and shouts. Within minutes the lunchroom clears, only a scattering of students remain.

What's ironic now that it's happened, and what I never really noticed before in any of my mental replays, is that the whole thing, the whole scene, is really just your typical high school prank. This, Vauxhall singing with Jimi doing his lame beat-box shtick, is almost exactly what you'd expect to see in an '80s movie. This is such a cheeseball *Breakfast Club* moment that everyone else but me and Paige is going to forget about it an hour from now.

My moment, it's such a cliché.

Vauxhall smiles, bows. "I'm Vauxhall. It's a weird name."

Paige says, "It's pretty."

I say, "Welcome to Mantlo." My voice cracks at every syllable.

Vauxhall, she says, "Thanks. I'll see you around, right?"

"Right."

On her way out she turns and looks back at me, her eyes sparkling in the cheap fluorescence. Paige puts a hand on my shoulder,
squeezes. "Don't."

She can see my body lurching, my muscles twitching to move.

To run and gush to Vauxhall.

"You will freak her out. She'll think you're a stalker. A freak."

"But not if I—" I try.

"You can't. Won't. You need to play it cool. We'll talk to Jimi."

I ignore Paige, say, "We're going to be in love."

Shaking her head Paige says, "You've been spoiling the ending
for a year now."

FOUR

After lunch, Paige and I are by my locker and I'm panicked.

"I don't know what to do now," I say to Paige.

She just shakes her head. "You need to calm down. I've never
seen you this freaked out. You've seen it all, dude. Just chill and let
the pieces fall."

"That's the thing. I don't know what happens next. I need a
concussion so bad."

"What happens next is you calm the F down and strategize.
Start this right, Ade."

Like most afternoons Jimi's in the parking lot smoking.

Like most afternoons he's got his sunglasses on, looking like
he's waiting for applause that will never come. Paige and I, we walk

slowly over to Jimi. We take our time because both of us want to get our story straight. Both of us know Jimi well enough to know how well he can manipulate a situation. Turn it on its head.

"You talk to Belle yet?"

"Of course not."

"She's going to be pissed. This is totally why you two broke up. I certainly hope you're not still following her around. That was creepy."

"I was never—"

"Yeah. Right."

With his back against Ben Kunis's Lexus, ashing into the car's hood intake filter.

We walk up to Jimi and he looks over his sunglasses at us and then looks around, over one shoulder. Then the other. Slowly. Wrapping it up, this scene, he stares at us hard and screws up his face like he's confused. Like we've just come from outer space and landed in a shiny ship in front of him. This is Jimi being dramatic. It's Jimi being a dick. He knows we're there to talk.

"So?" I finally ask.

"Who is she?" Paige prods.

"You mean Vauxhall?"

Paige rolls her eyes.

Jimi coughs out a plume of smoke. Chuckles. "She's quite a chick, right? We met in Melton's driver ed class at triple A. I was hitting on her hard and 'course she rejected me at first, but we became fast friends. The two of us cracking up over how giant Mrs. Melton's ass was. Platonic flirting really, but then you know how—"

"Yeah. You're the stud," Paige interrupts. "We get it."

"Anyway," Jimi huffs. "She transferred here for film. Believe it or not, Mr. McKellar is pretty highly regarded in the avant-garde film world. Who'd of thunk, right? To me he's just this stuck-up art teacher. Anyway, Vaux doesn't have many female friends. She's more the lone cowboy type. You could say she's one of the guys. Roughhousing and crazy. You know, kind of like . . ." He looks at Paige.

She crosses her arms and tilts her head. "Like a dyke?"

Jimi grins. "You said it, not me. Only she isn't gay. She's just what every guy dreams about: a hot girl who likes wrestling, loves collecting old comic books, and watches action movies. Hot bod too. Wild. Went swimming at Celebrity with her once and wow, what can I say. Given her tomboy behavior I was worried she'd come out of the locker room looking like that chick at the end of *Sleepaway Camp,* but she's totally—"

"How about her name?" I interrupt.

"Weird, huh? She says her parents are stoners and they got the name after the neighborhood in London. Hippies come up with the darndest things. By the way, how'd you like the intro? Vaux planned it."

I ask, "Why me?"

"—"

"Why'd she sing to me?"

Jimi shrugs. "I suggested that. Fun, right? Vaux is all about shaking things up. Making people feel uncomfortable or the opposite, totally loved. She's right there on the edge. Did she make you feel totally loved, Ade? Did she get you all bothered?"

I don't say anything. I know Vauxhall and I will be together, happy lovers, and so I don't say anything.

Paige asks, "So it meant—"

Jimi claps, flicks his cigarette off like it's a biting insect. "Nothing. Doesn't mean anything." Then he looks to me, eyes narrowed, "You don't know her yet, Ade. There's a lot going on. She's complicated."

"How's that?"

Jimi grins and shakes his head. "Look, players, I really gotta roll to Mr. Russo's. If I'm late one more time, he'll burn my ass on that trig exam."

He turns to go but then looks back, over his shoulder male model style, and says, "Oh, and she's left school already. So don't go trying to track her down. They say first day's best for ditching."

Paige spits onto the asphalt. First time I've seen her do that. "What a prick."

FIVE

Today, at home, I use what I call the side entrance.

It consists of me jumping the fence by the junipers and coming into the house via the sliding door in the study. I jimmy it open with this little tool, kind of like a flattened crowbar, that I keep hidden under the coiled snake of hose by the shed.

I do this because today there are three of them on the porch.

Three freaks.

They're on the porch for me. Each of them wants to hear a story. A story about how their life improves dramatically. About how in the future, they will find their lost loves or lost cats or missing charms or even their faith in the Lord Jesus. These people, I tend to find them in front of my house the way some people find strays.

Thing is, with the Internet, most anyone can find my mom's accounts, other church members' accounts, of my abilities. They type in stuff like "I need to know what will happen with my baby when she's a grandmother" and "Oh God, will they evict me next month?" and somehow, by some weird quirk of electronic routing, they wind up here.

Mom's at All Souls Chapel the whole night, so I eat leftover casserole in my bedroom.

The freaks, they leave around nine. Heads hung low, kicking at the lawn.

I settle in on my bed and replay the day's events.

So far, so brilliant.

There's a mirror on the back of my bedroom door and I prop myself up in bed and stare hard at myself. I see my mom. Only my hair isn't thinning out. If anything it's gotten bushier. But the perfect triangle nose is the same. The thin arched eyebrows. The full bottom lip. With Vauxhall's sudden appearance, I'm tripped up a little thinking about how I must look, all battered and broken.

I don't normally fix my hair or worry over zits, but I find myself looking in the mirror more and more often these days. Looking more and more closely at the scars. At the bruises. In mom's makeup mirror, I find myself trying to find the sunken spots from the dents. Tracing the scar tissue. The healed-over gashes and fractures. My nose, it's been busted more times than I can remember, and yet it's still straight. Went right a year ago but then busted left a few months later. All the damage works itself out in the end.

My face comes back together no matter how I break it.

Looking through myself, back at myself on the bed, my mind drifts to my ex-girlfriend, Belle. This is probably because I'm tired and the last time Belle and I talked, really really talked, we were sitting on my bed looking into this same mirror and saying ridiculous things to each other. She was drunk or high. With her it's always one or the other. I fall asleep hanging on that memory but I'm only under seconds before the phone rings.

"Hello, Ade."

It's a voice I don't recognize. A voice filled with phlegm. A voice like a third-generation dupe of a badly recorded rock show. I yell to Mom that I've got the phone.

"Who is this?" I ask.

The voice rattles. "You're in trouble."

"Who the hell is this?"

"Doesn't matter. I'm calling to help you."

I snicker. Loudly. Push my ear down on the receiver hard. "Who the fuck is this?"

Just ratty breathing.

"Okay. I'm going to hang up now, freak."

The voice on the other end, it laughs. The sound is nauseating. The voice ignores me, says, "So I had this woman come in to see me this afternoon. An old friend, but she's never had much in terms of work. Trifles usually. Or truffles, as the case may be. Stuff like that, pedestrian courses, I maybe can give her a week at the most. But today she comes in with a big surprise: thousand-year eggs."

"I have no idea what you're talking about." Getting angry, I say, "Is there a point to this phone call? You that creep across the street that the cops have been bugging—"

The voice interrupts, "Actually, they're only a hundred days old. The eggs. They're preserved in ash and salt and have a gray yolk.

Very bitter, salty, but exquisite nonetheless. But only one hundred days."

"This is really educational and all, but I think—"

The gargled voice, it gets louder. "Why I'm calling you, Ade, is because eating those eggs I had an superb vision. My client got what she wanted, and we're talking months in advance, but I also saw you."

"Me?" I laugh uncomfortably and know immediately that I shouldn't. This freak on the phone could be sitting outside in a car. He could be watching me from a rooftop right now. He wants this. He wants me spooked.

"Odd, isn't it."

"That's enough, I'm gone."

But I don't hang up. I can't.

Ten seconds pass. They're as long as visits with my brain-dead dad. And then the voice comes back in, swimming in through the static. "Here's the deal: You're at a reservoir. Maybe Cherry Creek. A few weeks from now. And something just terrible goes down. This is at night. This is really dangerous. You look frantic. Seriously, I'm worried—"

"Worried about what?"

"Just I wouldn't plan on going to the park anytime soon."

"Who is this? Tell me. Is this a joke?"

The sewer voice says, "This thing I saw, it's just the setup for an adventure, Ade. What I saw today? Well, that's the third act. Like a play, my friend. You know, first act introduces our hero, his or her situation, the usual background stuff. Second act is the longest, usually it's like second act part one and part two where all the action happens, where our hero is put in a weird situation, or has a conflict to resolve. And third act is where the shit hits the proverbial fan."

"Why are you telling me this?"

"You're the lone cowboy, Ade. I like that you're a fighter. You're scrappy."

I say nothing. Just breathe back slowly. Every heartbeat is cautious.

"I'll be seeing you," the voice says. And the line goes dead.

SIX

My mom is the reason that these nuts call me.

Why they appear on the porch.

What's interesting is that this one, this old guy, seems a bit more confident. The way he talked it's almost like he had abilities like mine. What makes me say almost is the fact that he's surely a nut. I'm convinced of this because of his voice. His phlegmy rattle pretty much insures that he's a freak.

I'm guessing he's a freak from The Fairlight Hospital.

It's this place my mom used to volunteer and they had a burn unit where she'd crouch down low with the third-degree guys, most of them bums who fell asleep downtown while drenched in alcohol and smoking and pretty much combusted themselves. These burned-up guys had the very same voice as the guy on the phone. My mom, sometimes she'd drag me along on her Fairlight Rounds (that's what she called it), had me hold the hand of some still sizzling hobo while she told him about the joys of Christ and the promise of eternal life. The way those crispy guys said "Amen" sounded exactly the same as the way the dude who just called said my name.

I have no idea what he's on about now, what this phone call meant, but I don't really want to worry over it. My time for worrying about the here and now is over. Long gone. If it doesn't have anything to do with Vauxhall and our future, than it's just chatter in the wind.

Me, I'm over the nut jobs.

Me, I'm done with the bozos.

What I need is to seriously kiss Vauxhall and then knock myself out.

CHAPTER THREE

ONE

Professor David Gore, MD, PhD
Department of Medical Physics
University of California San Diego, San Diego, CA

Dear Dr. Gore,

Thank you for your short note. I appreciate your taking a few minutes to reply to my letter and I can understand your doubting me. Comes with the territory.

Fact is, Dr. Gore: When I get knocked out, I can see the future.

Maybe my last letter wasn't clear but, really, the seeing the future thing is simple. Just a matter of complicated physics. It's changing what I see that's the tough one. I'm wondering (again) if you have any ideas on how I can change the future after I've seen it.

Like I mentioned in my last letter, I've tried it before. Maybe it's bet-

ter if I get specific: Last year I saw a guy I knew get killed in a car acci-dent. I did everything I could to stop it from happening. I knew the rules, but this was life and death and I wasn't just going to sit there and let it happen. I told this dude, told him everything I saw. He didn't believe me. For like three days I hounded him, practically begging him. I mapped it out for him, gave him a description of the car, of the people at the scene. Still, he wouldn't listen. Eventually, he showed up at my house, said he was going to get a restraining order if I didn't leave him alone, told me he had some friends who would kick my ass. Still, I begged him. He ran out of my house, flicking me off. I heard the bang three and a half min-utes later. Ran out to find him in the middle of the road a block away, run down by a red car. Vision came true and I made it happen.

See, me trying to stop it made it happen.

I'm haunted by it. And if I ever see something like that again, some-one being hurt or worse, I'm not sure what I can do. But I want to do something. I need to do something.

Dr. Gore, you're a medical physicist, an expert. I read your paper on "temporal disturbances" and chronic migraines and even though I didn't really get anything beyond the first page (just being honest), I figure if anyone can give me some good advice it'll be you. Here's to hoping!

Sincerely,

Ade (not Abe) Patience

TWO

Vauxhall's sitting a few rows over.

She is stunning in the dry fluorescence of McKellar's Art Room.

I'm staring at her so hard that I'm worried I'm drooling on my shirt. I'm worried that if she turns around and sees me, she'll just freak out. God, she is so incredibly beautiful!

Mr. McKellar is going on about the history of perspective.

It's the driest stuff I've heard in years and already half the class is nodding off. I can't imagine why Vauxhall would want to transfer to this class, this teacher.

Vauxhall does not appear bored by the perspective talk.

Head on her hands, she looks enraptured.

I decide to give it a go and actually pay attention. Mostly this is an act for Vauxhall. But I can feel my brain rotting away and only five minutes in I'm eyeing the edges of a stool in the corner of the room.

I'm thinking: If I take a running leap from here, I can nail my forehead on that stool and be out in seconds.

Buzz.

I'm actually tensing up, getting ready to leap, when something spins onto my desk. White cray paper, folded over four times.

It's from Vauxhall.

Try not to fall asleep, the note says.

I look at her and smile. I write back, *Gonna be hard.*

My heart is exploding. Her handwriting is exquisite.

Vauxhall writes back, her head close to the paper, hands tight on her pen. She writes, *He's actually pretty famous.*

The way she writes her *a*'s—this dollop of ink—is so freaking sexy.

I respond, *For boring students to death? Where's the art?*

She writes, *Ha Ha.*

Have I seen anything he's done?

Vauxhall writes, *Probably not. His stuff is pretty arty.*

I write her that I dig arty. I'm really into arty.

Like what?

I list the films Paige and I have seen at the Esquire. Mostly they're midnight movies. Stuff like *El Topo* and *The Rocky Horror Picture Show* and *Showgirls*. I write Vauxhall that I realize it might not be as arty as I thought at the time.

In her note back she laughs. No, really. It's a drawing of her, a little kind of thumbnail sketch of her face with her hair and eyes, and she's laughing her head off. That's her response. The drawing, it's honestly pretty good. Actually, I want to frame it on my wall.

Mr. McKellar decides its time for questions and he looks over at me, so I fold the note up and put it in my pocket.

McKellar asks, "What would art without perspective look like? Would it be primitive or would it be abstract? Has art improved with its invention?"

I stare back blank, my mind not even turning.

Vauxhall answers for me. She tells McKellar, this apparently brilliant instructor worth transferring for, that the answer depends on where you're coming from and what you're looking for. She tells him it's all in the eye of the beholder. She says, "Perspective is just another tool. If you're making something realistic or that's supposed to seem realistic, then it's a great tool. If not, then you can freely leave it behind. It's a relatively new thing, perspective. Medieval times it wasn't distance that was important but weight. The bigger something was, the more central it was, the bigger it was on canvas. They say it revolutionized art when perspective appeared, sometime in Italy, but really, I don't think it was such a great thing. Art might look more realistic, it's certainly easier to get, but it's lost that imaginative view. That childlike view of things that just opens everything all up. There's real beauty in seeing something the way it isn't meant to be seen."

The way Vauxhall speaks is jaw-dropping.

When we're packing up before the bell, and Mr. McKellar has drifted off to his desk, I turn to the brilliant and beautiful mind next to me and I say, "That was amazing."

My veins are drumming overtime as I'm speaking.

Vauxhall stands and bows. She says, "*That* was bullshit."

Before she leaves she asks me if I'm going to Oscar's party tonight.

"Sure," I say. I'm hoping it's not apparent I wasn't invited. Oscar's this really loud almost–frat guy who seems to have a party every other weekend. Both his parents travel, he drinks Red Bull and Jägermeister, and his liver is probably the size of Montana.

"Great." And she smiles.

That smile has me floating all the way to Paige's locker. And Paige can read it on me the way a dog can read the cheeseburger off your lips. She says, "You know, I've been meaning to mention that I don't think . . . Look, call it woman's intuition, but I think she's got something going on with Jimi."

"What? That's ridiculous. Since when do you have woman's intuition?"

"Eat a dick, Ade. I'm being serious."

"Nah, I've seen this."

I don't let on that I've got stress about Jimi.

I say, "We, you and me, are going to Oscar's party tonight. Vauxhall's hoping I'll be there."

Paige crosses herself. She says, "You been on airplane mode this whole time?"

"What the hell are you talking about, Paige?"

Hands on her hips, Paige says, "Just think it's funny how much you miss. It's like you're only half awake most of the time."

"No idea what you're talking about."

"I think they're together."

"Well, if they are," I say, winking, "it won't be for long, buzz kill."

Paige kisses me on the cheek. The peck, it isn't sweet. She smiles, says, "Not as though you'd remember anyhow."

THREE

The song has been sung in the lunchroom.

We've talked. We've laughed together. Flirted even, maybe.

This party is surely where we kiss.

Tonight, this party is the moment I have waited so many seasons for.

The frost is over and the summer has come. I spend an hour in the bathroom and I look over every inch of my face. This is prom and my wedding and my first real job all wrapped up in one. I make myself look and smell and feel as good as I can. I use the gel, I use the lotions, I use the aftershave, I iron my clothes, and shine my shoes. My stomach is an impossible knot.

First thing Paige and I notice when we hit Oscar's is that it's a costume party.

We decide to hang around outside Oscar's place and wait for more partygoers.

Maybe find some other idiots without costumes.

———

Everyone who walks in I scan like I'm an MRI. Trying to make out the shapes of the beneath the costumes. 'Course I'm not looking for tumors.

I'm looking for Vauxhall.

Paige has smuggled a half bottle of whiskey from her dad's liquor cabinet and we sip that while we wait, out throats getting chapped. Paige is chatty, but I'm too nervous to speak. When I do, it's just me saying stupid things and stuttering about how anxious I am. Paige finds me ridiculous.

When this guy named Jethro that Paige's friends with shows up, we walk in with him and his date. Jethro's a Mormon and is dressed like a nun and his date is some Filipino girl with braces dressed like a witch. Walking in, the two of them describe their newfound love of chicken tinola. We have no idea what that is but imagine it's something like what Oscar's place smells like. It must be pot and coconut milk.

Inside, I see Vauxhall first.

Of course I do.

This is exactly how fate and destiny and providence works.

She's wearing dark slacks. Innocuous footwear. A blue button-up shirt. Electric blue, no less. She's also wearing gloves. Black leather. And her face is entirely swathed in bandages. Bowler hat on. Shades on. Vaux's speaking damaged French to someone I think is named Bethany.

Vaux has a name tag that says, VAUXHALL, NEW GIRL.

A little light on the top of the tag, like an Xmas tree light, flashes on and off and on and off. This is Vauxhall as the cool mummy.

She's so relaxed. And it makes me feel uptight.

I can't keep my eyes off where her face should be.

So I push my way into the kitchen for a drink. I need something to loosen up before I talk to Vauxhall. Unfortunately, Heather Albine, Chris Lavoire, Liz Chin, and Gina Foley are standing around the cooler. These are bitches I hate being trapped in kitchens with.

I push in between them, reach into the cooler, and pull out a cider. Not my favorite, but I want something sweet because I'm sure I'll be swilling bitter wine later. I look around for a bottle opener.

"What do you think of her?" Heather asks me.

"Who?" I play it dumb.

"Who?" Liz laughs. "Who else?"

"Uh, yeah, she's interesting," I say, reaching around each of them, hands scouring the countertops looking for the bottle opener, desperate for the bottle opener. Gina has it. Has been holding it the whole time. She hands it to me and asks, "Ade, how did you get into the party, anyway?"

"I was invited. Me and Paige."

They laugh like jackals.

Gina says, "You three—you, lesbo, and the new bitch—are like a perfect team."

"How's that?" I ask, eyes narrowing.

Chris, she says, "You're all mutants."

"Why're you lumping Vauxhall in with . . ."

"Are you serious? Have you even seen her?" Chris snickers. "That crazy bitch is like the biggest—"

"Opposed to who?" I interrupt. "You ugly skanks're just jealous. Maybe she wasn't raised in Crestmoor. Maybe her dad's not a doctor. Doesn't make her any less—"

I stop when I realize they've all gone quiet.

Standing behind me, Vauxhall says, "My dad's dead."

Liz and Gina cringe, make sympathetic faces. Heather laughs uncomfortably. And then all four of them, moving like some trained acrobatic team, squeeze out of the kitchen in seconds. There was a magic trick and the bitches have evaporated.

"Friends of yours?" the mummy asks.

"Not at all."

I'm thinking right here is the real beginning.

The way this story really truly starts.

Standing here, looking at Vauxhall in her getup, I'm imagining how we'll reenact this story for friends years from now. In my mind I see us older and sophisticated, maybe at a restaurant sipping wine and eating strange cheese, and Vauxhall's covering her mouth and laughing and telling our friends, also mature wine drinkers, that we met for real, really met, at a costume party at some dude's house, some dude neither of us can recall. We'll laugh about that. I'm sure of it.

Right now, me getting all dreamy leaves a wedge of uncomfortable silence between us. Vaux breaks it by leaning in and saying, "It's not what you think it is."

What a great opening line.

"What's not?"

"My costume. It's more complicated than it looks."

I take a sip of cider, say casually, "Okay. Let me guess. Uh, a mummy?"

"Didn't see that coming." Vauxhall laughs.

"I got nothing."

She looks disappointed. "Why are you drinking that bitch fizz, anyway?"

The cider in my hand, I shrug. "Tasty?"

I'm leaning against the stove and put my right hand down on the range and while it's there, just fleetingly, Vauxhall puts hers on top. The touch is brief. I feel only the warm leather. The hand beneath is a mystery. I feel the shape, but without touching the skin, it's like touching a picture.

This is our first official touch, as brief and unexpected as it is.

And this is exactly when some asshole barges in with a bottle of wine, splashing it everywhere. His eyes are bloodshot.

He sees Vauxhall, his face twists into a mischievous grin.

"Sorry." He laughs. And turns and leaves.

"Know him?" I ask Vauxhall.

A silence follows. Both of us rocking in our shoes. I break the tension, ask, "Right, so, I think I should know, but what's the costume?"

"I'm Negative Woman."

"Who?"

"From *Doom Patrol*. Comic book. She has to wear bandages, otherwise this black energy spirit can fly out of her body and wreak havoc."

"I never read *Doom Patrol*."

"From the sixties. What do you read?"

"Usually new stuff. Recent stuff. Really, I'm more into the art."

"Oh. One of those."

"What do you mean?"

"Well, most people read comics for the story lines. The characters. They're like soap operas, only with big pecs and fancy suits and the ability to shoot electricity from fingertips. Then there are the people into the indie zines that are just like these examinations of human failing and stuff. And there are people like you. Nothing wrong with that. Nothing at all," she says, and I don't believe a word of it. She adds, "Personally, I like the most messed-up characters. The ones with demons. With secret powers that they can barely control."

"You that way? Have some sort of energy being inside you just itching to get out and tear the world apart?"

Vaux's bandage face registers nothing. "Aren't we all like that? All of us with this powerful person inside that we can hardly control but can't ever really let out. The consequences would be too great."

I shrug. "I'm not sure I do."

Vaux laughs. "You just might have lost contact with him. Or her."

"Her?"

Vaux laughs again. "Why not? Maybe you've got some out-of-control bitch deep inside you. Some hellacious chick who's just rearing to break out and break hearts and bring the world to tears."

"I don't think I do."

"That's lame, Ade. Come on, be clever with me for a few minutes."

I take another sip of my girl drink. "Technically," I say, "I'm a superhero."

"Technically?"

"Yeah. Totally. I can see—"

We're interrupted when Paige struts in. "Hey, guess who she is?" I ask.

Paige looks Vaux over, says, "The Question?"

Vaux shakes her head.

"Uh, some evil Charleston mummy character?"

"Nope."

"That one mummy from Marvel Boy?"

"Negative Woman."

Paige's face lights up. "Ooh, an obscure one. *Doom Patrol*, right? What was her name again?"

"Valentina Vostok."

"Damn, that's good."

They talk comics for twenty minutes. Bouncing from *The New Mutants* ("Is Wolfsbane the shit or what?") to *Avengers* ("A baby with Vision? *Huh?*"). I stand there transfixed. A butterfly pegged to a specimen board. They move on to school. Friends. Parents. Watching Vauxhall is like watching a mime. Her movements carry so much more weight since I can't see her face.

Paige asks about her name. I find myself leaning in. Physically trying to move myself close so I can hear every word even though the party in the background isn't that loud. I'm only an observer here.

A very biased one.

This story, I've been filling in the blanks of it ever since my first zit.

Vaux says, "My parent's named me Vauxhall Renee Rodolfo because they were told it was a strong name. They were told that giving a baby a strong name ensures that she will grow up to be a powerful woman like Sojourner Truth or Isadora Duncan. These women were powerhouses. They were revolutionaries. My parents were told this by their guru. They always insisted that my name is the strongest name they could find. Dad said, 'It's the *v* and the *xh* combo. Those sounds, they're like jumping into a lake of ice. You hear those sounds, and you wake up. That's real.' Bunch of New Age bullshit, if you ask me."

Paige laughs. "Hippies, huh? Mine too. Named me after an actress."

I say, "Hippies are so deluded."

Vaux continues like she's lecturing us. Only she doesn't talk down and keeps it simple. Part of me thinks her lines sound rehearsed. There's something very Jimi about it.

Vaux says, "My parents decided early that their daughter would stand out. They decided this the night they were married. At least that's what they've told me. What they say is that they were married on a cliff overlooking the Pacific in Baja. The stars were out and there was a man with a ukulele. There was a rabbi and a Buddhist monk. After the brief ceremony, they jumped off the cliff hand in hand and swam naked while the wedding party rained daisies down on them. As they swam they kissed and talked and my dad said, 'We will have a daughter. She will be incredible and have an incredible name.'"

"That's cool," I blurt.

"The word comes from Faulke's Hall. Faulke de Breaute was the captain of King John's mercenaries. Over time the word changed to Foxhall. And then finally to Vauxhall. Great example of how a word grows and letters migrate over time. How the *f* and *l* in flutterby switched places with the *b* and changed the word to *butterfly*. How the *day's eye* became the *daisy*. Mutation. Evolution. My mother once told me that the evolution of a word gives it its strength. That means it's tested. Proven. She said, 'Your name's migrated along the alphabet. It's grown and now, now it's your name. The last and final step to perfect balanced energy.' Said, 'You can tell the glow of someone influential a mile away. It radiates, darling.' You believe that?"

"Serious New Age shit." Paige shakes her head.

Vaux says, "Before Dad died, yeah. After, Mom got goofy."

"Sounds like mine," I say. "Dad too. He lives in another dimension."

"Like *The Twilight Zone*?"

"No. Like really. He's in a coma."

"Sounds bad," Vaux says. I can imagine her grimacing under the wraps. "I'm sorry. That must be really hard."

"I'm not sure if it is. We relate to each other the way trees or rocks or clouds relate to each other. Just sharing the same place. My mom thinks he's still in there, like trapped in a shell. Says she can talk to him and in his nothing to her he speaks volumes."

Vaux, under all her bandages, gives a look. A tilt of the head that suggest either she's confused or that she's feeling sorry for me. I'm guessing it's something more remote. Maybe even understanding.

Paige says, "Welcome to Ade's whole life."

Vaux laughs and I want desperately to pull the bandages off her face. Just to see her expressions while she speaks.

I want to see her lips move.

Her cheeks flush.

The chat group in the kitchen breaks up when a mob of frat guys from DU suddenly appears and raids the coolers.

Vauxhall stays in the kitchen talking. I go take a piss but then, when I get back to the kitchen, I can't find her and so I wind up in the living room on a couch talking to someone I don't think I've ever seen before about football. I know nothing about football. But he assumes I do because he's heard about my head injuries.

This guy, beer in his goatee, says, "I've just been assuming, you know. That's jacked up if it wasn't from like rushing a lineman and shit."

I don't correct him.

Goatee guy gives me another beer and we stop talking after that and I just sit there, in a drunken daze, and people-watch. I think I see my ex, Belle, but maybe it isn't her. Paige passes by and waves.

I'm not sure if it's what I've been drinking, but I don't want to get up. I want to stay right here and watch for my girl. I'm doing exactly what my mother always told me to do if I ever got lost in a department store. Just stay where you are. Just hang tight and wait. And again I'm playing through the rest of the night, planning my next moves, getting a bit sweaty thinking about when exactly we'll hold hands, when exactly we'll kiss, and what it will feel like to touch her.

To really touch her.

I'm daydreaming on the couch long enough to watch two people pass out and then, finally, I see Vauxhall again.

Thing is she's stumbling upstairs with Ryan Mar.

FOUR

Ryan's a guy I've seen in the halls maybe twice.

He plays basketball and wears red Converse shoes. They're making their way upstairs, Ryan laughing with his hand on Vauxhall's ass.

Her arm around his waist.

Her mouth whispering things into his ear.

And then they're gone.

For two seconds I think maybe it's just a prank. That or she's giving Ryan a tour. That maybe they're really just good friends from way back. But I'm not convincing myself.

I want to shout. To let her know that that's not me.

That she's got the wrong dude.

That, Wait, Hey! I'm over here.

What happens inside my stomach is something horrible.

Most of me screams out in tatters and my brain fizzles out into glitches.

I can't breathe.

This is not supposed to happen.

I stumble out away from the couch and drop my beer on the carpet. The way I'm swaying, almost vomiting, everyone backing away from me must be thinking that I'm on something really gnarly. That maybe my drink was spiked.

This isn't what I saw.

I find Paige in the garage talking on her cell. I tell her to hang up, that it's urgent. I tell her that I need to her to take me home, that I need to crawl under my house. I say, "I just saw Vauxhall take Ryan Mar upstairs."

When I say it I almost puke.

Paige frowns this sad frown and hugs me. "I was trying to tell you," she says.

"You were telling me she was with Jimi," I say. My voice all panic.

I'm getting angry. I'm burning up.

"I was trying to tell you that. And also—"

"That she's a slut?"

I want to just fall down in a heap. Curl up. Die.

Paige just hugs me again. Says, "I don't know, Ade. It doesn't—"

I get a crazy feeling and storm out of the garage and push my way to the bathroom. And I do the only thing I can think of that will stop the pain raging in my gut: I smack my head hard as I can against the sink.

There is a crunch and it's pretty deafening but nothing I haven't heard before.

The feeling, it hurts. The pain is like a flash of rain that washes clear a street. It's a shock of cold water and, honestly, it feels great.

Here is how it works, step-by-step: After my head hits, I fall back. I see the ceiling and the silly, ornate fan spinning lazy circles. I hit the floor, but it's like falling into water. I just sink down into it and the light fades. There's this cheesy-ass British TV show I saw once about some doctor dude who travels through time in like this blue telephone box and why it reminds me of what happens when I fall back into the floor is that the show opens with this pretty dope sequence of lights going down a tunnel to a sick synth riff. Leave out the synth riff, sadly, and keep the tunnel of psychedelic lights and you get a sense of what I'm seeing. And at the end of the tunnel? Well, it's like a curtain going up. There's like the swell of the symphony, only it's totally a drug-induced sort of rush, and then I open up my eyes to some future scene.

Not too long ago it was me downtown base jumping.

Now, I see myself on a beach.

This is likely after college and it's got that plastic sheen, that future fakiness.

I'm maybe in California, though I've only ever been there once when I was little, so it could be somewhere else. The sand is hot. My shoes are off. I'm in a wet suit. The ocean is wild, tossing up these enormous whitecaps. I can tell, just the way my chest is heaving and by tasting the salt water on my lips, that I've been in the water. I'm dry now, but judging by the fact that there's a surfboard in the sand beside me I'm guessing I was in there getting crazy. The sun is so high, so distant, it's like the earth has gone spinning off course.

This beach, it's not Colorado but, of course, I think of the phone call from the phlegmy dude. In the future, I laugh to myself. Whatever happens that he was stressed about, it's not that bad. If the dude's really a seer he's a super-sucky one.

Total crank.

Here, in the next decade, the warmth feels great. The sand too. But over the ocean there's a storm. Really dark clouds and fingers of lightning. This is why the waves are so big, the surfing so good. And probably, just because I'm such a future badass extreme sportsman, I'll bet I'm on this beach, at this very moment, just for these waves. Just for this storm.

These waves, my heart racing, I need to go back in.

I'm reaching over for my board when I notice the guy in the mask.

He's tall, young. Wearing jeans and a green wifebeater. The mask, it's one of those Mexican wrestler deals. Black with sequined flames around the eyes. Sequined white and red teeth around the mouth.

The guy says, "I thought I might see you here."

"Why's that?" I ask. My future voice is deeper. Raspy.

"The storm. The waves. This is totally your thing. Thirty-foot swells like this, you get guys from all over the country, hell, the world, descending on these beaches for a chance to ride one of those monsters. Go down in history."

"That why you're here?"

The masked man says, "Nah. I'm here to talk to you."

"So why the getup? Do I know you?"

"Not really."

"Well, if you don't mind, I think I'm going back out there. Can this wait?"

And the dude in the Mexican wrestling mask starts to say something, but the vision starts shaking. The sand is shaking. The world is shaking.

I'm pulled back through the tunnel.

Back through the lights.

Then I realize it's someone shaking me awake, shaking me out of my future stupor and back into the present. I'm not on the beach anymore, I'm on the floor of Oscar's bathroom and there is a burly dude with a ball cap pulled low over his eyes standing over me. He says, "I gotta take a piss, freak. Fucking. Move. It."

I can't stand from the strength of the Buzz, so the guy with the baseball cap just drags me out of the bathroom and leaves me on a throw rug in the hallway. My bottom lip is busted open, but all I can taste is cider.

Liz Chin finds me and rolls me onto my back. My vision's all distorted from the high rampaging through my veins and I can barely see her face. But I hear her just fine. She says, "How dare you do that shit at someone's house? During a party? You're sick."

I ask her to get Paige for me. "Please," I say, drooling.

She rolls her eyes and says, "Think your little dyke bitch is gonna nurse you back to health? You're pathetic, Ade. And by the way, your new girlfriend is sucking some dude's dick upstairs."

I close my eyes and focus on my high.

Everything in me has shattered.

The Buzz is all I've got left.

I'm floating in it until Paige shakes me back. She helps me up and takes me outside to the front lawn and then I collapse again.

She sits at my side crying, rubbing her nose on my sleeve.

She tells me that she hates me. She tells me that she wishes I was just dead sometimes. She says, her voice all breaking, "You're the most selfish person in the world."

FIVE

The Buzz lasts for about an hour.

It must be the alcohol–concussion combo but I'm pretty much unresponsive the entire time. Except for the twitching. When it wears off and I sit up, rubbing my eyes, Paige tells me that I was shaking like I was seizing. She tells me that a whole bunch of people asked her if they should call an ambulance and a whole other bunch of people told her that she should just put a bullet in my head. Paige says, "They told me I should just put you down."

"Thanks for defending me," I say.

"I didn't defend you," Paige says. "I just didn't shoot you."

I say, "Thanks for not putting me down. What time is it?"

"Two."

"Party still—"

"Yeah, but the beer's cashed, so most everyone's gone. By the way, she was looking for you and then she saw you and went back inside."

"Vauxhall?"

"She's over there."

Paige points over at a huddle of people smoking. Vauxhall's still got her costume on. She's a monster in the moonlight. I grimace and Paige notices. She pats me on the head and says, "You're not any better. You know that, right?"

"I have no idea what you're talking about," I say.

Paige laughs. "I'm going inside. Come in and get me when you want to leave."

I lie back on the lawn and stare up at the stars. The back of my head is still spinning and it's like I can feel the planet moving beneath me. The stars stuck and flashing and the soil whirling, me in the middle. I feel so much better. So much stronger.

"What're you looking at?"

It's Vauxhall sitting next to me. Her non-face all ghostly.

"Nothing," I say. "Space."

Vaux looks up. Shrugs. "You crack your skull open?"

"Heard about that?"

"Saw the blood. I don't understand why you're not in a hospital right now."

"I'm a professional." I manage to prop myself up on my elbow. I ask, "Any chance you're going to take off that costume?"

"I wasn't going to sleep in it."

"How about now? At least let me see your eyes. Easier to talk."

Vaux pauses and then takes off the shades. And then she takes off the hat and lets her hair hang down. Lets it breathe in the half-light. "How's that?"

"Great start."

And it is. Even with her face wrapped up she's still striking. And despite the emotional pain, I actually don't blame her. I'm disappointed but not mad. In my head I'm not ranting and railing about her being a slut. Maybe it's the head damage, but I'm not wanting to spit in her face. No matter how many dudes she hooks up with tonight or in the next week or month, the two of us will be together and in love and she will be mine. It's like a sour candy; this is just the bitter outer part. Eventual sweetness this way lies.

"Would you believe me if I told you that I've seen you before? That I've been thinking about you for years? Like in a dreaming sort of way?"

"Maybe. How many girls do you say this to?"

"Only you. You're the first. So, why'd you sing to me?"

"I don't know. You're cute."

With that, Vaux slowly unravels the bandages from her face. This is like a striptease but the payoff is so much better. She does it slow and teases something awful and part of me dies and is reborn with each inch of face she reveals. First her eyes. Then her nose and finally her lips and chin. She's amazing, in the night, under the stars. Her features aren't flattened by the fluorescent lights. Her skin breathes out here.

She asks, "What have you heard about me, Ade?"

"What do you mean?"

"You know, the rumors."

"I haven't heard any rumors about you, Vauxhall. Wouldn't matter, anyway."

She smiles. It's a heartbreaking smile.

But then I say, "I did see you with that guy Ryan a few hours ago. And . . ."

"Does that turn you off?"

I look at Vauxhall as hard as I can, push my eyes to see under her beauty. "I don't . . . don't think I'd be the right person to be judging you. It's not like I think it's, well, I just . . . Are you with Jimi?"

"What did Jimi tell you?"

"Nothing, but other people have said that you were."

Vauxhall nods. "It's complicated. A long story, but the short answer is that we have a connection but I don't think I love him. If that makes sense."

I swallow and it hurts. "I think it does."

The last few jags of Buzz go rattling down my nerves and my eyes roll back into my head for a second while I just let the feeling surge through me. The overwhelming peace of it like falling asleep but never sleeping. I don't know how long I'm like this when Vauxhall says, "Hey. Come on." And her voice shakes me back into the present. She is so incredibly soft in this light. Then, looking back at Oscar's house, she asks, "Want to go to the roof?"

"Okay."

We make our way back upstairs not saying anything.

Of course, I'm thinking maybe she's going to do with me what she did with Ryan Mar. Whatever exactly that was. Part of me, the lower part, is excited at the thought, has been sleepily dreaming of this. The other part, upper, doesn't want it to go down like this. Really doesn't want this.

But just being in Vauxhall's presence I'm getting goose bumps again.

It's like she's radioactive. Like there's a Geiger counter in my chest that's pinging violently the closer I am to her. This girl is not only beautiful and deeply funny and clever and complicated and so freaking flawed and hooking up with random assholes, but something tells me she's also like me. It's the same thing that tells me that we will be together. It is inevitability. Going upstairs I'm giddy with expectation, the same way I felt when I went into Black Bart's haunted cave at Casa Bonita for the first time. Scared. Jazzed.

Up the stairs she's in front and I can't peel my eyes away. Despite the boxy suit, I catch glimpses of feminine shapes beneath. A calf. Thigh. Ass cheek. It's intoxicating but over so quickly.

Now the party is just ten loud people. They're falling over each other. Lying in sleepy piles. Guys are copping feels. Girls are crying and talking too close to each other, face-to-face, like they might kiss or they're sharing each other's breath.

"Good view on the roof?" I ask.

"Sure," Vaux says. "Mountains sometimes."

"You come up on Oscar's roof often?"

"—"

Vaux and I make our way to a porch on the second floor and from there to a ladder that rocks back and forth when she climbs up.

"Not sure I'm in the best state to be climbing ladders," I say, trying to hold the ladder steady as I climb.

Over the roof, Vaux looks down at me and smiles, says, "I'm completely wasted and I made it. You worried you'll fall? Maybe hit your head?"

SIX

On the roof we can't see shit.

Just trees and the Christmas lights of distance houses and the haziness of stars. The roof slopes hard and the tiles are loose, but Vaux leads me over to a spot where the roof isn't nearly as angled and I sit down next to her and lean back on my hands.

She lights a cigarette and offers me a drag.

I take it even though I don't smoke.

Vaux starts with a story about how when she was little, her father bought her a jumbo-sized copy of Winsor McCay's comic strip *Little Nemo in Slumberland*. She tells me all about how the drawings just sucked her in, how even then it looked like cinema to her. Forgotten and neglected cinema. She tells me she identified with the princess who was always lonely. "As a kid," she says, "I'd think of my dad as King Morpheus. Only he was really sweet but just as magical. He'd made this whole thrilling world for me to play in."

"Sounds nice. That's a lot like my dad."

"A dreamer, huh?"

"You could say that."

Vaux switches gears, asks, "How'd you get it? Your ability?"

I laugh, nervous. Ask, "What are you talking about?"

Vauxhall says, "You know."

Still being coy I ask, "Did someone tell you some—"

"Hitting your head and walking away from it the way you do. The way your eyes are rolling around in your skull like you're high as a kite. I can see there's something more going on with you, Ade," Vauxhall says. "Besides, your friend Paige told me that you can see the future. And even if you don't believe me that I believe that, I do. I can see it. I can read it on you. So, please, tell me how it happened."

This girl, I want to explain everything. I want so much to laugh and cry right now. But I relax and just start talking. "An accident," I say. "Just a fluke."

"Typical origin story, huh? Radioactive spider bite, gamma rays, the usual."

"Not that spectacular."

I tell Vaux it went back to dissecting toads in eighth grade. I tell her that before we could even get started, before I'd even sat down at the lab bench, scalpel in hand, I accidentally stepped on Kevin Harris's new shoes and he caught me with a fist on the right side of my face, just below the orbital socket of my eye. I say, "I went spinning into Vanessa Katz and then tumbled over a lab stool and wound up on the linoleum. My forehead hit first and my skull bounced. Went black for only heartbeats, but in that darkness I saw something. Like a short film or a trailer for a movie. A young woman and an older man meeting. It's hard to recall the details now but what I overheard was that he'd been lost after an accident. Something with amnesia. Or maybe he was in hiding. It was on the news. Anyway, they ran into each other at a food court and hugged and sobbed and sputtered in front of the Chick-fil-A."

Vaux says, "Classy."

I tell Vaux about the Buzz. I tell her how, for me, at first, it was like being over-caffeinated but in the best way imaginable. I say, "It was a breaking-the-laws-of-physics high. That first time I was sure I was beaming light. Everyone could see it. Kids in the halls stopping to look at me. Pointing me out across the basketball courts. I was radiating some heavenly light or something. The Buzz lasted until the next morning and then melted away, like how your body melts back into itself after a hard workout."

Vaux nods, staring off into the non-view. She says, "I know that feeling."

"You do?"

"Yeah, that so strange?"

"Uh, no. I'm just surprised is—"

Vauxhall does this finger-twirl thing, says, "Come on, don't leave me in suspense. Tell me the rest of your story."

"Okay. So, two days after the knockout I was at the mall with my friends and I saw the girl from the vision. I sat down in the middle of a record store and watched the dream come real and the players took the stage and it was acted out exactly as I'd seen it. Every detail. The tears. The intense smiles. I couldn't breathe. I hurled when I got home."

"Must have been amazing," Vauxhall says. "The power of that."

"After that it was just me chasing the Buzz around. It's harder to start a fight than you'd imagine. I said some of the worst things I could think of to the worst people I knew and still came up empty. What it came down to was me going bat-shit crazy just for the thrill of a ten-second ride into the future. Something I shouldn't be able to do. Something that no one should be able to do. It felt wrong but so right."

Vauxhall puts her hand on my shoulder. Squeezes it. This is the first time she's intentionally touched me, and there's an electric current. All the hairs on my arms stand up. I can feel each and every one of them.

What's really funny is how open I am about my ability. How I'm just letting it all spill out. Then again, I'm talking to the only person I've ever really loved.

Vaux asks, "What do you see when you knock yourself out now?"

"Decades out. I need to push it to get the Buzz stronger."

"What's it like, your future?"

"Clean, fun. I don't have any lasting head injuries or any brain problems. At least not that I can tell. It's what's been keeping me doing it, really. Knowing that I end up fine. It's funny, but in the future, I'm like this daredevil. Kind of a *Jackass* sort of dude."

"Like what?"

"Jumping off buildings. Stunts. I have no idea why."

"And you're not like that now?"

Up on the rooftop with an invisible city spilling out in front and all our peers asleep or rocking drunkenly beneath, I sigh and say, "I'm looking forward to it but, sometimes, I worry I'm out of control. Even now. I mean I know that last summer I was out of control, but I'm not sure when, if, I'll ever really get under control. Some of the stuff I've done, I'm not really proud of. Most of it, thankfully, I don't remember."

This is a lie. I remember a lot of it but I don't want her see me that way, to think of me that way. Not now.

Vaux can see I'm holding back. She says, "I was out of control for a while too."

That thought, her kind of out of control, it has my stomach sinking.

She says, "I did some really . . . regrettable things."

"I'm sorry."

Vaux reaches into her purse and pulls out this tiny digital video camera and then flicks it on and says, "I think we'll start here."

"Start what?"

Her face half hidden by the camera, its lone little red eye now her right eye, she says, "This is the first take, the first fourteen minutes, of my new film. Not sure of the title yet, but we'll get this. Free-form at the moment."

Awkward under the camera's stare, I ask, "What's it about?"

"About when the past meets the future. I've always said that by the time I was seventeen I'd have made a feature-length documentary film."

"So, do I—"

"Just act natural," Vaux interrupts. "Tell me about your family. About your childhood. What you liked to do as a kid. Your best friends. Your first kiss. Tell me about who you used to be."

I ask, "Used to be?"

Vaux nods. "Don't you find that who you used to be is always more interesting than who you are?"

"Not really."

The camera says, "Then you just haven't thought about it enough. Tell me something weird. Something that will give me some glimpse into you. More about your mom."

I say, "Dragonflies."

"Huh?"

"My mom, when I was six, just after my dad started drinking, before she found All Souls Chapel and was still working at the bakery, she got totally obsessed with them. The Green Darners. The Mosquito Hawks. Darning Needles. Dragonflies. Russian folklore has it that dragonflies are devil's knitting needles. Romania they're horses possessed by Satan. Sweden they weigh the souls of the damned."

"Spooky."

"Mom dragged me all over the foothills looking for them. We had this Corvair. Blue and dented everywhere by some cataclysmic hailstorm in eighty-nine. We called it Pineapple Face on account of the dings. The way my mom drove it was like one of those centrifugal force rides at the state fair. The kind you stand up in and it spins around and plasters you back against the walls. I always loved those rides. Love how it takes a few seconds longer than you expect for the force, or whatever, to hit, just a few seconds longer of stillness before your stomach catches up. Those seconds are magic. Mom driving the car was the same way. She'd turn lanes so fast, without signaling, that I'd see it before I felt it. My stomach was still in the other lane for a few seconds and then whoosh, it'd come sliding back smooth as silk."

"Sounds fun in a really stupid sort of way."

I laugh. "Only times she'd slow down was when she saw a dragonfly. She'd pull the emergency brake right there, right in the middle of the highway sometimes, and jump out and chase after them with the nets she had in the trunk. Then she'd hold what she caught in front of me and say, 'Aeronautic marvels. It's the wings. Two pairs. Two pairs and they can coordinate those and move them so fast that's it almost against the laws of physics. Almost.' I always tested her. 'Which one is that, Mom?' 'Shadow Darner. *Aeshna umbrosa*. Like ambrosia. The foodstuff of the gods.' It was fun back then but now, now it's pretty obvious how crazy she was. Is."

Vaux, taking her eye from out behind the camera, says, "You're a dream. Go on."

And she films and I talk. I talk until nearly dawn, when the lights of the city that we can't see are fading out, blending in with the light of the sun. I talk through my childhood, but it's like it was a movie I saw. Not something I really experienced. I keep coming back to me now.

Then I take the camera and put the questions to her.

Watching Vaux in flickering green light, her face glowing, she tells me stories about her father, how he would get her stoned and take her to rock concerts ("Summer I turned fourteen we hit five shows, even traveled as far as Topeka to see Bowie.") and how they used to see *The Rocky Horror Picture Show* every Friday night for like two years. Said that she was practically raised in that movie theater by squadrons of drag queens and Monty Python–quoting geeks.

She's tells me stories about her mother. About her cousins. Extended family. What foods she most likes. Which ones she hates. Her favorite colors and what they mean to her. Her favorite clothes. Why she loves movies. What music she despises. She goes ballistic with politics. Cries about chimpanzees and Amazon destruction. She laughs about her period. Recites Baudelaire. And she sings a number from *Grease 2*, something about reproduction.

Vauxhall makes it clear that this theatrical thing, it isn't just an act. It isn't like the way Jimi does his show for attention. The real Vauxhall is on the outside. Her heart right there for anyone to see it, to touch it. Any emotion crossing her, it's suddenly out in the open. I've never met anyone so unafraid of talking. She'll mix it up with everyone.

Vaux also tells me that she has only a handful of friends.

She tells me that a lot of people, well, they hate her.

Girls in particular.

Mothers, teachers, coaches, authority figures. All of them give her bad looks.

She says she's not lonely. That she's fine not having tons of friends. She says she doesn't give a shit. She's tough that way. Vaux tells me her dad trained her. She says, "That's exactly the word for it, too."

"How's that?"

She says, "My dad was just so antiauthority. He was always giving the finger to the man. Calling out the establishment. Hippie stuff. At the dinner table, he'd go on these long-winded rants. Wind up hoarse from shouting. He told me to never shut up. To never stifle myself. Always express and never regret."

"Cool."

"Yeah. Only he was just outspoken. Didn't ever act on any of it."

I say, "Not like you."

"That's sweet."

Vauxhall is silent for a minute and for that minute it's just us and the whirl of the satellites above us. And then Vauxhall takes my hand and holds it in hers and she looks at me with eyes as wide as I've seen them and says, "The reason I hang out with Jimi is because he's one of the most beautifully fucked-up people I've ever met."

"And that's attractive to you?"

"The things his mother did to him," Vaux says. "She made him run for miles until his feet were blistered, she made him swim in an ice-cold lake until he was blue and shaking uncontrollably. I can't let him deal with that alone. He needs me. Right now, he really, really needs me."

"And what do you need, Vaux?"

She's quiet. Breathes in, breathes out. "I just need someone to let me be myself."

Vaux sighs, puts her head on my shoulder, and just keeps it there. The way I'm sitting, the weight of her head is pushing me back. Slow-motion toppling me over. But I stay, even with my head still kind of whirling from the hit I took in the bathroom, I stay. Eventually, my shoulder is numb. My hands are numb. Hell, even my back is numb. But I don't dare move. I want her here.

The sun's long been up when Paige yells up at us.

She tells us she's been sleeping for like two hours and it'd be nice if we could leave. She tells us the house is just filled with passed-out people and she's missing her bed. Paige says, "Doesn't your ass hurt being up on that roof all night?"

Vaux and I clamber down from the roof and my ass does hurt.

Before I walk Paige back to the car, I tell Vauxhall I had a wonderful time talking to her only I whisper it because I'm hoarse from talking. I tell her that I'm anxious to see her documentary. Vauxhall smiles and waves good-bye, says, "When it's done, I'll be sure to show you first."

We don't kiss. We don't even hug.

The most intimate relationship I've been in and we don't even touch each other.

SEVEN

Just as we're pulling out onto Grape, I see Vauxhall catch a ride home from Chris Hirata.

In the car, as they're driving off, Chris has his arm around her shoulders. I can only imagine what they'll be doing next. I do. And then I'm sick because I do. I'm so ready to go home.

Whole drive to Paige's the both of us are super quiet. Almost comatose. At one point Paige asks me if I had a nice time up on the roof.

I say, "Yeah. Incredible."

"And the Jimi thing?" she asks.

"True. Maybe a problem for the time being, but I'm not too stressed."

"You look stressed."

"Just tired. I've seen it all, remember. All good."

When I drop her off, before she steps out of my car, Paige gives me a kiss on the cheek and tells me to take it easy. She tells me not to think too hard about it. She says, "You took a nasty hit tonight, Ade. If I were you, I'd just rest. Take tomorrow off, okay, champ?"

I shrug. "Okay, babe."

A few blocks from my house, at a red light, I pull down the mirror on the sun visor and take a look at my jacked-up face. All the usual bruising is there. The usual cuts and scrapes. I've got a nasty welt on my forehead and it's swollen out like a gourd.

I'm not ready to go home, so I just drive. The sun is blinding as it balloons up over the apartment buildings and McMansions near Wash Park. I drive past school and realize the reason I'm not ready to go home is because I'm thinking too much about Vauxhall. I'm jealous of Chris and Ryan. I want so badly to rewind time and kiss her on that roof. To convey that I can't wait for it to just happen in its time. That she can be herself with me and me only. That Jimi isn't special. That Jimi is just sick.

I need the Buzz again. I need it terrible.

Fact is: The future is just so damned addictive.

And cars are so easy to crash.

Used to be, only two years back, before I could drive, that skateboarding or biking or even just walking into things was the easiest way to propel myself into the future. But the collateral damage was heavy. Mostly broken bones and busted-out teeth. Looks seriously suffered. I wore helmets and even padding but still I'd come away with way more bruises and cuts than I'd hoped. Got so that sometimes, bad times, the high would be hardly worth it. And then came the car. Give me an empty street and a wall or a telephone pole or even a tree and I'm on my way to not-yet land. I'm very careful. Cars are big. Fast. What I do, it takes practice. To not really really wreck the car takes serious skill.

And this morning, at five to six, that's just what I do.

There's this spot just off Hale Parkway, back in a neighborhood, with a low wall and a telephone pole. I angle my car just right, just so, and I'm able to hit it going twenty. I'm adept at this, making it so I do minimal damage to my '96 Honda Accord but ensuring that my head rebounds off the steering wheel like a basketball.

Only it doesn't just rebound but it snaps back and in the hollow part of my skull, my brain goes bouncing and the blood starts flowing. I see the tunnel again. It looks the way Vegas would if it were rolled up into a tube. Walls of light, flashing and glowing. And in the walls are shapes and figures but nothing exact, nothing definite. The edges here are all worn down, the colors reduced to static.

Another concussion.

Another vision.

Actually the same vision. I'm back on the California beach with the storm crashing against the sky and the waves getting higher and higher as the sun glows dimmer and dimmer. Again, there's a surfboard at my side. Again, the wet suit. Again, the salt water taste on my lips. It's like I'm starting over again.

And what's really crazy is I've never had this happen before. Of the barrels of visions I've had, I've never seen the same thing twice. Sure, I've been in the same place before but never at exactly the same time. What's going on here makes no sense.

My feet in the sand, I'm assuming that wires were crossed.

Or maybe this isn't the future but a memory of the last vision.

Maybe I'm not unconscious enough to throw my mind forward.

I grab my surfboard and stand up. Start walking to the waves. And as my toes hit the cold water, I start thinking that maybe this is different. The guy in the mask last time said that he expected me here. Maybe I try to surf these storm waves all the time. Maybe this is just another of one of my yearly trips to the coast.

But then again, maybe not.

Sitting across from me, on a big red towel, his head angled down, his eyes burning the air between us, is the masked man. He's here, again, only this time the Mexican wrestler mask is red with flames all around it. He's staring me down and with his index finger on his right hand, he's motioning me over.

I walk to the edge of his towel and sit in the sand. What makes him stand out this time isn't the mask so much as it's the white suit he's wearing. The guy is sitting cross-legged, he is filing his nails.

"Back again, huh?" I ask.

The man says, "Actually, I'd say you're back again."

"You've been waiting?"

"Not long. I had a feeling you'd be back and so I came 'round to see."

I look up and down the beach. It's lined with surfers watching the clouds and the waves. The sand is being whipped up down near a pier and it blows in little funnels. The sky is getting really dark.

"Cutting to the chase," I say with my again deeper voice. "What exactly is it that you came here to see me for? Is there some sort of problem?"

"Yes." The masked guy's eyes narrow. "Big problem."

"And?"

The suited wrestler pauses. "That's the thing, you're just not ready to hear what I have to say. And I don't mean the you that's here on this beach, I mean the real you. The kid you. See that storm?" The man looks over his shoulder at the black broccoli clouds.

"Couldn't miss it."

"The closer that storm gets, the more sense this will all make. I'm guessing that when it's right on top of us, truth's going to just spill right out and you'll be ready to understand it all."

My throat tightens. I'm confused. "Is this the future?"

"Yes, but I'm not in your future."

"You're not? Then . . . ?"

"Ade, I'm in your mind."

There is a flash like lightning's hit the water near us but when the brightness of it fades away I'm no longer on the beach. I'm back in my car and the sun is scorching down. It's flattening the whole world out.

Back to now. Return to regular programming.

I'm confused.

This future that I've seen now more than once, which is, in itself, totally bizarre and inexplicable, has got me shaken. Who is this guy with the mask? Isn't he in the future? It certainly looks like he is. Could he really be in my head? I hope not. And how? That's just fucked up. Maybe I'm dreaming him? Maybe in the near future I spend a lot of time on a beach tripping.

Fact is: I need to stop stressing and just enjoy the Buzz.

One thing I've learned after doing this so many times, after seeing what comes next so many times, is that no matter how strange the future seems, it pales in comparison to the present. This masked dude, whatever. This joker, I'm already over it.

And I need the Buzz so badly right now.

EIGHT

Sucks that I'm snapped out of it too soon by someone knocking on the windshield.

It's my ex-girlfriend. Angry, I lean forward and my broken nose just lets loose like a faucet. Belle's seen this before. Plenty of times.

She's sitting on the hood of my car smoking a cigarette and wearing the very same outfit she wore when I first met her. The leather boots. Black skirt. White dress shirt. She's got her blond hair slicked back and if it weren't for the hastily applied makeup and the scars on her arms she'd be perfect for a sexy temp or a trampy accountant.

Belle watches me intently, takes a long drag, and then says, "Pop the trunk."

I do, though the Buzz has my head fogged and I almost pass out reaching down for the trunk pop lever. Belle slips off the hood and comes back with my emergency med kit. She slips into the passenger seat and opens the box and pulls out some gauze and white tape and pours a little hydrogen peroxide onto the gauze. "Lean back," she says. I do. She wipes my forehead and I can hear the peroxide foaming up over my left eye. Belle's face very close to mine, her breath cool on my forehead, she says, quietly, "You didn't say anything."

"About what?" I ask, feeling a loose tooth with my tongue.

"About the girl," Belle says. "It's kind of a big deal, right?"

"Oh, right. Right."

"I got a text. Everyone's talking. Why didn't you think to call me?"

I just shake my head.

"It's six in the morning, Belle. On a Saturday. What the hell are you doing here?"

Belle smiles. "I followed you home from the party."

"You were at Oscar's? I didn't see you."

Belle laughs, more to herself than to me. "Yeah, what else is new."

What Belle isn't saying and what her eyes are is that she's monumentally jealous. This is what I thought she was dreading. My fault, really, first time we ever hooked up I told Belle about my vision. I told her about the girl and it made Belle a bit crazy. Totally understandable. Frankly, it was pretty lame of me to mention it at all and not a bit surprising that every time we were together, at the movies or at Piggies at the Tivoli or at Paris on the Platte or INXS, she was always looking over her shoulder for the girl with brown hair and green eyes. The girl I told her way too much about.

Of course, I was looking for the girl too. We'd be making out in those leather chairs at the Cherry Creek Mall beneath the cylindrical elevators and I'd be hardly into it because my heart was racing thinking I'd seen my vision girl step into The Sharper Image. I can't even tell you how many times I'd pause our conversations to chase after a shadow, how many times I canceled our dates or forgot to show up because I was sure, so freaking sure, that Vauxhall would appear at any minute.

Who in their right mind could put up with that?

Amazingly, she did. For a while she seemed okay with it. Honestly, it was like Belle was just that happy to be with me, just that happy to have found someone she could really bond with even if it was temporary. To be fair, when I wasn't distracted, things were decent. We did have some nice conversations. We laughed a ton. Made out well together.

Then, October, Belle split. Shocking thing was that it wasn't because of my future fascination, wasn't even because of my being an emotional retard, it was something even I didn't expect.

But right now what I thought was jealousy at first has grown into a whole different sort of animal. Far nastier. Far crueler. Right now, her face in my face, Belle says, "Funny name, Vauxhall. Is that foreign?"

I say, "I hear it's a neighborhood in London."

"Okay. So this is it, right?"

"I . . . I'm not really sure—"

Belle leans in and then tapes a folded piece of gauze on my head with the white tape. When she finishes, she takes a penlight from the kit and shines it in my eyes, one at a time. Then she sits back and says, "Of course this is it, Ade. The future never lies. You told me that."

I shrug.

Belle says, "If I could charge you for the number of times I've bandaged your ass up, I could buy myself a new car. I'd be even richer if I got a dime for every single time I told you that you were sick. And dangerous. And messed up. You know that? That you are, right? Wonder if your new girlfriend knows?"

I say, "You're just jealous."

"Please. You're an addict."

"That what you think of me?"

"That's what everyone thinks of you, Ade. Everyone but this new girl. She'll come around soon enough. Seriously, I feel sorry for Vauxhall. Unless she likes being neglected and watching her boyfriend beat the shit out of himself for some impossible high, then she's in for a lonely time."

Fact is: Belle didn't leave me because I was waiting for someone else. No, she left me because the future I was waiting for didn't show up.

October and we were downtown walking the mall. It was one of those fall days when it feels like it's about to snow, when the air is pregnant with frost. We had hot chocolate and were reading books at the Tattered Cover. She was acting distant. I asked her if there was a problem and she led me upstairs over to the self-help section, where there was a couch. She sat me down and laid it all out simple: "Nothing you've seen, not your vision girl or any of the other future stuff you've knocked yourself out for, has happened. I've got to tell you, Ade, you're the lamest psychic I've ever met."

I told her I wasn't a psychic.

"Divinator, prognosticator, whatever. You suck."

And it hurt. It hurt most because of what she said next: "It didn't bother me that you were always drooling over your doodles and notes about some girl that you'll probably never actually see and it didn't bother me that you're always passed out or barely there, what bothered me was that it was for nothing. You live the life of a rock star but you can't sing, you can't play guitar, hell, you're not even a keyboardist. You suck, Ade, and I'm done wasting my time. I'm going to find the real deal."

Today, in my car, she lights a smoke and repacks the emergency kit.

I ask her not to smoke. "Gives me a headache," I say.

She laughs at that and then gets out and stomps out her cigarette the way she'd stomp out a spider. "This is pretty monumental, Ade. I'm shocked—"

"Yeah. Crazy, right?"

"Crazy." And she says it like the word's stuck to her tongue. Like it's caramel.

And then she leans in and kisses me on the cheek. Then she puts a finger to her lips. She fakes embarrassment. "Can I still do that?"

When we were dating Belle was very conscious of kissing me. Any chance she could, any moment my mouth was free, her lips were on mine. Halfway through a conversation, my mouth full of food, trying to yawn, and Belle's lips were on mine. Being in public not only didn't matter, it spurred her on. On the leather chairs at the Cherry Creek Mall with moms pushing strollers past us fast. In the back of the movie theater with people shushing us, whispering, "Can you keep it down?" I'll admit I wasn't just sitting there letting it happen. My hands were everywhere. An hour with Belle left me exhausted, my lips chapped, my hands aching. There were times I'd get home at night and find my face smeared with makeup, lipstick smudges like slashes across my cheeks. I would find bruises in the oddest places, bruises that looked like fingerprints behind my knee, on my collarbone. And the hickies. Good God, the hickies.

Right now, literally crashed out in my car, I ignore Belle's comment, her kiss, and walk her over to her ancient Accord. She gets in and rolls the window down, says, "It's a good thing I follow you around all the time, isn't it? Otherwise the cops would be all over you."

"You should really just transfer to Mantlo."

"Just to be closer to you, right?"

"Of course."

After we broke up Belle basically vanished. I'd see her at parties here and there and the part of me that was still pissed at her would ask her stupid things like, "So did you find your messiah yet?" She'd pretty much ignore me. Act as though I was being too immature. Also she was drunker and higher than ever. People were whispering things about designer drugs, about hard drugs. Not a month later and she was showing up at odd times wearing all manner of trendy clothes and wiping her nose all the time. She'd berate me with stories about the artists and designers and hackers and drug dealers she was circulating with. "You can't even believe the lofts these people inhabit," she'd say. "It's sick, bird!" Soon she had an older man at her beck and call, it was rumored he drove a Benz and was a banker, but none of us ever saw him. Certainly did keep her knee-deep in gifts, though.

The end of last summer, after all the brawls and the bruises and the incident at the bowling alley, I got in kind of a weird place. After July, after meeting Borgo, I cooled my jets briefly. Focused on something else for a few weeks. Focused on Belle. End of August I saw her at a pizza joint with her dad and she looked so different. She was trashy and brilliant at the same time, like a million-dollar gutter punk. After I'd finished dinner I hung around until she left and then I followed her. Creepy, yes, but necessary. Kind of I missed Belle. I needed to know what was going on.

I trailed her like a true detective.

I went slow. I swerved in and out of traffic. When she pulled into a parking garage on Welton, I paused behind a Dumpster and watched her go into an apartment building. Then I ditched my ride and ran in after her, saw her duck into an elevator and took the stairs pausing at each floor to see—cautiously as ever—just where she was getting off. And, of course, she saw me.

Belle reeked of pot and her eyes were watering fierce but she stayed staring at me. Me, hiding behind an ornamental plant, and looking so guilty. There was no hiding it. I just stood up, waved, said, "Hey, Belle. Yeah, I was following you."

She made this snicker sound and actually put a hand on her hip like this was a scene in a sitcom. "Ade, how embarrassing is this for you?"

"Pretty embarrassing."

"Why are you following me?"

"Just wanted to see what you've been up to. I saw you at the pizza place, noticed how different you're looking, and figured it might be an interesting mystery to try and solve. You know, Junior Detective style. So what are you up to?"

"If you had any real abilities, Ade, you'd already know."

And with that she flicked me off and marched down a hallway.

Flash forward to now, my body swimming with good vibrations, and only girl ever to call me a failure for not delivering a future where I leave her for someone else. Belle is, sitting here with the thick eyeliner and the drop-dead body, the one girlfriend I've had who left me for not being me enough.

As she gets out of the car, Belle winks at me and asks, "You okay to drive, Ade?"

"Sure," I say. "Professional, remember?"

Belle blows me a kiss and walks back to her car and peels out.

Woozy, I nod.

Slowly. Drunkenly.

The Buzz pummeling me into bliss.

NINE

I get home in a record forty-five minutes.

Normally it takes me ten but I'm delirious enough from the knockout that I have to pull over every few blocks and close my eyes to stop from seeing double. Most of the way I go ten miles an hour.

Thankfully, I can use the front door. Too early for the freaks.

At home I doze off in front of the TV for the whole day. Eat nothing. Drink a soda. Mom's at All Souls and doesn't get home until night. She wakes me up off the couch, turns off the tube, and sits down on the rug and sobs at the sight of me.

"Bad this time?" I ask.

Mom nods.

I try and stand, but just fall over. Pass out. When I wake up again Mom's putting a cold compress on my head and holding a mirror to my mouth. "To make sure you're still breathing," she says. "Your left pupil, it's almost totally blown out."

"Greater than six?"

"It's like ten millimeters, Ade."

"Damn."

Mom makes beef with snow peas and sesame cauliflower and I eat dinner lying down but puke up most of it. Mom, with a bucket at the ready, says, "I don't even know why you bother eating in the first place."

"I saw her again last night, Mom."

"That's wonderful."

"It was. But complicated."

"Ummm, women are always complicated."

I move the conversation forward to avoid hearing more biblical passages.

"Mom, you ever worry about the fact that I failed most of my classes last year?"

She pats my head. "No, baby. This, this is just a stepping-stone to the better you."

"Better?"

"The you with Christ."

On the back of the pantry door Mom's got this black velvet

painting of Jesus she picked up at a flea market in Pueblo. In this painting, J.C. is young and vibrant and he's got a halo of sunbeams around his head. He's sitting on a lawn and kids are sitting in his lap. Kids of every color and creed. All of them total stereotypes. The Native American kid, he's got a feather in his long black hair. The white girl, she's blond with blue eyes and rosy cheeks. The black kid, he's got an Afro and a multicolored African robe on. Mom's always loved looking at this painting. She says that the one white boy, the kid with brown eyes and sneakers, is me. The one white boy, he's closest to Christ, sitting right in the middle of his lap. Sitting with his head right at Our Lord's heart. Even if I get old and frail and miserable or if I'm strung out on drugs and wasted away with my teeth gone or a drooling vegetable from all the concussions, Mom'll still see me as this one kid. To her, I'll always be right there with Jesus.

Tonight I don't try to say anything about Mom's obsession. I don't make a crack or sigh like I usually do. Just try to clear the puke taste from my mouth by swallowing so many times that I'm all out of spit and my mouth is dry. Mom, hands on my head again, fingers in my hair, says, "You never talk to your dad about this, do you?"

"No."

"Why not?"

"Because Dad isn't alive anymore, Mom."

"When was the last time you went to the hospital to see him? You remember, used to be that you'd go every day after school. Pedal your bike all the way, cheeks all flushed, huffing and puffing. Your shirt so sweaty I'd have to wash it twice to get the—"

"I was in middle school, Mom. That was years ago."

Mom puts on a frown. It's disappointment more than anything.

"What if I told you that he needs you? Right now more than ever, Ade. He cares about you. It's just that he . . . he's kind of lost out there. He's in limbo and needs a voice to guide him back."

I give in. Sigh loud. "I went to see him four months ago. And it wasn't Dad. Not the dad I grew up with. Not the one who taught me how to ride a bike or do a flip turn. Not him, Mom. Not that guy. That guy is like this emaciated thing. You know, like when the mad townspeople crack open the crypt to stake the vampire and they find . . . well, they find something like what's lying in that hospital bed."

Mom has tears forming but wipes them away before they can run. "Ade, you're being very cruel . . ."

I lean in, give my mom a hug. Hold her tight and in my arms she shakes. Then I say, "It's hard for me. I don't like being reminded of who he used to be. I'm not sure what to believe, either. I'm not sure that he's there. I know you think he is. That maybe talking to him will help him, but I'm not so convinced. You know what Dr. Ruby says. She says that Dad's not actually—"

"I know," Mom sobs. "I know." And then, pulling herself away, straightening herself out, pushing back her hair and her glasses, she says, "We can go visit him together sometime. That would be nice, wouldn't it? If we go as a family?"

I nod and then notice a text on my phone. It's from Jimi.

It says: *Meet me at 9. Ellis.*

It's already half past eight.

"I need to go. Can you drive me?"

My mom gives me a frown

Then she produces the Revelation Book from under the Coffee

table and flicks a pen out from behind her hair. I fill her in on the vision and, just to get her jazzed, I add a detail about some random surfer dude being pulled out of the ocean by the lifeguard in Christ pose. It works. Mom's hands are shaking as she writes it all down. I do not mention the guy in the mask. I know that will just send her into a fit. When I'm done, and when Mom stops scribbling, I ask her if she'll take me to Ellis Elementary, explain it's for a school project. She laughs. "Don't try and trick me, Ade," she says. "You have a date or something?"

"No. Nothing like that."

Mom asks, "How do you plan on getting back?"

"I'll get a ride. Don't stress."

"You're in no shape to be going anywhere, Ade. No shape at all."

"Mom . . . come on. Scout's honor I'll be careful. Just a school project."

She gets up, gets the car keys, and then throws me a sweater. Says, "Proverbs 21:31: 'The horse is prepared against the day of battle: but safety is of the Lord.' You keep that in mind, okay?"

"Sure, Mom. Always."

TEN

Mom drops me a block away, near the playground at Ellis Elementary School.

Jimi wants to meet up here 'cause he can skateboard and do rail slides without being hassled by the cops. This is a typical evening for Jimi. Skating and smoking and sipping from this silver flask he claims he stole from his mother. What's inside is rum, he claims, but I'm sure it's vodka.

When I see him he's tying to jump a two-foot wall that rings the playground but he keeps missing, his deck smashing, him falling. Him cursing and spitting and stomping on it. I yell out, "Hey!"

He asks, "Been here long?"

"Minutes."

"But long enough to see me jack up that jump, right?"

"Yeah."

Jimi takes a swig from his flask. He's wearing flannel even though it's sweaty hot. He looks me over, says, "I like the headband. The gore really adds something to it. Honestly, I wouldn't recognize you without a shiner."

"So, what's up, Jimi?"

Taking another sip and wiping his upper lip with his sleeve, Jimi says, "I just wanted to tell you that Vauxhall, well, she's mine."

"—"

"I know you, Ade. You're a screwup. How are you even still in school?"

"'Cause I'm special."

Jimi chuckles. "Yeah, helmet special. More like you've got some connections or everyone just feels that sorry for you. Good karma is all."

I sit down on the wall Jimi's been trying to jump. "That's the only reason you asked me to come over here?"

Jimi sits down next to me. Hands me his flask. I take a swig. It's vodka.

He says, "Just because she sang to you, just because the two of you spent a romantic evening together, it doesn't mean you're suddenly in like Flynn. Get it? She's fragile. Doesn't have friends outside of a few guys and even them, she's not someone a lot of people—"

"I get it, Jimi."

He takes another gulp of alcohol and leans in close. It is over-dramatic the way he does it. It's Theater 101 and the way he narrows his eyes has got me irritated. He says, "You can't get so uptight about it."

"I'm not uptight about anything, Jimi. I don't even—"

"We're living in the future, buddy. People want what they want. They go out and get it. Love something and you set it free, you know? That's what you do. But when people hear about her with guys at parties. Sometimes girls. Her just, well . . . it freaks people out. The whole slut thing starts up. The whole—"

"What exactly are you trying to tell me?"

Jimi takes another swig, makes another cough. He shakes his head. "She's a drama kid. She's loud and in your face and at the same time she's secretive. She's trying to change. She's looking for something new."

"You love her or something?"

"No. No. But I respect her. I want her to do what she wants. Truth is, the girl has been all over me for the past year. She just can't get enough. Does that make you mad?"

"Mad?"

"Yeah. Sick to your stomach? Queasy? I know you like her, Ade. I can tell."

Part of me, it wants to run screaming and tearing my hair out.

Jimi picks up his board, messes with the wheels. Says, "If you haven't already, you'll fall in love with her. Despite yourself you will."

"You didn't."

Jimi's like, "Maybe I did, for a while. But I can tell she's into you."

"Into me?"

"Intrigued by you."

I try not to smile, but it's hard.

Jimi slaps me on the back, slams down another swig of vodka, and says, "You want to hang out with her? Be close to her? Well, you and me are going to have to become close buds. That okay with you, Ade?"

Of course it's okay with me, but I don't answer right away. I mull it over. Actually, I make it look like I'm mulling it over, but really my mouth wants to scream out yes a thousand times. In my mind hanging out with Jimi is only hanging out with Vauxhall. In my mind he will just slowly fade away. Overzealous actor that he is, he will be on the cutting room floor in no time. To Jimi I say: "Of course."

Jimi gets this big shit-eating grin and says, "How messed up you are is funny. You remember when you and me and Paige and that guy Larry went to see that one movie, the one that was kind of like a Western but was all sorts of mystical and crazy? You remember that night?"

I don't. "What movie?"

"You don't actually remember going? This was only like in July or something."

"—"

"Well, Vauxhall was there. She was sitting two rows behind us."

"What?"

"Yeah. I don't think you guys met then, but she's been around for a while. Just new to you I guess. Don't know how you could forget that movie, it was fucking nuts."

I try not to let my face show just how crazy that makes me feel. I'm sure if someone else were listening right now, someone like Paige or maybe my mom, they'd say I'd missed the forest for the trees. Or something. They'd say that all my knocking myself out, all my diving for the Buzz, has gotten me so messed up that I missed meeting Vauxhall by months. Months. Being who I am, being aware of myself, I know that's a lie. I'd never miss her. Not in a million years would I miss her.

Fact is: Jimi's just a jealous prick.

He takes another swig from his bottomless flask and gets up and kicks his skateboard down, does a slow circle around the playground while I watch. He comes back and pulls out a cigarette. Him lighting the cigarette with a Zippo is the same as him doing everything, anything, else. It's an act. A pose for a reaction. It's as though Jimi can see photographers camped out in the trees around the schoolyard. This is for them as much as for me.

"I wonder what she'll learn about you, Ade. What secrets she'll uncover."

I say, "There's not much."

Jimi gives a brash laugh. "Oh, I'm sure there's plenty. How 'bout we find out?"

ELEVEN

First of all, I'm stressing about the car being stolen.

There is no way that Jimi can afford this vehicle.

"It's a sixty-nine Dodge Dart Swinger," he says, grinning in the rearview. "Been customed with a hopped-up 340 and a Pertronix Ignitor and a, uh . . ."

Jimi's flailing. In the mirror, I can see the act fade.

"Anyway," he says, staring me down, "it's freaking fast."

And then there's the fact that Jimi is driving sixty down Monaco, weaving in and out of traffic, tossing cigarette butts out the windows, talking on his cell, making faces at me, and grabbing Vauxhall's thigh so tight the marks of his fingers are still there in the skin of her.

Just past Eighth Avenue, Jimi tells me that where we're going is secret. He tells me that a guy like me, a guy used to doing crazy things, should have no problem with. He says, "I think when you see it, you're going to just drop a load in your pants."

Vauxhall just turns to me and smiles. She asks, "Did you hit your head again? Looks fresh."

I just shrug. "Force of habit."

Sitting behind her in this speeding death trap, I can't describe how good I feel. The air is warm and it's rushing in the windows and it's blowing Vauxhall's long hair as though she were blow-drying it herself. The smell of her hair, something citrus and something almost chocolate, has me twitching like too much caffeine. The smell of berries in lemonade. Of freshly cut cucumber.

Her past is her past. Even if it was last night.

Right here, right now, she's mine.

I'm in this car for three reasons. Number one is that Jimi is a maniac. This car, the way he's driving it, this is all just a reminder that if I ever want to see Vauxhall the way she is right now, I need to be here. I need to be right beside her, otherwise the future I saw, of us together, it'll be after she's gotten out of the hospital or out of rehab or divorce court. Number two is the fact that the future is the future and forgetting what I just said about number one, I know we'll be together. Consider me anxious enough for that future that I'm willing to spend time with Jimi regardless of the risks. That leads me to number three and that's the easiest: Vauxhall is magnetic. She's as magnificent as Jimi is dangerous. I'm basically a moth to her flame. Damn the consequences. Damn her hooking up with Ryan and Chris and God knows who else.

She will be mine.

Barreling through a yellow light on Seventeenth, Jimi says, "What you need to understand, Ade, is that we're all products of our environment. The mark of a true genius, a true rebel, is someone able to not only overcome all the bullshit that's been thrown at them, but to turn it around."

And with that he spins the wheel, Vauxhall gasps, and the car careens across two lanes of traffic onto Twenty-third. Jimi slows up only a little, the trees are thicker here, branches dipping down low over the street, and I can feel the coolness of them breathing out their moisture as we sprint by.

Jimi says, "The secret of life is simple: Only you matter."

We left the park only an hour ago.

Jimi handed me a beer when we got into his car and I pretended to drink it but really only sipped it. When we pulled up to Vauxhall's house and Jimi jumped out, I got out to slide into the backseat and poured the rest of the beer out onto the lawn. Jimi was in her house long enough for me to have a good look at it.

The house, it was where the love of my life had been sleeping, eating, showering, dreaming, crying, laughing, singing, living. I didn't want to think of the other things she might have been doing. The house was small. Nestled between two larger houses and hidden behind blobs of shrubbery. The walkway up to the front door was cracked, the cement coming loose in large chunks here and there. I could imagine Vauxhall, the child version of her, skipping there, playing jacks, jumping rope. There were two lights on inside the house. One was clearly the living room, though the shades were pulled shut. The other, maybe a bedroom or office. In my mind it was, of course, Vauxhall's. A single window—I imagined it had one of those little knobs you turn to wheel it open—that looked out over a quiet, dark neighborhood. I could see Vauxhall sitting at that window, her chin in her hands, watching the sun set and the clouds move in. I could see her sitting there, sighing, and wondering what the rest of her life would be like. If she'd get married and have three kids. If she'd become a doctor or an artist. I could see her with her eyes closed, the rain on her face as it splashed through the screen, breathing in slowly, inhaling the ozone and the sweetness of the soil.

Right now, sitting behind Vauxhall, her feet up on the dashboard, toenails painted light blue and chipped, I only imagine she has her eyes closed and is breathing in the night the same way. I want so badly to put my hand on her shoulder.

My mission here is to make us happen. To make this work.

My mission here, and I'm totally seeing it like I'm an Army Ranger or something, is to make sure that whatever is going on between Vauxhall and Jimi and anyone else doesn't go any further.

My mission, outside of the Buzz, is being Vauxhall's right hand.

And right now, I even go to move, just a finger to touch her hair, to touch where her hair has been caught up in the seat, when she says, to me, "Jimi's not a guru or anything. You have to take most of what he says, at least like ninety percent of it, with a truck-load of salt."

Shouting back, I say, "I'm guessing more like one hundred per-cent of it."

Jimi, lighting a smoke, coughs. "That's true." He hits the brakes and brings the car to a sudden halt under a cypress tree and turns around and looks at me, narrows his eyes, "Maybe I dress it up too much. Like make it a bit too—"

"Forced?" Vauxhall laughs.

"I was going to say 'intellectual.' But anyway, definitely don't take me too seriously, Ade. I'm bad for your health in large amounts."

Jimi turns back to the road, slams down on the gas, and away we go again. Vauxhall, however, turns back to me and winks. She mouths: He's. Full. Of. It.

I nod. I smile. I'm not sure what else I do.

"By the way," Jimi says, staring straight into the soul of the night, "I borrowed this car from a friend of mine. I didn't ask him, but so long as it gets back in one piece, should be fine. Actually, he's just a neighbor. Not technically a friend."

Where we stop the car is nowhere.

It's at the end of a dead-end street. Houses on either side, a fence in front. And beyond the fence is pretty much nothing. Just darkness. Not even the flicker of lights. Jimi halts the car and jerks the keys loose and then jumps out and walks to the fence. He lights another smoke and turns around and motions for me and Vaux to get out.

Vaux gets out slow. I get out slower.

"So, what are we looking for?" I ask.

Jimi takes a long drag and then pulls out his cell phone. He says, "We have one minute and twenty-two seconds. I suggest we get over the fence."

" 'Til what?"

He doesn't answer, just flicks his cig into the shadows and smooth as a spider climbs up and over the fence. He is engulfed in dark. Vauxhall takes my hand, my heart hiccups at the touch. Her skin so soft, so warm, and she holds my fingers tight. Right now, I'd jump into the Grand Canyon.

Vauxhall smiles, says, "Come on." And she goes over the fence.

Jimi says, "You got fifty-seven seconds, Ade."

I go over the fence. Not easy like Jimi. Not smooth or fast like Vaux, but I make it. On the other side, it's just weeds and darkness. We walk. I follow the blue light of Jimi's cell phone. I'm looking around but seeing nothing. Hearing nothing but the crunch of weeds under my shoes, the scatter of pebbles, and the rush of wind.

Only there isn't wind.

Just sound.

Jimi says, "We got twenty-two seconds, kiddos."

"What is that noise?" I ask.

Jimi laughs. "Noise. Just noise."

And then he stops. I run into his back. He puts a hand on my shoulder and says, "Just sit still. Right there. Feel that?"

And I do. Vibrations. The earth moving beneath us like the thick bass from a lowrider. I can feel my intestines jumping. My heart fighting back with its own beat.

"What the hell is going on, Jimi?"

Vauxhall is not with us. She's standing about ten feet away and I can just make her out by the faint light that at first I think's coming from Jimi's phone but it's not. It's white light and it's getting brighter by the second. Bigger and brighter. It's behind us. The rushing noise, it's as loud as a building coming down.

Jimi grabs my shoulder, holds me tight. Says, "Fifteen seconds."

Of course, it's a train behind us. I hear the conductor pulling the horn down hard.

But there is no squeal of brakes. The conductor, he's not trying to stop.

I'm shaking.

Breathing out fast.

Jimi can tell, he says, "Ten seconds, dude. Hang tight. This is going—"

But I can't hear the rest of what he says. The noise of the train is the noise of a thousand trains. It is the buckling of the world. It is the ripping-open of the sky. And the light, it's like we're floating out into the sun. I remind myself that I will live. That I've seen myself in the future. That nothing can happen right now.

Jimi pushes on my shoulder.

The train horn is the yell of a dinosaur. It shakes the air.

There is dust in the light around us like bubbles deep underwater.

I tell myself that I will live. I tell myself not to think that maybe the visions have been wrong. That I saw Vauxhall and she's here now, watching me. That she's here now and any second Jimi and I will jump out of the way.

Only we don't.

The train is on our heels.

The sound of it has turned me to jelly. I can't feel my feet, the vibrations of it are that numbing. I'm standing on a jackhammer and Jimi, the suicidal nut job, is grinning.

Hand on my shoulder, he pushes me down hard.

I close my eyes ready for the impact. Ready to feel my bones shatter and ready to see myself spray off into mist. I grit my teeth. I tense up. And I count it down.

Four . . .

The light is blinding, even with my back turned. Even with my eyes closed.

Three . . .

The rumbling has me deaf.

Two . . .

The rails whip around like snakes.

One . . .

Nothing. I open to see the train just to my left on a second track. It's passing maybe a foot from us, maybe a half-foot from Jimi. The train rattles by and Jimi lets me go. I stand there for a few seconds, my body twitching as it comes back to life, and then collapse on the rails.

It takes five full minutes for the train to pass. I know 'cause I time it on my cell phone. Jimi stands, looking over at me, smiling. Sometimes laughing. Sometimes shrugging. Saying things I can't hear.

What has me worried, though, more than the thought that Jimi almost just got me killed, is that for a few flashing seconds I actually was kind of psyched at the thought of getting the World's Greatest Concussion.

Me spinning off the front of that locomotive at a million miles an hour, can you imagine how many hundreds of years into the future I'd see?

How crazy the Buzz would be?

When the train finally passes, and my hearing returns, Vauxhall walks over and sits down next to me. She gives me a hug and having her close is like diving in a cool pool. And right there, my brain kind of has a freeze-frame moment. With Vauxhall's arms around me I don't care about the concussion that I missed. For the first time in a long, long time I actually want to be slowed down with all the other fossils around me. I want to be right here with Vauxhall in this instant.

Vauxhall, stepping back, smiling, says, "That was the nine-twenty Rio Grande on its way to Cheyenne."

I ask, "Why did we just do that?"

Jimi walks over, sits next to us. He lights another smoke, the red of it casting demon light on his face, and asks, "You close to your family, Ade?"

"Yeah, I guess. . . . Seriously, though, Jimi. That was the most—"

He interrupts, "How close?"

"I don't know. Close. You know, I love my mom and my dad and whatever. What are you trying to ask me? Would it be something worth almost dying for?"

Vauxhall whispers, her lips only an inch from my ear, "Just humor him."

Jimi says, "I don't think you're that close. I can tell it."

"Fine," I say. "My mom's a bit of a freak. Religious stuff. My dad, he's in a coma."

Jimi nods slowly. "You're like us. Abandoned."

"No." I shake my head. "No. My dad was in a car accident. He didn't—"

"He was a drunk, right?"

I just stutter. "He was drinking, but he didn't—"

"Your dad chose the bottle over you. Worst kind of abandonment."

"Wasn't like that at all, Jimi."

He ignores me, says, "I've been tracking my dad. For years, I've been slowly but surely, step by step, tracking him down. He left me, my mom, back when I was just a little kid. Not even two. He just up and vanished. I was able to kind of make a life for myself, able to avoid a lot of the traps other kids like me fall into. And how I did it was by keeping myself focused. Focused on one thing."

Vaux, whispering, says, "Ask him what the one thing was."

"What was the one thing, Jimi?"

Jimi takes a drag. More drama. Drags it out. He says, "At the end of most Westerns, the good ones, the spaghetti ones, there's always this scene where the good guy and the bad guy come face-to-face. Just mano a mano in a dusty street. Vultures overhead. Harmonica on the sound track. Tense. That's it. Confronting my dad. The big showdown. Ka-boom."

I nod. Not sure what to say.

Vauxhall, beauty at my ear, breathes, "Just make him think you're interested."

Jimi tells me that his childhood was the stuff that people write bestselling memoirs about. He tells me that his mother used to torment him mercilessly and when she died he kind of felt guilty that he was so elated. He says, "It's the past that makes us who we are, Ade. It's not destiny, I don't like to use that word. But your parents lay down tracks for you to follow. Most of us don't ever get off them. Most of us don't need to."

"And the train?" I ask. "Why we almost died?"

"Metaphor. Allegory. Past sneaking up on you. I'm not sure what, but I thought it was a nice touch. Train was like ten feet from you, dude. You weren't ever really in danger. Just thought you were."

Vauxhall murmurs, "He planned it out for like a week."

Jimi stands up, reaches out a hand, and when I take it he pulls me up. Pulls me up fast. Then he hugs me hard. Tight, the way football players do after a game. He says, "Welcome to the club, buddy. What do you want to do next?"

I say, "Sleep."

Jimi laughs. "You'll sleep when you're dead."

Vauxhall stands up, puts her arm around my shoulder, and says, out loud this time, "It's a three-day weekend. Nothing but open road out there. We have a car, lots of friends. Why don't you come along? We won't bite. Promise."

Of course I say yes. Mostly I want to be around Vauxhall. But part of me also wants to be around Jimi. I'm not sure why. After tonight, after finding out he's touching the girl I've been writing about for years, I should be head-butting him into unconsciousness. The guy's an asshole and like a lot of assholes he's also just crazy enough to be wildly entertaining.

"Okay," I say.

Vauxhall jumps. Giggles so sweetly I can't help but break out grinning.

"We'll leave tomorrow, after school," Jimi says.

And I think it's funny that these two actually care about going to school.

"What do you have in mind?" I ask.

Jimi says, "Really, I only have two modes: vengeance and party. And, in a twisted way, I think one just leads to the other. It's party time."

CHAPTER FOUR

ONE

Professor Susan Graham
Department of Experimental Physics
University of Colorado, Boulder

Professor Graham,

A family friend of mine, Dr. Reginald Borgo, suggested I get in touch with you about a certain school project I'm working on. I'm a junior at Mantlo in Denver, so it's nothing major. Not a dissertation or anything! (I'll admit it's an attempt to salvage my grade, but it's a long, ugly story.)

Anyway, this thing I'm doing (a "thought experiment") is about seeing the future. I realize that's such an old sci-fi movie deal, and probably a standard for Physics 101, but I'm really trying to add a few new wrinkles to the idea and wonder if you might be able to help me flesh some of them out better.

Dr. Borgo suggested I just lay out the hypothetical, so here's the gist: I've got this "subject" who can see the future, only he/she can only see it when he/she is unconscious. The future the subject sees can be way off in the future or very near—this depends on a kind of focusing, but is not really important. Let's say that our subject, when he/she looks out into the distant future, sees only good stuff. I mean, he/she sees himself/herself living a very normal, enjoyable life totally devoid of brain damage (from repeated concussions (the whole knocking-out thing) and having succeeded in his/her work despite not being a very good student (getting kicked out of school three times, suspended on a monthly basis, etc). Oh, and the future can't be changed. What he sees happens. Always. So, that's the "thought experiment."

I've got three guesses on how the future winds up so cheery:

1. He/she isn't really seeing the future (though this is frequently contradicted by those times when he/she sees the near future and it comes true, down to the letter).

2. He/she is really seeing the future and everything just worked out right for the subject—e.g., the whole "concussions are really terrible for you over the long run" thing was exaggerated. Also, that school—at least high school—isn't as necessary as everyone seems to think. College too.

3. He/she is really seeing the future only something big happened to change it. Like divine intervention.

What do you think? Am I missing some variables here?

Sorry for the long letter and thanks again, in advance, for you help.

Sincerely,
Ade Patience

TWO

What I am is dead tired.

Dead. Tired.

The good thing about having a mom who only thinks about the future you, the one she knows will be successful, is that the you right now isn't nearly as important. The me right now is almost extraneous. According to the future I've seen, not getting good grades isn't such a big thing. Not having perfect attendance is par for the course.

I'm literally lying on a desk when Paige finds me.

Not lying there with my head on the desk. My head cradled in my arms. No, I'm lying on my back, my eyes shut, and I'm pretty sure I'm snoring something gnarly when Paige shakes me awake.

I sit up groggy and first thing I notice is everyone else is gone. Fourth period, speech, and the classroom is now empty. I missed the whole thing. Whatever it was we were discussing.

"Time is it?" I ask, trying to get a crick out of my neck.

Paige just shakes her head at me.

"Seriously, though. Is school over or . . . ?"

"You only missed lunch."

I swing my feet over the edge of the table, stretch. "What's funny," I say, "is that I don't think I've been this delirious after a concussion. This is like, it's like being the most wasted ever."

My best friend, head still shaking, she tells me I'm pathetic. She tells me that if I was a true friend I would consider limiting myself to just the concussion. She says, "Real friends, they don't keep adding on damage. Real friends know where to quit."

"Did I mention the thing about Vauxhall and . . . you know?"

"Yes. Several times already. Makes perfect sense."

"Of course it does."

"Both of you're junkies."

To this I just give her a hug and ask her to help me to the bathroom.

Why I'm so dead tired is because I haven't slept in days.

That's actually not quite accurate, I did get about three hours of sleep on Sunday but that was post-concussion, so I'm not actually sure it counts as sleep. It was more like just plain unconsciousness. And a good ten hours or so was spent in a daze. Not sure if a daze counts as sleeping.

My arm over Paige's shoulder, my feet scuffing, dragging, I tell Paige that she can think of this as an experiment. I tell her that, really, it's one of those experiments where everyone involved is blinded to what's actually happening. I say, "And I think I'm close to a breakthrough here."

"Breakthrough, huh?"

"Yeah. You see it's like that game Mouse Trap."

"The one with the little plastic mice?"

"Right. And the whole trick of it is to set up this complicated trap and catch the little plastic mice . . . no, wait, maybe the trick is to not get caught. . . ."

"Anyway . . ."

"Well, whatever it is, this is like it. Except the mice are me and Vauxhall and Jimi and you are somewhere in there too. No, I'm the trap and Vauxhall is that . . . What the hell am I talking about?"

Pretty much, it's been the Me, Vauxhall, and Jimi Show. The past three days have seen us doing just about everything together from eating to sleeping and I'd be lying if I didn't say it was incredible. The parts I can remember, well, they were incredible for sure.

It began last Friday, after school, when Jimi ambushed me in the parking lot. He drove up beside me in his neighbor's car, the way you see it happening in movies, me walking quickly, the wheels of his tires turning slowly, and he rolled his window down and waved me over. I went. Vauxhall was sitting in the backseat reading a paperback book. Jimi told me to get in. He told me to get in fast and not to think about it. He said, "Thinking about things kills them."

I got in. He sped up and out of the lot and we were off.

Halfway to Boulder, on 36, I asked him where we were headed. I'm not sure why I waited so long to ask. He smiled and said, "We've got many things planned for you, grasshopper."

We didn't actually make it to Boulder but stopped in Louisville at a guy named Roger's house. Really it was his parents' house and it was massive. One of those McMansions that spring up outside of the city, the kind that look so new and sterile you can't imagine anyone really living in them. They're like big, empty waiting rooms. Waiting rooms in fields, in cul-de-sacs, below mountains. At Roger's there was a party. Enough booze for a cruise ship full of people but less than a hundred of us there. We ate hot links and greasy chips. There was a keg. There was pot. I woke up on the couch in Roger's basement to find the moon nearly down and stumbled upstairs to find the house empty. Everyone was on the lawn shooting off fireworks and I pulled myself over to a lawn chair, slumped down into it, and watched Vauxhall move, talk, laugh, drink, in the kaleidoscope carnival light. Someone walked over to me and punched me in the shoulder, said, "You dog, you. What's her name?"

I said, "Vauxhall."

This random guy, he said, "Yeah, right."

Whole time Vaux and I didn't really talk. Just a few words here and there. Really it was just me observing her, the way I had been for the past two years. Only this time up close. This time in person. At the party, she moved through the crowd the way a leaf moves down a stream. Caught up swirling in conversations here and there, spinning for a time, and then washing free and moving on. There were times she'd vanish for an hour or two. Sometimes with Jimi. Sometimes not. When she was gone the party would pretty much stop for me. It'd be like someone turned down the music or turned on the lights. The empty chatter would rush back in. I'd sit on the couch and pout. But then, Vauxhall would return, sweep me up, and introduce me to someone, laughing and nodding and splashing white wine on all the carpets.

Today, with the hallway empty, and me falling asleep between footsteps, Paige sweeps me up and walks me into the bathroom.

She sits me down on a toilet and says, "That's all I'm helping. This is gross."

"Do happen to have an energy drink or—"

"No."

"Coffee?"

"No, Ade."

"Okay." And I close the door to the stall but open it up again quickly. "Hey, Paige," I say. "You should probably not be in the men's room."

After Roger's place, things got weird fast. We didn't go back to

Denver until Sunday night. We were camped out in a field, some random, desolate place that was beautiful the way only empty sky and empty land can come together and be beautiful, and sitting on the hood of Jimi's car. I was bumming about how Vauxhall and I still hadn't found the time to talk. Mostly it was Jimi doing the talking and the two of us listening.

And whatever had developed between the two of them, it was obviously deep. Deep enough that often times they'd just give each other sideways glances and then nod knowingly. They had whole conversations, long detailed discussions, with just a few looks. A shake of the head. An eyebrow raised.

I felt like a ghost.

THREE

It all ended last night around two in the morning when I found myself back home, sitting on my lawn, Jimi behind me, his head on my shoulders, and Vauxhall in front of me, sitting between my knees.

The three of us a totem pole to the over-partied.

Jimi fell asleep. Was doing that little stop-start, head-jerking thing that people who are way overtired do when they first drift off. I didn't bother moving him because I didn't want Vauxhall to move. Even though I was losing feeling in my feet, I didn't ever want to move.

Sitting there, the night chirping around us, cars throwing occasional light, Vauxhall, not turning around to look at me, said, "So, what did you see this time?"

"Nothing. I didn't go under."

The beautiful creature between my legs laughed. "You missed?"

"Ha, ha. Very funny."

Vaux asked, "You choose what you see? Like if I were to ask you what will happen to me in five years? Or will I win the lottery?"

"I don't really have much control over it."

Vaux turned to look back at me. "Prove it."

I said, "You'd need to knock me out."

Vaux turned away, shook her head, and even though her shirt was buttoned up high I caught a glimpse of cleavage. Part of me suddenly got very warm.

"I hate to say this," I said. "But I've actually had a vision about you."

Vaux sighed long and loud. "Is that so? Sounds like a pick-up line. Or are you just really trying to make me knock you out?"

"I've seen you before. Two years ago. I had this vision of you coming into the lunchroom and singing. Just the same as you did the other week. And—"

"What?"

"I don't . . ."

Vaux looked back at me again and asked, "What else did you see?"

"Us in love. Riding off into the sunset."

Vaux said nothing.

"Yeah. A little weird, right?" I felt really stupid.

Then Vauxhall got up, pushed Jimi off my shoulder, and he slid down to the grass in slow motion but didn't wake up. With him there snoring in blades of wet grass, Vauxhall stretched and looked up at the stars for a few heartbeats before looking down at me, me looking up at her beautiful face, and the world just paused there. The moonlight, the stars, even the passing headlights of the cars all focused in on Vauxhall and illuminated her exquisiteness.

I asked her, "Why are you with him? He's such an—"

"Asshole?"

"Yeah. Did I mention this before?"

"You did. Maybe I chalk it up to bad-boy attraction. Us girls are kind of hardwired for it. Lame, I know. But with him there's something more. It's not love. For me it's really not. We just have this thing that—"

I interrupted, "He also said something about you trying to change."

Vaux shook her head. Sighed. "What if I told you that I was like you?"

"I—"

"Like you, Ade, only I don't see the future. And I don't need to knock myself out. What if I told you that for me it happens with intimacy? With sexuality?"

"Okay."

"You don't buy it?"

"I do." I was being entirely honest. And right there, that moment, dawn was just around the corner and the both of us were so exhausted and hung over, suddenly everything made sense. The reason she and I were meant to be together wasn't because I was obsessing over her for so long, it wasn't that she found me irresistibly charming and funny, it was that we were cut from the same cloth. Whole time I'd been wondering about others like me, she was waiting only a few years away. It was so Hollywood it made me want to laugh.

I asked Vaux, "What do you see?"

"The past." She closed her eyes. Her eyelids fluttered, delicate and soft as moths. She said, "Would you believe me if I told you that I can see the past, see deep inside someone's history, when I'm with them? Would you believe that the thrill of it, of seeing their past, their hidden history, their stashed away ideas, I get this crazy high?"

I cleared my throat, nodded. "I would."

"You have that high?"

"The Buzz, that's what I call it. That's why the bathroom at Oscar's. That's why the handful of concussions this year. Not so good for my memory, terrible for my future prospects. But . . . it's miraculous."

Vauxhall nodded. "It is. Anyway, that's why I'm with him. Jimi's past, his hidden history, is so crazy that it gives me the most unbelievable high every time I look into it. Each act of abuse I uncover, it helps him and it helps me. I'm like the shrink who can get inside his head and clear away the sins, pull down the cobwebs, and let in the light. He needs me, and I admit that I like the feeling I get from it. Is that wrong?"

"No, it's not wrong. And the other guys?"

"It's the same thing. I'm helping them, Ade." Then she smiled at me and her teeth were so bright and wonderful and she said, "It's good to know I'm not alone."

God, how I wanted to kiss her right then.

"Me too. You're the first person I've ever met who can—"

And that's when the crack came.

I felt something hit my head, something super hard like a two-by-four or a tire iron. I've been hit with both of those before and this felt remarkably the same.

Anyway, it was concussion time again.

What's funny is that I was shocked that I wasn't on the beach with the masked dude again. Instead, after diving down the tunnel of swirling light, I wound up at home. At home with my mom and some of her All Souls Christ friends sitting across from me. Like grilling me or something. Also there was a projector and a slide show on.

Strange. And thankfully short.

And that only meant the Buzz would be really weak.

I woke up in the back of Jimi's car with the Buzz already fading from my system.

I was in my boxers, a ratty blanket covering my legs. Vauxhall was in the front passenger seat looking down at me with worried eyes. Jimi was in the driver's seat smoking.

Vauxhall asked, "Are you okay?" And then she punched Jimi in the arm and told him he was a dick for hitting me. She told him he could have killed me doing that. She said, "Sometimes I think you've completely lost your mind."

Jimi said, "Isn't it what he does?"

Turning to me again, Vauxhall asked, "Seriously, though, are you all right?"

I nodded, rubbed the back of my head, and felt a serious knot buried under the hair. "What the hell did you hit me with, Jimi?"

"A baseball bat," Vauxhall said. "Oh, God, I'm so sorry, Ade."

I told her I'd be fine. I'd hit myself with worse before.

She laughed uncomfortably.

"So, Jimi, why am I in my boxers?"

Jimi asked me, "What did you see?"

And that's when I noticed he was wearing my clothes.

FOUR

"Why are you wearing my clothes?"

Jimi didn't answer. He threw his cigarette out of the window and then scratched at his chin and pulled a notebook out from the glove box. He opened the notebook, took a pen from his pocket, turned to me, smacked his lips, and asked, again, slowly, "What did you see?"

"I saw the future. I saw myself at home. Boring, really."

Jimi asked, "How far out?"

"I don't know. Weeks, maybe. I wasn't focused, I wasn't trying, and when I'm not trying I only see a little ways out. Could have been months."

He wrote that down. Then he asked, "Can you make it sooner?"

"Make what sooner?"

"The future you see, Ade. Can you see something in, like, days?"

"Maybe, but I can't control it. Why, Jimi? What's—"

He shushed me and held up the notebook. On the cover, it read THE BESTIARY. Jimi said, "It's a catalog of the worst sorts of creatures: parents." He wasn't laughing when he said it. He added, "My whole childhood, right here. Everything I can remember. Everything I can't. But what happens next, after today, after next week, that seems pretty important to know too. I'm hoping you'll help me see it?"

"I can only see my own, Jimi. I don't think I'll—"

That's when I threw up. All over the back of Jimi's car.

And then, thankfully, I blacked out. Happens. When you've

had as many concussions as I've had, blacking out is almost second nature. Throwing up too.

When I woke up I was inside my house, fully dressed, lying in bed with my mom hovering over me, dabbing my head with a wet towel and singing that one hymn about being in the garden with Him.

When she saw I was awake she stopped singing. Smiled.

"Was I dressed when I got in bed?" I asked.

Mom made a funny face. An uncomfortable face. She said, "Yes, dear. Of course you were. Just like you are now. Your friends just dropped you off, said you'd . . . well, they said you'd had an accident. But I know . . ."

And then she went off to get the Revelation Book. I stayed in bed totally confused, unsure of why I was so messed up and not really certain if what I remembered happening had really, actually happened. I decided, right before falling asleep, that I needed to see Dr. Borgo again. And, for the first time in a very long time, I wondered if my future, the one my mom was so eager to chart out, could somehow be wrong.

Be totally, absolutely wrong.

But right now, sitting on the toilet, my only thought is what I'm supposed to do next; I yell for Paige to come back into the men's room. I yell for her to help me up again. I yell, "I'm not naked or anything, you can totally come in here."

She opens the door to the stall and says, "I never left, dumbo."

"Can you get me out of here? Was I going to puke or something?"

"I think you had to take a leak."

I screw up my face. "I'm totally confused. By the way, you seen Jimi or Vaux today? Were they at school?"

"No," Paige says.

She helps me up and on our way out of the bathroom she tells me that this is officially the last time she's going to help me like this. She tells me that even if I got totally crippled and was in a wheelchair the rest of my life she wouldn't ever help me to the bathroom again. She says, "But I'll give you a chance to redeem yourself."

"You love me and you like cleaning up after me. If you didn't, you would have nothing to bitch about. I add the spice to your life."

Paige laughs. "Promise you won't do your thing. At least a week off?"

Fingers crossed behind my back, I say, "Promise. By the way, did I tell you that Vauxhall is just like me? Isn't that freaking crazy? The two of us just these beautiful, messed-up psychic beings? How—"

"Yes, Ade. You told me. I'm very happy for you and I really hope the two of you wonderful junkies have a great future together."

"Ouch."

CHAPTER FIVE

ONE

Quail Telephonics
Denver, Colorado

To Whom It May Concern:

So, I've been getting these calls. Really it's only been two, but they've been bizarre enough that I'm kind of getting stressed out about them. The first was roughly two weeks ago. Old, raspy-voiced guy on the other end of the line telling me that he saw me in a vision (!?) and that my life was in danger. Only, he didn't seem that concerned about it. Freaked the hell out of me, if you'll excuse my French. Wrong number, everyone said. Prank call, they told me.

But it happened again last night—Thursday, September 24—and it was the same guy. He knew my name. He said much of the same stuff as last time. That he saw me in a vision and that my life was in danger, only this time he went further, he said that what he saw scared him. Said it would be at a reservoir again. A battle royale, he said. Someone will die. He said, and I'm quoting here, that "what goes down is almost biblical." So I started suspecting my mom had something to do with it, but that's just paranoid thinking and I don't want to be That Guy.

Anyway, why I'm writing is because I'm wondering if you'd be willing to help me out here. I don't think this is anything for the cops to get involved in, but I'm hoping you can maybe track the calls. Maybe trace them for me? Caller ID it just shows up as "unknown" and star 69 doesn't get me anything but what sounds like a fax line.

Thanks for your time. Let me know!

Ade Patience

TWO

Paige and I go to Rock Island.

It's this dance club down on Fifteenth in LoDo and they've got a dark dance floor (tonight the DJ's spinning '80s industrial) and in the basement some pool tables and a few ragged chairs to kick your feet up in.

We head to the basement. I drink some Coke while Paige dances to one of her favorite songs, that super-annoying metal cover of Madonna's "Like a Prayer," and then we pulls chairs over to a corner and just sit and chat. Paige all sweaty and me with a knit cap pulled low over all my damage and Band-Aids.

It's fun to be out just the two of us like old times.

I've made Paige a promise that I won't hit my head and that I won't try and find out what Jimi and Vauxhall are doing. "This is just us," Paige says. "You need to take a break."

Of course, that doesn't stop me from proceeding to spill everything that's been going through my head for the past few days.

She, of course, couldn't be more happy to hear it all.

"Wait a sec, you've got some nasty old man calling you about some beach and maybe you drowning and you've also been seeing some gnarly cat in a Santo mask, also on a beach, telling you some sort of existential nuttiness?"

"Yeah, that's basically it. And also, Vauxhall has powers too."

"Right and I'm actually not surprised, in the movie, the movie of your messed-up life, that is exactly what would happen," Paige says, "But going back to the other stuff."

"Okay."

"Maybe it's some sort of sign? You know, maybe it's like—"

"It's someone screwing with me," I say.

"Who?"

"Honestly, I don't really care. I mean I do, but not really. This guy and the old man, they're just symptoms of the same thing: looking too hard at what you don't understand. You see that's really why I haven't gotten so upset about it. What I've learned from seeing the future is that you can't interpret it until it happens. What I'm seeing is just a hint of something, just a tiny edge of something. You ever hear about the blind men and the elephant?"

"What? Is this a sex joke or something?"

"Don't be nasty. It's basically like this: Three blind men each put their hands on an elephant. One says, 'This animal is like a snake,' 'cause he's touching the trunk. And another says, 'This animal has wings,' 'cause he's touching the ears. And the last one says, 'This animal is like a tree,' because he's touching the legs. Or something. Anyway, they all get it wrong because they can't see the whole picture. Get it?"

"Yeah, I get it. But that's a lame excuse."

"No. It makes perfect sense. I'm not going to stress because—"

"Why a luchador mask?" Paige interrupts.

"Maybe he's Latino? Maybe he just digs Santo?"

Paige looks very serious. "Could be that he's a time traveler."

I laugh. "No. Just supposed to look that way. Just supposed to look crazy."

"How? I mean maybe there's someone else out there jumping in on your visions? Your future? That is like so *Star Trek* it's sick."

"Nah. It's just that I'm only seeing part of it."

"Maybe it's just that you don't recognize him 'cause he's young now. Or maybe under that mask he just looks like a total freak. Maybe like a cat-man or a Neanderthal. You know, something totally otherworldly?"

"Like you used to, Paige?" I laugh.

She elbows me hard. I wheeze.

"How about the old man calling you?"

"Irritating is all," I say. "Super irritating. Sometimes these freaks find me. Remember me telling you about that one woman who called—" And I want to say more, but Jimi and Vauxhall come strolling out onto the patio and strike up a conversation with a dude with a Mohawk I feel like I've seen before.

I shoot Paige a look, mouth: I. Had. No idea. They'd. Be. Here. Seriously.

She just shakes her head and rolls her eyes. "Like boomerangs," she says.

Vaux and Jimi don't notice us, amazingly. They go over to the bar and somehow Jimi finagles them drinks, real drinks, and then they sit and talk and laugh with the Mohawk guy, who they also get drinks for, and then, when the Sisters of Mercy come on, they go out onto the dance floor. The way Jimi dances has me laughing in my soda. Actually, it's so ridiculous I've got Coke bubbles coming out my nose.

He's spinning around in his big black sweater. He's got high-top sneakers on to boot and he's wearing mascara. The scene could have been edited out of some goth teen movie. The worst is that he's mouthing along with every song. Every. Song.

Paige, of course, reads his lips. ". . . sing this corrosion to me . . ."

And he whirls all dervishly.

". . . you like an animal," Paige says.

I tell her that, unlike before, I can actually hear the music. I tell her that I'm not deaf. I say, "Paige, it's not like reading his lips when the song is actually playing really loud is impressive. If he were wearing headphones, then maybe."

Paige grumbles a bit and then asks me why I'm not over there with them.

I watch Vauxhall dance. She moves like she's in water. Her limbs and her hair in perfect motion, her face sliding in and out of the light and the expression, her eyes closed, is ethereal like a photo on an album cover.

"Aren't you like the Three Mouseketeers now?"

I shake my head. "Just to be near her is all."

"Nah, you're having fun."

"Maybe I am."

"So?"

"So, that." And I point over at the dance floor where under a steady throb of green and blue and yellow lights Jimi and Vauxhall are kissing. It's more Jimi kissing Vaux. Her eyes are still closed and she doesn't look that into it. But it's happening regardless. They're making out on the dance floor right in front of me.

Paige says, "How much does it suck that apparently there's only a few places to go in this city? I mean, it's like, I dunno, fate or something."

I tell Paige that she isn't helping. I tell her that maybe this would be a really great time for her to just shut up and go dance or get drunk or something. I say, getting out of my chair, "Ooh, look at the time. You know what I need to do."

Paige gets super pissed. Yells something nasty.

I don't want to hear it.

As I push my way through a crowd that's pretty much materialized out of nowhere, up the stairs to the larger dance floor where two girls in neon with crazy dreads are dancing spastically on a stage, I run into Belle. She's with some old dude and she waves to me and the old dude, this dude with a graying goatee and a shaved head, just nods over his super-thick-framed black glasses. What a dipshit.

Belle says, "What are the odds?"

I say, "I'm obviously in hell."

"Life of a scryer, huh?" Belle retorts.

"What the fuck does that even mean?"

And I push past her and her beau.

I find two East football guys near the back of the club. Both of them wearing jerseys. Both of them big guys. I walk over to them, say, "You guys need to step outside with me."

One of them, a black guy with a mustache, asks, "What is this?"

I say, "I need to talk to you both."

The black guy laughs. "Fucker's high."

Paige finds me, pulls me aside, says, "Don't. Really."

She has this horrible depressed puppy look. "Seriously, let me just give you a ride home. I'll just drop you off and that will be that. Cool?"

I shake my head and walk back over to the East dudes.

To the other guy, the white guy with two different-colored eyes, I say, "I've heard of women like your mom. Pretty rare, huh?"

"What'd you say?" He gets in my face.

Behind me, Paige shouts, "Don't answer!"

Again, the big guy says, "What the fuck'd you say?"

The BPM of my pulse ratchets up.

I can taste the anger on this dude's breath.

"Just ignore him!" Paige yells.

A circle of gawkers is forming around us.

"Yeah," I say to the white guy, my eyes narrowing, face preparing. "Takes a lot of acrobatic skill to take two dudes at once. I mean, how else do you explain those jacked-up eyes, you—"

And he plugs me right there.

Fat fist slams into the left side of my face. Zygomatic bone. I hear something snap and then black. The resulting concussion is swift and furious. Precious black. The vision sweeps and I'm back spinning down the passageway to my future.

The Buzz is glorious.

I'm free.

Where I am is back on the sunny beach. The surfing beach in maybe California. Thing is, the sun isn't shining now. I still have my surfboard and I'm still wearing a wet suit and my eyes are still crackly with sea salt, but now the sky is completely clouded over and the lightning is close. The boom of thunder even closer.

I feel the first drops of rain on my skin when the man in the Mexican wrestler mask lays a hand on my shoulder. He squeezes. I turn around to get a good look and he's there in all his wrestler glory, his mask all purple and shiny.

"What is your deal?" I ask him, sounding much older.

This is surely the future.

"You're still not ready, Ade. Wires are still crossed. Still foggy."

"This is just a waste of my future."

My hands curl into fists and I'm about to knock him on his back when he says, "Storm's here, Ade. Right on top of us. You still haven't woken up. Going to take a lot to turn this around. Only you can deny the past and stop the future."

What happens next is crazy.

What happens next hasn't ever happened before: I skip ahead, leap over decades, and see myself as I'll be when I'm old enough to have a kid just about my age. I'm in front of a mirror and I look down and I see something really upsetting, something that makes me want to scream, but it's hazy.

The image, it just gets all warped and dark.

Blacker than black.

THREE

I come to in an ambulance, just Paige at my side.

The EMTs have oxygen on me and one of them is prepping a saline IV and just about ready to put it in my arm. I hate needles and ask him not to. I mention to him that I've been in enough ambulances to know it's not necessary, but he just tells me to lie back and does it anyway. The whole rest of the ride I'm puking my guts up. And I hear howling, but Paige doesn't hear it. The EMTs don't hear it.

And I black out again, but this time, nothing.

Just matte black and silence.

At the hospital, it takes me two hours to wake up. But I do. And I'm woozy but okay. My mom shows up shaking, hanging her head, her eyes all wide and bruised looking. She's brought the Revelation Book and she dutifully records the college vision. I add a little side note that in the trees, I saw a mourning dove. When she's finished, Mom closes the book and puts it in her lap and smiles through her tears, says, "We're getting closer all the time, baby."

My voice all scratched out, I ask, "To what?"

"The end," Mom says so quiet I can barely hear it.

Paige leaves in the morning. All night she sleeps on the couch next to my mom and anytime a nurse comes in, she jumps up and listens intently. Before she goes she cries on my chest and tells me that I'm breaking her heart. She tells me that I'm really the most selfish person she's ever met. She whispers, "This is the last time."

The doctor, she tells me I'll need physical therapy. She tells me

I'll need some serious medications. She shakes her finger at me and says, "You should be locked up."

I ask her why she has to blame the victim.

The doctor, she says, " 'Cause we've seen you in here eight times this year."

I wish I could say I remember those eight visions, but I'm sure my mom's got them charted out on her wall. Each of them embellished just for her. The ones I do remember were the ones I squeezed the most Buzz out of. The one with me paragliding over Detroit at night. The one with me crashing a Ferrari into the back of a semi truck. And the one with me tightrope walking over Times Square. All of them meaningless outside of the adrenaline. What's funny is that lying in a hospital bed right now I'm kind of wondering what else I could have seen. Why only the action? It's like a child skipping through his favorite movie. What about the other parts? Why haven't I ever thought of this before? Where else has the guy in the mask appeared?

When my shrink show up he asks to be alone with me and my mom bows out. Sitting on the edge of my bed, Dr. Borgo asks me if I knew how bad things got.

I ask, "Worse than any other time?"

I am of course talking about the bowling alley incident. The time Borgo and I first met. My very first really really bad head injury.

It was last summer when the shit officially hit the fan and the Buzz dependence started. If I went a week without a concussion my skin would be crawling. I was sure, convinced, that if I went a month without hitting my head and riding the high, I'd die.

Mom was happy with every vision.

I pretty much walked the whole city and wore out three pairs of shoes. The whole time just looking for fights or jumping in front of cars or stealing candy from kids with big dads, big body-builder dads. I'm not an aggressive person, not a violent or angry guy, and most of the time I'd just throw out verbal abuse to get someone to throw a fist.

People I knew, people like Paige, all got summer jobs. They worked the cash register at the Hungry Elephant at the zoo. They were lifeguards at the JCC. Mowed lawns in Cherry Hills. Had internships they thought would get them into that one special college far away from their parents.

Not me.

Every day Paige would call or visit me at the hospital or bring cookies over to my house. Every day Paige would say, "Next time you're going to die" or "Next time you'll be in a coma."

My summer job was getting my ass kicked.

Kicked from Broadway to Wazee. From Speer to I-70. There was a fight with five bums in the parking garage just off Paris on the Platte. A full-fledged mêleé with skaters on the Auraria campus. A hospital visit after a smackdown with gang-bangers near City Park. Fights with factory workers. With Air Force cadets. With bar backs. With strippers. With drunks. And with football players in a bowling alley.

It was last July, I'd spent the day all jacked up downtown and had taken the bus home but decided to stop at Monaco Lanes Bowling Alley for a soda. It was freakin' hot out and I was exhausted. Maybe a little confused.

I got a Coke at the bar and sat and watched people bowl. Didn't take long before I was itching for the Buzz again. Like really frantic. Started a fight with these football players from TJ, they kicked my ass all over the place and the fracas ended with me getting conked on the dome with a bowling ball. I wasn't ready. I wasn't focused. Smash. Crash.

What I saw in the darkness didn't seem far off at all. Maybe only days. I was standing in the middle of a street watching the aftermath of a car accident near my house. This guy from school, a guy I'd only recently met, Harold Vienna, was lying in front of a red car. He looked like he was asleep, only one of his legs was bent backward the wrong way, the way it shouldn't bend. There were people getting out of their cars and covering their mouths to stop from crying or screaming or both. I couldn't move. My heart had slowed to just this hollow thud, like when you hit the side of an empty can. Just metal in my chest.

And I woke up in the hospital.

The Buzz was pitiful.

Mom was bummed the vision wasn't focused, wasn't far out, but she was sympathetic. She said to me, "Isaiah 40:26: 'Lift up your eyes on high, and behold who hath created these things, that bringeth out their host by number: he calleth them all by names by the greatness of his might, for that he is strong in power; not one falleth.'" Paige didn't quote any Bible, she cussed me out.

Dr. Borgo came to see me the second day I was there.

Still in my hospital gown, still in bed, feeling sick still from the vision. Back then Borgo had a goatee to go with his black-framed glasses. He's a black guy and with the goatee he totally looked like Malcolm X. I told him that and he shrugged. He looked me over, asked some questions, and then leaned in and whispered, "You see anything?"

"Like what?" I asked him.

"Like things that haven't happened yet."

I wasn't sure if he was for real, so I said, "Maybe."

"Thought so. How far out can you see?"

"Mostly years. Decades."

"But you can see sooner?"

"Yeah. Sometimes weeks. Hours one time."

Dr. Borgo put his head on his fist, like how a shrink should look thinking, and said, "And you prefer one over the other, right? The further-out visions, right?"

I nodded. Face just blank, splotchy with bruises.

"You get a certain, well, feeling?"

"Feeling?"

"You get high from the visions, Ade?"

I nodded again. Mouth so dry.

"And the further out in time you see, the greater the high is, the stronger the high? I'm guessing that you control how far out you see by focusing. Pushing down, the ciliary body changing the shape of the lens. That's how you do it. Just the same as normal seeing."

I sat myself up in the hospital bed, asked, "How come you know all this, Doc?"

"I've seen people like you before. Only a few. It's considered dodgy to research psychic phenomena, but there's a group in Toronto studying it. Another in Omaha. Ten years ago I met a man who could see a couple weeks into the future if he held his breath and passed out. He was the best of the bunch, but there are others, some of them very young. Most of them can't really see, they just get impressions, like random—"

"I see everything. Crystal clear, like in a movie."

"I believe you."

"What about these others, are there any here? That would be amazing to meet someone else who could do it. That would just be—"

"I don't know. The ones I've met, and it's only been a handful in a dozen years, had real problems. They weren't what we'd normally consider well people. A lot of them go crazy. A lot wind up on the street. Ranting and raving like—"

"How come I've never heard of anyone else before? How come I've never heard of you before? I've been in this ER like twenty-three times."

Like in a movie, Borgo picked my chart up, flipped through it. "Twenty-four," he said. "Looks like almost ten this year."

"Yeah. So?"

Dr. Borgo laughed. "I like to stay on the edges. Honestly, it's risky for me to talk to other physicians, other researchers, about this. They assume, before I even get into the meat of it, that I'm a quack. That people like you don't exist. I'm at peace with that. Not looking for fame."

"What are you looking for?"

"Just knowledge, Ade. I'm fascinated. Curious."

"Me too."

And he told me about research that had been done in Canada in the mid-70s. About how the government had recruited people like me, people with divination skills, to lead some new armed force and how it all fell apart and was buried because of the precognitor's addictions. He told me that it's a quirk of nature. He told me that my ability, in the minds of most scientists, is a parlor trick, even if it's real. He said, "Space-time continuum's a bitch, you can see but you can't change. Ever heard of Cassandra?"

I shrugged.

"Greek mythology. What you've got, I've been calling the Cassandra syndrome. The god Apollo gave Cassandra, daughter of King of Troy, the ability to see the future because he thought she was beautiful. Nice gift, right? Wrong. She wasn't interested in him. So like any pissed-off immortal Apollo cursed her something terrible. His curse? No one would believe her predications and she couldn't ever change them."

"Yeah, that's what I've got. But nothing about a high in that."

Borgo smiled, "The high's a modern addition."

And later, just before I left the hospital, he gave me an illustrated book of Greek myths. He told me to call him whenever I wanted. He told me that he would help me so long as I kept him in the loop. He said, "Stop by my office from time to time and let me run some tests. Just humor me."

That's when I told him about my vision, about Harold. I asked him if he thought I could stop it. If he thought I could change things.

He just said, "Sorry, Ade."

"Well, I'm going to try."

"Best of luck. See you soon."

I've seen Dr. Borgo a whole bunch of times since then and he never asked how it went with Harold. I'm glad for that. What he did do was hook me up to all sorts of machines. He did blood tests. Breathing tests. Sleep tests. He talked the school district out of placing me in special ed twice. This guy, my own personal mad scientist, is the sole reason I'm still in school.

But maybe not anymore.

Right now, the look on his face is super grim.

Right now, my own personal physician in crime tells me that

he's read over the MRI of my head and that it looks ugly. Very ugly.
He tells me it's serious. Says, "Ade, feel on the back of your head,
a few inches back from your left ear."

I try. "There's a ton of gauze."

"A lump?"

"Lump?" I go and feel, probe. Each touch and my skull is jumping. Definitely a lump. "Yeah. Lump detected."

"The docs had to drill a hole in your head to relieve the pressure."

"Pressure?"

"And repair a blood vessel."

"—"

"Yeah, Ade. You were knocking on death's door."

"Sounds familiar."

"Not like this. This, this was you just about ending up a vegetable. They thought you might be paralyzed. You almost got a
colostomy bag. And I would be willing to bet that if you'd have
had so much as a pin or a feather hit the top of your head, you'd be
dead. Kaput. You came as close as you probably ever will and honestly, despite the fact that I am still in awe of what you can do, if I
ever see you like that again, I'm gone."

"Gone?"

"Gone. You can get someone else to talk to your principal."

FOUR

I got home from the hospital with my head wrapped the way Vauxhall's was at the party.

My mom dropped me at home 'cause she had to go to the church.

Some emergency. Some lost soul had shown up desperate and Mom heard the call. When she heard the call, she had to go. Just had to.

Being at home alone, after everything, I was on edge.

On edge in a way I haven't been before.

The phone calls.

The masked dude and his threat.

It was almost too much. I half expected a cat to come cater-wauling out from my bedroom and give me a heart attack right there. Blow my blood pressure up so high I'd have some red geyser coming out of my neck. Or maybe it would be an old man with a sinus problem and a cell phone and a knife. Or a Mexican wrestler with his greased-up arms ready to just crush my bones on the living room carpet. So I was tiptoeing around. I was eyeing every door. I was reminding myself of where my baseball bat was. Of where a tire iron might be found.

I was ready for the cat.

The geezer.

The luchador.

What I found was Jimi Ministry.

He was sitting on my bed, once again wearing my clothes, my jeans, my sweatshirt, and he was tattooing himself. He had one of those little tattooing irons, the ones with the little needle that buzzes up and down like a dentist's drill, and he was sitting on the couch, feet apart, grounded, putting little final touches on a bicycle remark-ably similar to the BMX I got when I turned eight in black ink on the skin of his left arm. When I stumbled in, my mouth open, he stopped and looked up at me calmly. Said, "You're dreaming."

And then he got up, pulled the sleeve of my sweatshirt down

FUTURE IMPERFECT | 141

over his inky arm, and walked out the front door. Left the door wide open and I watched him make his way to his car, just loping along like he didn't have a care in the world, and not looking back once.

I know that I freaked out.

I did pinch myself, as if that would help, but really I couldn't decide if what I saw was happening then or later. If it was really happening right there in my house or if I was seeing something that wouldn't happen for twenty years. And yet that didn't make sense either.

None of it made sense. Hence the freakout.

I ran outside after Jimi, hands all whirling in the air, and I was shouting. Shouting all sorts of crazy stuff. My head hurt. Hurt bad. I limped back inside and then passed out on the floor of the kitchen staring into the grill on the air vent over by the washing machine.

It's night now.

I've been drifting in and out of sleep. The way my head feels, the way my eyesight is all fuzzy, I'm half convinced that I imagined the whole Jimi thing. I've been told that it's amazing what you can see if you want to bad enough. You can make yourself see just about anything.

Fact is: I'm losing it.

Fact is: I've lost it.

Looking at myself in the mirror, my swollen face sticking out pink bulges between the bandages, my head looking twice the size it should, I decide that maybe the Buzz isn't worth it.

Glorious as it is, maybe it's just not worth all the damage.

As much as I love it, Dr. Borgo's right. Even though I don't ever see myself jacked up in the future, maybe it's because the damage just takes longer and I haven't seen that far out yet. Maybe just beyond the horizon of what I've seen, I'm serious effed in a wheelchair and drooling and shitting my pants. Maybe just a few seconds after the furthest I've seen there's me rolling on the ground as my brain just dribbles out my head.

'Course, there is another possibility.

Maybe what Borgo's right about is convincing me. Could it be that the reason I don't see myself messed up in the future is because I quit right now? Because I will never go to the ER again? Because I won't have another concussion? Dr. Borgo didn't say it as fiercely as he could have: I need to stop because this isn't a life.

FIVE

Set up in bed, Mom brings me a bouquet of flowers that she found on the porch.

Who would ever send me flowers?

My first guess, and already my head is swimming, is that it's from the phlegmy old dude who's been calling. I'm not sure why, but that's the first thought that comes to my head. I even go as far as worry that the flowers might be poisoned. Read about that once in a magazine, these poisoned flowers that killed some reporter in Russia. But that's stupid, right?

My second thought, well, it's most likely Paige. Or Belle. Maybe it's Belle trying to send me a message. What would the message be?

Ah, but there's a card.

The message is written backward, so I have to get up and hold it up to the mirror on the back of the door to read it. Even though the handwriting's pretty, I'm guessing the message is nasty. If it's from the geezer prank calling me, then it's gonna be a nasty limerick or a curse. That's it. It's going to be a curse. Belle cursing me.

Only it's not.

The note, it says: *Negative Woman fell in love. Her powers, the negative energy, got out of control and she was worried she'd hurt the man she loved, so she gave her powers up. Really, they left her. Negative Woman was pissed at first. But then, she realized she didn't need the negative energy, she realized she was better off without it. That made her very happy. What would make you happy, Ade? Love, Vaux.*

Once again, I'm sure I'm still unconscious. I'm sure this isn't happening now.

What would make you happy, Ade?

The room isn't as plastic as it should be. There aren't any black-light blues.

Love, Vaux.

I do pinch myself. Hard. Really really hard. And it hurts. Hurts enough for me to know that this is real. That this is right now. Jimi was in my house just hours ago tattooing himself. Vauxhall wrote me a letter. This is the moment right here.

Love, Vaux.

The future has come.

We are going to be so in love.

I'm saying it right now: I'm quitting.

No more concussions. No more Buzz.

Being with Vauxhall and not being brain dead would make me happy. Knowing that I don't need the Buzz because Vaux is kissing me would make me happy. Not having an overripe melon head would be nice. Not having to shit in a bag would be wonderful.

After a few painkillers, with the last birds singing outside and Mom rustling in the kitchen, I have a revelation.

I realize that I don't know a single person living in the now. The here.

Me and Vaux have it the worst. Her and me, we're chasing down highs everywhere but now. Her stuck in the past and me racing into the future. Neither of us caring about anything else. And I think about my mom and how she's in the future too. Her life is all about the distant prospects. The Rapture. The Return. She loves me dearly, but in some ways, really in many ways, I'm just a looking-glass into that distance. And Paige, I think about how she just longs to leave high school and her parents and find someplace that will accept her for who she is. And Jimi, him hunting down his dad like his dad was a stray dog that bit him, obsessing over something that might never ever happen. And I think of everyone at Mantlo, everyone out for the next big thing, the next big score. All of us, we're not living for right now. For all of us, life is just one step to something better.

Not for me now.

Not anymore.

SIX

I've been "sober" now five hours.

This is, naturally, when Vauxhall calls my cell. I answer with a squeak, must be the concussion or maybe the fact that my throat is sandpaper dry. Vauxhall says, "Hey there, you okay?"

"Yeah," I say, clearing my throat. "I'm a pro at this."

"That's really sad, but I get it. I know why you—"

"The high. Buzz, that's why."

"Not me?"

I'm silent for a few breaths though I don't mean to be. It's telling.

Before I can say anything, Vaux says, "Let me make it up to you. Will you go see a movie with me next weekend? Saturday night?"

"You and Jimi?"

"No, just you and me and maybe two friends. A double date."

"Double date, huh?"

"Yeah. I'll pay."

"Okay. I'll drive."

"Great. Hey, can I ask you a question? Did you see anything? I mean the last time, the time you went to the hospital? I'm not going to tell Jimi or anything, I'm not . . . Just so you know."

Closing my eyes tight, I relive the hit, the spin, the future, and then tell Vauxhall what I saw. I tell her all the details, down to the color of the masked man's mask. I say, "And he turned to me and told me something kind of poetic and that was it. Over."

"What exactly did he say?" Vauxhall is fast to ask.

"Uh, it was like denying the past to—"

"Change the future?"

"Yeah, right. What? Is that some movie quote or something?"

It's Vauxhall's turn to be quiet and it's all static for what feels like a whole movie's worth of time. Then she says, "I saw him, the scary guy in the mask. When Jimi was a kid. He was there ten years ago. Jimi's sure it was his dad."

"What?" My head starts to hurt. A headache creeping up.

"I didn't think much of it other than it was really strange."

"Messed up is what it is. How is that even possible?"

"I don't know, but Jimi is keen on it. He thinks it's his dad."

"His psycho dad?"

"Yeah."

"How? How could he . . ." I clear my throat. My head is pulsating, I close my eyes tight to push the pain back inside. "You gotta get rid of that guy, Vauxhall. Seriously."

She says, "I can't, Ade. We have—"

"He's using you, Vaux."

Vaux laughs, it's all uncomfortable. "I'm helping him."

"He's dangerous, Vaux. This dad thing . . . I'm worried about you."

"Every day, he gets better. Every day, I help him see and help him—"

"Don't lie to yourself, Vaux. You do it for the high."

Vaux goes cold. She says, "Okay, I'm going to hang up now. . . ."

Only she doesn't.

We sit in silence for as long as it takes for a plane to fly overhead, for the rumble in the sky to go dead. I say, "You are so much better than Jimi. Deserve so much more. Vauxhall, you're incredible. I've been in love with you for two years now. I've been drawing pictures of you ever since I saw you. Been trying to come up with your name. Trying to remember every detail about you. I'm going clean for you. Stopping for you. Doc's making me take the next week off from school to recover, but when I get back, I want . . . I want you to go clean with me."

And that's when the line goes dead.

CHAPTER SIX

ONE

Dr. David Gore —

I don't know why you're insisting on doubting what I'm telling you. And I find it really offensive that you've taken to calling Dr. Borgo a "quack." What's that about? What if I called into question the degrees you have listed on your business card? The FRCSC thingy after your MD, for example? Or how about your FACS? Whatever that means.

Fact is: You just don't like the fact that you're stumped by this.

I also take offense at your suggestion that I'm a paraphrenic. I had to look up what that actually meant though I was sure right off the bat that it wasn't good. And it certainly isn't. Couldn't have you just called me a schizophrenic? Or said I was delusional? I think you need to take a moment and do some (what Dr. Borgo would call) old-fashioned self-exploration.

Anyway, your attempt at trying to ruin my day has failed.

Later.

Ade Patience

P.S. I've been considering keeping your name in my mind the next time that I happen to receive a concussion, just in case I can see something about your future. You know, something juicy.

TWO

Paige keeps her fourth-grade class photo on her dresser.

When you look at it you can't believe it's the same person. The Paige in the photo looks like someone who'd been kept locked away for years. Someone who never saw sunlight. Who was fed with a tray slid under the door. The Paige in the photo is blond to the point of hurting your eyes. She looks off to the side, her eyes so milky blue you'd swear she was albino.

The Paige I know today is nothing like this feral girl.

She is lively and popular and she's dyed her hair black. Now when people take pictures of her she looks right in the camera and gives this big smile. Now it's the smile that's blinding and not her old weird ghost face.

I'm over at her place, it's one in the morning, and I've spilled my guts, and I've informed her that I'm done. That I'm ready to stop the concussions and quit the Buzz and mostly it's because I just want Vauxhall to myself. "I want her to go cold turkey with me. I mean, she can have sex with me and all, but not—"

"That wouldn't be cold turkey for her, then."

"All right. All right. You know what I'm saying though, right?"

"That you don't like her being with Jimi?"

I nod.

"That you don't want her to be a slut."

I nod.

"That's romantic," Paige says. "In a junkie sort of way."

"I'm ready for this. To stop. It's the first time in a long, long time."

"And you'll stay clean how?"

I shrug. "I just won't need it."

"And Vaux?"

"We need to convince her."

"We?" Paige sneers. "Actually, you need all the help you can get. You talked to her? It's been almost a week?"

I say, "You know she avoided me all week. Said hi via text maybe twice. You know, the verbal equivalent of that little arm punch like you do. That let's-be-friends-right-now arm punch. That I'm-totally-uncomfortable arm punch."

Paige looks disgusted. "I don't give you arm punches."

"You do. But anyway, I think we're still going out tomorrow."

"Right, the date. What do you think Jimi will think?"

"He won't know."

"Hell he won't."

"He won't care."

"Hell he won't." Then Paige hugs me, tight. Says, "I just think it's so freaking cool that both of you have powers. I mean how crazy is that? All this time you've never met anyone else and, wowsers, the girl you love is another genetic freak like you!"

"Like I *was*. I quit, remember? Haven't had a concussion, not even a slight rap on the head, for over a week. For me, that's monumental. Anyway, I'm also going to swim. Join the swim team. I don't have to compete or anything, but my doc thinks it'll be good for me. Used to be a pretty good swimmer. First practice is tomorrow afternoon."

"On a Sunday?"

"It's like tryouts."

"Won't your brains leak out?"

"Ha. It's been over a week since the hospital, Paige. I think I'm safe to swim."

"No, seriously, swim team is good. Good start."

"That's what I thought. Chicks dig swimmers, right?"

"Honestly, Ade, even if this whole true love thing doesn't work and Vaux ends up turning tricks on Colfax, it would be nice to not be worrying about you every week. It'd be super nice not to have to patch you up."

Then she turns on the TV and makes some cheddar popcorn. We watch this crazy Mexican soap opera that involves pirates and it takes my mind off things for about fifteen minutes. First commercial break and Paige just hugs me out of the blue.

This girl, damn she's my Holmes.

Fact is: I knew Paige before I met her.

I could see in the Vauxhall vision that we were friends. I took things slowly. We sat next to each other last year in Mr. Paul's social studies class. Really it was a front for long, dull lectures on economics. A lot of kids left the class within the first few days and Mr. Paul seemed totally unfazed, as if this happened all the time. Paige and I were two of the ten who stayed. Me mostly because I knew she was the first step toward meeting the girl from the vision. We bonded over our shared love of H. P. Lovecraft and comic books. Our shared fascination with water (being in it, watching tanks filled with it brimming with colorful fish, swimming across it, staring longingly into the depths of it). Our shared interest in Sylvia Lorne's impossible cleavage (one warm day, when Sylvia was wearing this outrageous V-neck, we estimated the length of the crack to be an astounding ten inches).

Boobs and horror, pretty much the stuff friendships are made of.

And it goes without saying that her parents, Bob (collar up) and Linda (tattooed eyebrows), don't accept her. That they don't even try. Paige would love a shouting match. Screaming fits. Slammed doors. Even being kicked out of the house would be a blessing. It would mean Bob and Linda care enough. Just enough to reject her. They don't, though. Paige is merely a teen going through a phase. In her parents' minds she'll be a punk rocker next and pierce her nipples. Then she'll go to college and become a hippie kid. Maybe hang out naked with dreadlocked black guys. This is all a phase. After school she'll straighten out completely. She'll follow Linda's footsteps and get a career in advertising. Marry young. Marry wealthy. Have kids. Raise dogs. It makes Paige sick and I can't count the number of times when we're just hanging out that she'll stop mid-sentence and look like she's either going to scream or punch a hole in a wall. When that happens I just hug her or punch her shoulder.

Grabbing a handful of cheese popcorn, I say, "I'm really quitting, Paige. Really. There's going to be a new me. You're totally going to be surprised."

"I believe you."

"I'm serious. Really, it's a new day for me."

"I believe you, Ade."

I ask, "Just like that?"

Paige mutes the TV, says, "You've never wanted to quit before. I've begged you for years. Since we first met. You never once said you would. Never once made a false promise. Ade, you love trashing yourself, but if you love this girl more, well, I believe you. But . . . how much of this is because you don't want her with Jimi?"

I hold up my thumb and index finger about an inch apart.

Paige shakes her head.

"Fact is," I say, "if the guy died, I don't think I'd go to the funeral."

THREE

Because Mantlo doesn't have a pool, we swim at Celebrity Sports Center.

It's the perfect place to make a change. To get away. Celebrity has a massive pool, three water slides, twelve bowling lanes, an arcade and even bumper cars. They say it was originally built as a training center for employees on their way to Disneyland. Once you're inside, it's like being in another world. Something vaguely Caribbean without the poor people and the trashed-out beaches. Around the pool and water slides are fake rocks that bristle with fake plants. It's hot and steamy and the water is suspiciously bright blue.

We've been here for like two hours. Everyone swimming lesuirely before things technically get started. I've just been doing my thing.

Swimming fast and then slowing down and blowing bubbles, kicking too high, kicking too loud. I'm like a kid in here.

And then Coach Ellis blows his whistle and ushers us to the food court.

"We're gonna reflect," he says.

Technically it's meditation. We find a spot between two fake rock ledges and lay our towels down on the Astroturf. Then we stretch. After stretching we lie down, close our eyes, focus on our breathing and imagine we're not lying on ketchup-stained Astroturf. At first I imagine the Great Barrier Reef from pictures I've seen. Bright blue-green water, shot from above, and in it undulate these ribbons of coral and color. I imagine flying over the reef, dipping down every now and then to skim my feet along the warm water. Meditating this way, my mind feels clear for the first time in God knows how long. Here on the Astroturf I'm not anxious or itching to knock myself out at the bottom of the pool or against a telephone pole on the way home. It's glorious.

I swim in the fourth lane.

It's clear immediately this is the lane reserved for those of us who need a little extra time. Those of us who need the encouragement. That's why Beverly Morrison is in lane four with me and the other slowpokes. She's the carrot. Has this killer body and wears the skimpiest swimsuits imaginable. And usually it works, but I don't feel like swimming fast to be right behind her. I don't notice her at all. I swim leisurely and finish after everyone else, languidly splashing down the lane and I can feel Coach's eyes burning into my back.

Fact is: I don't care.

I'm obsessing over Vauxhall the way I obsessed over the Buzz.

At first, it's just me reliving the past few weeks. I pore over every word, every glance. It's like a film I watch in my head. Only better because I cut out all the bad parts, the parts that make me want to curl up in a corner. In my movie, I see Vauxhall smiling and laughing and being ridiculously brilliant. Underwater, mid-stroke, I laugh with sheer pleasure.

Maybe that last knockout shook something loose?

I'm about fifty meters into a two-hundred-meter crawl when I take a deep breath and kick down to the bottom of the pool to touch the bottom. I run my fingers along the black line painted there. It's slick, seamless. I replay the vision of Vauxhall singing in the lunchroom just the same as I saw it. Her and Jimi walking in and then speeding things up and seeing her on the table singing, cutting to when she's eye-to-eye with me and the world is revolving around us. I move through it quickly.

When I open my eyes I'm about fifteen inches from the wall and about to eat tile.

I pull back. Blink hard.

I worry my teammates are watching me. That they're swimming in place, faces puffed out under the water, watching me lose my mind at the bottom of the Celebrity swimming pool in the shadow of a fake rock cliff. In my head I sigh and swim to the surface. Everyone else is at the other end of the pool listening to Coach. He's yelling. He's pointing at me as I swim back.

"What's going on?" Coach has his hands on hips, leaning over with his whistle dangling a few inches from my face.

I shrug, water running into my eyes. "Just not feeling it today."

"Not feeling it? It's the first day, Patience."

"Yeah. Sorry. I dunno. I'm going to try hard, though. Just maybe not—"

Coach's interrupts. "You sick?"

"No."

"Why don't you get out and take the rest of the night off. While I don't think you'll be a star or maybe even third tier, we need bodies on the team. So you're good." He smiles, but it's not meant to be a nice smile, this is Coach mocking me. Before turning away he says, "I'm just impressed you bothered to come at all."

I towel off and sit on one of the many lounge chairs lining the edge of the pool and watch the others swim. I watch them but don't really see them. I'm zoned out thinking about the line at the bottom of the pool. Seeing Vauxhall's smile everywhere I look.

In the locker room Garrett Shepard whips me with his towel and makes a crack.

All I hear of it is, ". . . with this retard."

Garrett, he's the type of guy who will be arrested doing something completely inappropriate with a drunk girl. The type of guy to go to college and make as many women as possible very unhappy, very embarrassed. This guy, he is the epitome of everything I hate about jocks.

I finish getting dressed and walk over to him. "You have a problem?"

Garrett laughs. "Yeah. I do."

"And what's that?"

"I hear your girl's always in heat. She's just craving it all the time and yet she's hanging around with you. With a fucking retard."

Sighing, I say, "I don't feel like fighting you tonight, Garrett."

"Oh, really? You don't?" His face almost cracks with overexaggeration. "You don't like me talking trash about your new girlfriend?"

"Not my girlfriend yet."

Garrett scans the room, his teeth out and gleaming. "Yet? You hear that? Yet. Oh, right! I forgot she's riding the joke of that theater homo."

"Leave it alone, Garrett."

Garrett steps closer. "From what I hear, all the fights you've been in you've lost."

"Most."

"This going to be another one?"

"No."

For the first time in my life I get really, truly angry. I've been mad before. I've kicked holes in walls before. I've wanted to smack people silly before. And sure, I've had too many fights to count, but I've never actually been this angry. I've never wanted to kill someone the way I do right now. The way I see it, there's a volcano exploding inside me, lava spilling just under my skin, and the only way to let it go, to let it flare out, is to do something aggressive.

To do something vicious.

Garrett brushes his hair from his eyes and looks over at Mark Cullman. Mark shrugs. Garrett turns to me, probably with another smartass remark about the mentally handicapped or maybe a jab at Vauxhall, but he's not able to say it because my fist is in his mouth. His teeth are rocking back in his gums and he stumbles backward and falls.

The thud, I'm sure, can be heard even at the bottom of the pool.

The benefit of having been in as many fights as I have is that I know when a fist is coming. It's like catching a fly. You watch a fly, see how it darts when your shadow slips over its own. Compared to flies, people are the slowest things on Earth. Fists travel like paint drops. Even if Garrett had been ready. Even if he'd had a fist prepared it would have been no biggie. I've tempered away those reflexes that say flinch, that advise my body to duck or swerve or jump or dive. If a car smashed into me right now, I'd be perfectly relaxed.

Hot-tub relaxed.

And, honestly, it disturbs me.

FOUR

Our date is a foreign movie because Vaux only likes art films.

She won't see "mainstream crud," so we're driving to the Chez Artiste on South Colorado Boulevard, a place I've seen hundreds of times but never been in. From what I hear, the seats don't recline and the screen is something just a tad smaller than Roderick Burgundy's home theater.

This movie we're seeing, last time it was in theaters we hadn't been born.

I pick Vauxhall up but don't go inside of her house or meet her mom because she's waiting for me on the porch.

The sun's just setting, the sky still blue but bleeding out fast into night.

There are stars but none of them are twinkling, so I'm guessing they're really planets. It's cool and dry with a breeze that's picking up all sorts of floral smells and lawn scents. The whole scene is everything you imagine a first date might look like.

Vaux is wearing jeans and this crazy, frilly kind of blouse. It's blue like the disappearing sky and it's so loose and thin that looks lighter than air. Underneath she's got on a tank top. Black. Her shoes, they're open-toed. Her nails, purple. Vauxhall's hair up and her eyes gleaming under mascara, she's a combination rock star and vacationing princess.

She gives me a big, long hug and looks me over. "You smell like chlorine."

"Joined the swim team. Thought it might, you know, do something for me."

Vaux smiles. "You really scared the shit out of me last weekend. Someone called me in a panic, told me you were dead. That just killed me."

"I know. I'm sorry."

"I was worried we weren't going out tonight. I kinda showed up here not knowing what to expect. I realize I upset you when we talked last, but really, I was just trying—"

She shushes me with a finger to my lips.

Vauxhall tastes of coconut.

On our way to the theater she fills me in on who we're meeting.

She tells me I'll love them, Clyde and Ambrosia, and that they're from her other school, the one she ran away from. And Vauxhall tells me that Clyde is really into the occult. She says, "You two will really hit it off."

"Sounds like someone I know."

Clyde is five inches taller than me and has hair all the way down to his ass, slick like a horse's tail. He's super friendly and Vauxhall was right, within minutes the two of us are laughing loudly about palm readers and pyramids. Ambrosia looks like her name, all long curls, narrow Eurasian eyes, and a nose ring. She talks slowly like she's drugged and touches my elbow or arm or shoulder every time she speaks.

Both of them smile big at me. Clyde even gives me a hug.

He says, "Been a while, dude."

"—"

"Right?" Clyde screwing up his face.

The way I look at them gives them pause. Clyde shrugs to Ambrosia. Ambrosia shrugs back, this their little private language, and then we head into the theater. I overhear Clyde whispering, "Looks just like that one guy, doesn't he?"

Before we sit down, Vauxhall tells me she saw this movie the first time with Ambrosia. She tells me they were both really toasted. "Ambrosia was freaking out about it for like a month," she says.

Clyde says, "First time I saw it I freaked too."

I ask if I'm the only one who hasn't seen this more than once and Vauxhall pats my head and tells me that it's okay. She tells me that it was a rite of passage for them. She says, "You're lucky to be seeing it for the first time. I wish I could see it over again like that."

"Hope I'm impressed," I say, and then the lights go dim. I lean over and ask Vauxhall if I know these two. Like, "Have I ever met them before? They're acting like I have."

She says, "I'm guessing they're just stoned."

The movie has something to do with a bookstore owner and a gangster. The bookworm is having an affair with the gangster's bruised wife and there's a chef. The whole thing is very arty and colorful but gruesome as well and I'm pretty sure one of the main characters is eaten. I don't really watch the movie because I'm too busy watching Vauxhall watch it.

Every time there is a scene shift and a flash on screen, as the light changes, in that brief moment I watch Vaux smile or frown or look concerned. She's seen this movie before, but you'd never guess that from her expressions.

Twice she catches me watching her.

Twice she smiles and blinks and grabs my hand and squeezes it hard.

After the movie we sneak up onto the roof of the theater where we can lie down on the pea gravel and watch the moon spin toward the mountains. Vauxhall and Ambrosia talk about the movie (Vauxhall: "If only Gaultier designed costumes for all movies." And Ambrosia: "Wait until you see his baby movie.") while Clyde grills me on the whole divination scene.

He lets me know he met my ex once. Says Belle came on to him. Says, "She's crazy." And then he props himself up over me like he's going to try and kiss me and whispers, "She's kind of hot too, though. In that crazy kind of way, you know?"

I mention to him that Belle and I dated. That she's crazier than he knows.

Clyde nods and lies back, chew it over, and then asks, "Tell me about seeing the future? You do that with psychedelics or some combo of designer stuff?"

"Who told you that?"

"Only everyone, dude."

"And you believe—"

He jumps in. "Cut the crap. Just tell me how."

"Just hit my head is all."

"Must be hardcore side effects."

"I guess."

Clyde laughs, this chest-deep hearty grandfatherly laugh, and then he's like, "Dude, I met you at a party last summer. We totally talked for like two hours. I can't believe you don't remember any of that. You told me all about your head injury vision thing. Seriously, dude, you don't remember that at all?"

I explain that I don't. It's true. Sitting up and looking closely at Clyde, there's nothing remotely familiar about him. And what's odd about it is that he's an instantly memorable character. Someone you would never forget. Ever.

Slapping me on the back, Clyde says, "Concussions. Can't be good, dude."

We go to Watson's, this ice-cream parlor/soda fountain place that's supposed to be like something in the 1950s. Vauxhall shares a float with me. The two of us like the dogs in that Disney cartoon drinking from the same frosty mug. She laughs so loudly that it startles me when she does. We laugh so much that by the time we say bye to Clyde and Ambrosia, my sides are aching and my throat is dry.

I drive to Wash Park and we walk around the lake. There are other people out even though the moon has vanished. Near the playground we sit on a bench and Vauxhall asks me about why she was in my vision. She says, "Tell me why you think it was me?"

"Destiny? Fate?"

"You believe in those things?"

Ducks spin lazily in the lake. Bats dart above us. Cars backfire.

"Not really. You?"

Vaux mumbles something. Her face smooth like it's under fili-gree.

She asks me if I'm disappointed.

"With?"

"Me. Two years you've been waiting and here I am. Me, not your dream girl."

"You're even more amazing than I imagined."

"And?"

I shrug. "What else?"

She reads my sincerity, smiles. "Nothing. Give me a hug."

And what's crazy is that all we do is hug.

It's brief, but just having Vauxhall's body that close to mine is exhilarating. Feeling the warmth of her, the shape of her, pressed against most of me, I never want the moment to end.

Vauxhall says, "It's so private. The most private thing."

I realize she's talking about the other guys. All the other guys.

"You love any of them?" I ask.

Vauxhall shakes her head. "In some way. That bad?"

"No. I don't—"

"It's the stories inside them. Each and every one has something hidden, something like a tumor inside them that's eating them alive only they don't know it. Me, I find that tumor, I bring it to light. I change their lives. And these guys, most of them just melt into nothing. They become children again."

"And the Buzz. The high."

"Right." Vauxhall smiles and closes her eyes briefly. "The high."

"If you didn't have the high. Would you . . . ?"

"—"

I clear my throat. "I don't want to end up eighty by the time I'm thirty-five. I don't want someone to be changing my diaper. I want to remember all this."

Vauxhall looks at me, her bottom lip trembles slightly like she's going to say something heavy but then she swallows that back down and says, instead, "Are you asking me to stop?"

I shrug. "I'm just telling you what I'm doing."

"I'm happy for you, Ade. Really happy."

"But you're not going to . . . ?"

Vauxhall looks like she's holding back tears. Her face is all scrunched the way a dam scrunches into a valley to hold back a river. She shakes her head. Says, "I'm not sure I'm ready. I want to be. Really want to be. But—"

"Vaux, those guys, you ever think that maybe what you tell them they don't really want to know? You ever think that stuff's hidden for a reason?"

Vaux shakes her head. "Not at all."

"And how about the fact that maybe they don't care about what you tell them? Maybe they're just happy to get laid? Maybe they just want to grab your tits and . . . I know it's harsh, but maybe they—"

"You haven't seen their eyes," Vaux interrupts.

"Okay. You're right."

Vaux, "Ade, it's beautiful. Not about the sex. Or the high."

I say, "I believe you."

But I don't believe her. I know her too well already.

Vaux hugs me. Holds me tight to her, so tight I can almost feel her heart beating through the cacophony of mine. And then I go in to kiss her and she turns away biting her lip and shaking her head. She says, "I want things to be different with you, Ade. I don't want the same thing."

FIVE

We sit in silence.

Far away a car backfires or someone is shot.

I turn to Vaux and put a hand on her knee. It's gutsy but it feels right.

She doesn't pull away.

I say, "I know that I love you."

Vaux's eyes don't widen. Her lips don't quiver. Her cheeks do flush, though. She says, "I don't know what I can say to that, Ade."

"You don't have to say anything. I just want to say it."

"Two years, huh?"

"Two."

"And you're sure I'm the girl. I mean you've never been mistaken before."

"I'm sure."

A tear forms in the crease of Vauxhall's left eye. Just a bubble at first, but it spills over and down her cheek quickly. Just glides down. And I want to reach up and wipe it off with the softest part of my hand, but I don't.

She lets the tear go. Says, "You don't know how hard it is for me. To be me."

"—"

Vaux clears her throat. More tears fall. "Do you want to know why I transferred here? Why I came to Mantlo?"

I ask, "Not for film?"

"Not just for film."

Vaux stops there and cries. Openly. Tears pour down her face and spot her shirt and I sit watching, starting into her eyes. My hand still on her knee, I squeeze it. Vaux turns away. Wipes her face with the back of her hand and laughs.

Vaux says, "You won't believe it, but I came here to quit."

"Quit?"

"Like you did. Cold turkey. Abstinence. Hasn't really worked, though."

"Why didn't you tell me the—"

"You saw me at the party," Vauxhall says. "I'm weak."

"You're not. Not at all."

Vaux smiles, tears bending around her cheeks. "That's sweet, but I am. I thought when I came to Mantlo that things would be different. Different people. Different scene. The pressure wouldn't be there, you know? But it's already started. I can just feel myself slipping back . . ."

"—"

"My last school, I was kind of run out," Vaux says, wiping her nose with the back of her hand. "Not like you see in movies or anything. No pitchforks. No torches. It was psychological. Over time. Really, it was a small group of girls, just five bitches, but the principal wouldn't take it seriously. Not the teachers either. Not the parents. No one tried to stop the name-calling. The torment. They called me 'easy' at first. Like that's genteel. Didn't last long because then it was 'slut' and 'whore.' Even my friends, people I went to school with since kindergarten, were saying horrible things about me. This is out loud. This is in the hallways they're saying it. Shouting it. At a party, once, a group of guys tried to rape me. I'd avoid lines because inevitably some guy would try and grope me. They all acted pissed when I'd shout them off. They'd say, 'Why so suddenly stuck-up?' and 'What sort of tease are you?' I was going home crying every day. Not wanting anything to do with school. Sobbing on the bus to—"

Vaux closes her eyes. Takes a deep breath in.

I don't know what to say. My heart lurches around. It's vulgar the way it's moving. "The world is full of bastards. It seems like every third person I ever meet is revolting. Stupid. Bitter. There are these families of these people. Generations of them. I'm not sure we'll ever be able to really get away."

I squeeze Vaux's knee again.

I say, "No one could hate you. You're amazing."

Vaux laughs. She says, "It's my body. It was made for my ability. For me to do what I do. You can't even imagine what it's like living with this body. Before the high, it was only torment. Being a guy, I'm sure you don't get it. I've been whistled at since I was twelve. Stared at. Spat at by girls. These . . ." Vaux puts her hands on her breasts and squeezes.

Part of me faints dead away.

She says, "When my boobs started to develop, my mom sat me down and told me how it was with her. All the same stuff, only it was in the sixties and men didn't have the social pressure to behave themselves like they do now. Battle of the sexes couldn't be more true."

I lift my hand from Vaux's leg.

She puts it back. Says, "I got the nastiest looks from girls. From the jealous ones who still wore training bras. There were other girls like me, though. Girls betrayed too early by their bodies. A clique of us, all these girls in big sweatshirts and coats. Scarves and frumpy dresses. My friend, Carla, she was the first the boys really noticed. They moved in like jackals. She was too aware of the attention it got her. Just the year before not a single boy would talk to her, but then, boom! And she took advantage of it. Let them touch her so long as they took her out. So long as they stayed friends. Not me. I didn't let my body cheat me that way. It pushed out and I pushed back. Back then, and this will sound crazy, but the boys, they all called me stuck-up. They said mean, wicked things but the opposite. I didn't cave. Then I met a boy I liked and we kissed and I felt something. This was freshman year and we dated for about two months. He was a senior. Things got . . ." Vaux pauses, asks, "Is it okay for me to talk to you about this?"

Already I can feel the muscles at the back of my neck straining. I just clench my jaw and nod.

Vaux gives me a smile.

Sitting there, my hand on her knee, she talks to me about the first time she got together with her first real boyfriend. How afterward she felt this rush, just barreling up her body and slamming into her brain, and how she saw, with this ex-guy in her arms, she saw him in this plane crash as an infant. How even though his brain was barely developed enough to process the memories, they were still there almost as fresh as if it had happened yesterday. The high, Vauxhall explains, afterward, it was like spiraling up into the sky and then over the sun and crashing down into cotton candy. Everything of her was vibrating. Everything felt alive.

Vaux says, "We broke up a week later. And then, I just needed to be in that place again. To have that feeling again. Parties. I'm embarrassed by some of the things I've done. That I still do. But I . . ." And she shakes her head.

"I know," I say. "I know."

Vauxhall asks, "Want to know why I sang to you?"

"Of course."

"When I first walked into the lunchroom I saw you sitting with your friend and the first thing I thought was that you were incredibly cute. Only all jacked up with bruises in a prizefighter sort of way. I saw you sitting there, with Paige, and I got jealous. It sounds silly, but I wanted you all for myself the moment I saw you. I wanted you—"

"You saw me and thought, Hmmm, wonder what's in that dude's past that he doesn't know about?"

"No."

"What, then?"

Vaux's face relaxes, the tears stop. "I don't know what it was, this feeling, this flutter, but when I saw you, I knew you'd understand me. I knew you'd help me. Maybe you'd even love me."

"I do."

"I know. At first, it scared the hell out of me."

I get closer. So close I can feel the warmth radiating off her skin. "And now?"

And now we kiss.

Finally.

Vaux's lips are softer than anything I'd ever imagined. Moist too. They are perfect and as my lips sink into hers, it's like I'm swimming. I'm pushing through the crystal water around the Great Barrier Reef. I'm slipping into a shallow sea.

Looking deep into me, Vaux says, "Were you scared to stop?"

"Yes but not for long."

Vaux whispers, "I'm scared."

"I know—"

"And really anxious."

"I'm here for you. I love you."

And we kiss again. Hard.

What happens in my chest is hard to describe. It's something I imagine only happens in the deepest parts of space. It's when a star collapses. Or is born. A supernova flowering into existence. What happens in my body is nothing short of miraculous. Every fiber connecting to every muscle and every tendon and every bone. All of it comes alive. All of it hums with a beautiful energy. A song.

This is magic greater than any concussive high.

My head clearer than it's ever been, like it's floating up into the sky, gliding over the treetops and scuffing roofs.

And then we leave.

On the doorstep to Vaux's house, I don't try to kiss her. I just hold her hand and look her in the eyes and tell her I'll see her soon. I tell her to sleep tight. I say, "I'll never leave you."

An hour later, at home, lying awake in bed, I'm trying to will every cell in my body to remember the feel of her, the weight of her, against me.

My pillow is a terrible stand-in.

CHAPTER SEVEN

ONE

Dark Lord von Ravengate,

Cool spell. Thanks for sending it over. Not sure exactly what it's supposed to do, but if I am ever threatened by anything spooky while I'm out, it's good to know I've got backup. Supernatural or not.

You know, you raised some good questions. Here I've been asking all these experts to help explain this thing to me, why I can do what I can, and all the answers I get are vague. You're the only one so far who's given me any "definitive" answer, even if it's not what I was expecting to hear. I suppose you're right: It doesn't really matter how I got the ability or if anyone believes me. I need to just accept that.

What if it really is a parallel dimension? That's a new suggestion. Not even the physics prof came up with that one. It's a good idea, but I don't like it. Not because it doesn't make sense but because, in the long run, it means that I will just end up a vegetable. If what I see is just

another me in another, parallel place, then that's jacked. I'm jacked.
Let's hope that's not true.

I wish I could help you more, Heinz. But my schedule, what with
school (I know, I know) and my mom and this whole new blossoming
romance, I just don't think I could man the booth at the mall with you.
Thanks for asking, though.

And if I ever do see crimson, enflamed sigils, you'll be the first per-
son I call. Seriously.

Rock on,
Ade

TWO

Not even Garrett can disrupt my good vibes.

Swim practice is like bathing in energy. The pool is warmer
than it's been in years. Decades maybe. I ignore Garrett's stares. He
even has the gall to point at me and then make that finger across
the throat slashing gesture like he'll really do it. The guy's a shell of
his former stud self. I've knocked him back to grade school.

Coach Ellis has pretty much given up on me.

Already. But still he lets me practice with the team because it
gives him someone to hate. Someone to compare and contrast his
best swimmers with. Me, I'm his foil. I'm his example of how not
to be.

For me, swimming's just a super-nice workout.

I get home and want to take a nap, my body aching from the
tension of the past few weeks, but Mom's beaming and tossing her

car keys up in the air and catching them. Something I don't think I've ever once seen her do.

"Want to go out to dinner?"

"I'd love to."

On our way out, we pass four people walking up to our front door. They've got folding chairs and a cooler. These freaks are going to wait it out, it seems.

Mom, she sees them but says nothing.

"Where do you want to go?"

"I'm fine with anything."

Mom shrugs. "A friend at church recommended a place on Colfax."

We have dinner at Good Friends. I just talk. Words stumble out. Mom listens intently, bits of her salad falling off her fork as she leaves it shivering just below her chin.

At one point she's nodding to herself not talking to me.

Not listening.

Eyes glossy and her head nodding rhythmically. It's like she's had a stroke. I ask her if she's okay and she says, "Ade, I really do think it will happen soon. Can't you just feel the energy in the air?"

"Yeah. No. What will happen soon?"

"The rising up. The end of our earthly bonds. I am so looking forward to seeing your grandmother again. I'm sure she's excited as all get out to see you too."

"Sure, Mom. It'll be swell."

By the end of the meal Mom's eaten maybe a third of her salad. Most of the time she's just spent mumbling to herself, pointing at my plate, telling me to eat up, and laughing at awkward moments in response to something funny only she can hear.

I haven't seen my mom like this before.

I imagine Mom before the divorce, when Dad still loved her. When she still loved him. I remember her laughing and having fun, her not concerned about eternal salvation but about how I was doing in school and what movie I wanted to see on the weekend. This mom, the one rambling and lost in front of me, it's clear why Dad vanished.

The ride home we're going slow because I'm tired.

It's raining hard. The road is a river and I can barely see.

But I'm so tired on top of it.

I want to pull over. I want just take a break.

I think about asking Mom to drive, but figure we're close. We must be only a few blocks from home. That's when it happens, my eyes close down. We're somewhere just past Eighth Avenue and I stop seeing.

I hear the crash before I wake up.

This, me crashing the car on accident, is completely new.

The sound is like a wave and I imagine it rampaging down Monaco and sweeping over cars and ripping hedges loose. The night sky sparking as the streetlamps topple over and split. Next comes the crunch. My head meets the wheel despite the seat belt, despite the fact I'm only going thirty. I can't see her but I know Mom's hands are clasped in prayer, her face as content as when she's fast asleep. For her, this wreck could be a one-way ticket to salvation.

The tunnel.

The lights.

The swirl.

The darkness.

The exit.

My eyes open again to night and stars.

I know immediately it's the future. Same waxy sheen. Black-light blues. I'm guessing it's soon, though. Maybe weeks away. I'm not focused on anything, not expecting anything but darkness.

I'm on a beach. Maybe the north end of the Cherry Creek Reservoir.

I get the fact that it's the same place the gruff old man on the phone mentioned.

The obscene phone caller, maybe he wasn't just a nut.

I'm thinking now that maybe I should be worried.

Should have been stressing earlier.

Could it be he knew what would happen?

The smell is strong. Strong like a marsh. Still, I can smell the rubber on the tennis courts above the reek of water. And I home in on it like the million moths that crash through the night to the phosphorus light of the courts. I follow the rise and fall of the water. Just the sand. The soft collapse of the lake. The wind in the reeds. The buzz of insects. The moon is only a sliver, just a scythe.

What's really weird is that I don't feel like me.

I mean that my skin is mine. The muscles, the weight of me, it's all the same. But inside, I'm angrier than I've ever been in my life. I'm seething. Furious.

My hands are fists. I'm walking to the tennis courts.

And then I'm not.

Like in a movie, there's a jump cut. Like the reels got mixed up or the projector skipped. Suddenly I'm not walking to the tennis courts but kneeling in the sand, my knees in the cold water of the reservoir, and my hands, well, my hands are around Jimi's neck. His face is under the water. His arms are thrashing. His legs kicking.

But I'm bearing down hard. My arms out straight, locked. My fingers, they're white from blood loss. Jimi's face, it's white too. His eyes are so bugged out.

There is surprisingly little noise. Just the kick of him in the sand.

Very little noise until he goes slack. His arms drop. His face stops contorting.

Me, I'm still raging.

I'm shaking. I'm so furious, so pulsing with hate, that I throw my head back and howl into the night like some kind of animal. I try to walk away and just fall over facing the lake. It's as if there was never anyone else here but me. Just the hum of the lights, the buzz of the insects, and the slow lap of the lake. Jimi's feet sticking up out of the water.

It's weird, but I'm not surprised when the guy in the Mexican wrestling mask gives me a hand, helps me up. Jimi's dad, he's wearing a tuxedo and his mask is white. He helps me up, pats me on the back, and says, "You tried."

I'm still shaking, ask, "Tried what?"

"To stop this. Storm's here, Ade. It's begun, you are almost ready."

"Do you know the guy I just drowned? Is that what this is about?"

The luchador nods slowly. Says, "You don't know the half of it."

And then the vision ends.

Back to black and then white and then the now.

The road comes into focus first. The trees. The streetlights swaying.

Mom and I, we're still on the road. Car idling. It's late enough that no one else is nearby. We've hit a tree and the only sound is the steady drip of fluid from under the car and the hazard lights tick ticking. My body is vibrating from the high of the Buzz. And even though it's a weak Buzz, it's been so long I'm really feeling it.

Mom, next to me, is fine. Her head still bowed in prayer, hands still clasped.

The front of the car is dinged, but the tree, a thin pine, got the worst of it.

I tell Mom that we're okay. I tell her to open her eyes. I say, "Look."

She does it slowly, looks out into the darkness at the skinny tree I've made a mess of, and then over at me. She smiles, tears beading her eyelashes, and runs her hand through my hair. It comes back to her slick. Dark.

Mom says, "You're bleeding."

"I don't feel it. Probably old."

"It's okay. We'll get it fixed. Are you—"

I say, "I'm fine."

She says, "I'm okay too."

I say, "Let's just drive home."

Before leaving I inspect the damage and find only a few scrapes, one busted headlight, and the bumper split. Not bad. Getting back in the car is difficult because my legs are shaky. My body's jittery with the Buzz though the infusion is slight. I put the car in reverse and as we back out into the street most of the tree comes with us. We drag this teenage fir tree down half a block before it's cut loose.

At every intersection, every red light, I see snippets of the vision. I hear the phelgmy chuckle of the obscene phone caller, the guy who predicted this. Him telling me to avoid the reservoir. That sends so many little quakes down my spine that I look like I'm spasming for a few blocks. And, of course, I see Jimi's face in every streetlight. His eyes in every pair of taillights.

And every time I hit the gas my stomach goes up like we're on a log ride.

The way home, the night around us is pretty much silent, outside of the scraping of the bumper on the asphalt. Close to home there are a few scattered dog barks under the near-constant hum of the streetlamps, but I only hear the muffled screams of Jimi going under. Sometimes so loud, I jump.

When we pull in the driveway, the freaks on the porch notice and run over, but I gun the car and slip into the garage before they're onto us. Nice thing we have a fast garage door.

Again my mom says nothing about them.

But getting out of the car, Mom asks, "Did you talk to baby Jesus?"

"No, Mom." My heart is thudding and my head swimming still from the Buzz. It's been a while since I've felt it this strong. It's overwhelming. Like when I first tried chew and almost puked from the jolt of it.

"What did He tell you?"

"Nothing, Mom. I didn't talk to baby Jesus."

I realize I'm shaking. Goose bumps pebble my skin.

Mom puts her hand on my thigh and squeezes it. Just like I do when I'm mothering her. And she sighs and mumbles, "It's fine to be humble. All comes out in the wash."

I kiss her on the forehead before she creeps inside the house. She's still crying when I leave. She just lets me know that she's so proud of me for being who I am. For sticking to my guns. For my faith.

I hit the garage door button, pray I don't hit anyone, and then jam the car into reverse and peel out. I'm guessing, just based on the sound of tires squealing, that the neighbors are all calling the cops.

A block away I call Vauxhall.

My voice, it's shaking. Breaking.

She mentions that she's out with Jimi, that they're at Twist and Shout, and she asks if maybe I can meet them in front of East, just on the lawn there. She asks me if it's okay that Jimi's around.

And I say, "I'm guessing he's going to want to know this anyway."

THREE

Jimi's leaning against a statue.

Something like a column in the middle of a fountain, only there's no water in it. He's leaning there as though he's taking a break from filming. Lighting a cigarette and exhaling so slowly that the smoke just makes a cloud around his face. Of course, he's got cowboy boots on and sunglasses and the neon lights are reflected in them as though he painted them there.

When I see Jimi, as I'm walking over across Colfax, all I can think is: Maybe it wouldn't be such a bad thing if I killed this dude.

I mean, the guy's a dick. Would anyone other than Vaux really mind?

Vauxhall comes walking over to me, she's dressed in black, has a sweater on. She hugs me and then looks in my eyes like she can read me. And she can, whatever she sees it makes her bottom lip quiver. That quiver, I've got to admit it makes me feel good. She's scared. She's worried. She cares.

Vaux asks what happened.

I say, "Something very bad."

Running her fingers along the bruise on my forehead she asks, "What'd you see?"

"Death."

Jimi strolls over leisurely. He flicks his cigarette over his shoulder and then takes his sunglasses off and folds them slowly, carefully, and puts them in the front pocket of his jeans. Then he cracks his knuckles, this fucker. He says, "Hey, Ade. I can see you've been busy."

"Jimi," I say. "I just saw your dad again."

He isn't fazed. "Ah, and how's Poppa Ministry?"

"He seems fine."

Jimi smiles. "Vauxhall's told me that you've been seeing him. That he's been way out and close in. He's spooked, Ade. He's onto me. To us. I have a feeling that the Ministry family massacre will be going down soon."

"Sooner than you think," I say. "I saw you drown."

"Drown?" Jimi chokes. "Did you say drown?"

"Yes."

Vauxhall's mouth is hanging open. She's shaking her head.

Jimi shrugs. "How?"

"I kill you."

And Jimi busts out laughing. Taking in deep gulps of the night air. The sound of his laughter is surprisingly loud. It's what you hear in a theater in surround. I'm surprised there aren't cars screeching to a standstill. Doubled over in pain, his laughter is nearly violent. And it takes him a long while to regain his composure.

After clearing his throat and snorting back snot, wiping his mouth with his sleeve, Jimi says, "*You* kill me?"

What I feel is anger. Not like any anger I've felt before. It comes racing up from my gut like it's on fire, like I've just gargled down battery acid. My skin is buzzing, becoming unfocused on me. I want to gnash my teeth like an animal.

Vauxhall can see it in me. She can read it the way you can read the dangerous movements of a dog or a snake. She says, "When, Ade? When does this happen?"

"A few weeks from now. Maybe sooner."

"Where?" Jimi asks, hands up.

"Reservoir. Cherry Creek, I'm guessing."

Wiping his forehead, Jimi says, "And my dad was there, huh?"

"He was."

"And I'm guessing he didn't try and stop you?"

"He didn't."

Jimi looks at Vauxhall. He says, "Not going to happen."

"What I see always happens, Jimi. Always," I say.

Jimi does a farmer blow into the grass at his feet and then puts an arm around Vauxhall's shoulder, says, "If that were true, Ade, then I doubt I'd have had visions of me banging your girl here for the rest of the year."

Vauxhall looks appalled, her mouth drops open, and she pushes Jimi away.

I close my eyes tight, the rage is so intense.

My body vibrates like a flame.

It's so unnatural, like I've had plastic surgery or something.

Jimi guffaws hard again. Eyes tear up again. He says, to me, "You, Ade, live in the shadows. You're so removed from the real world that you wouldn't even know what it is to really—"

And he stops short because I tackle him. The two of us go crashing into the fountain, the cold, dead-leaf-choked water spilling over the side in sloshing waves. I'm on top of him, pushing my fists into his face, into his stomach. I'm hitting his shoulders, hitting his forehead, his eyes. And I'm kicking. With every molecule of my body I'm trying to beat him into the concrete of the fountain.

I'm not doing this for long. Jimi gets his legs under me and kicks me back, out of the water, out of the fountain, and I fall back hard on the sidewalk, my breath rushing out in one big dying-fish gasp.

Vauxhall's not at my side immediately. She's standing there in shock.

Jimi pulls himself up, rancid water and decaying leaves falling off him like he's some swamp monster stepping out of the bayou. He steps over to me. Breathing hard, his chest rising and falling so heavily, he looks at me and then wipes his nose with the back of his hand. He says, sounding so tired, "You're exactly what I expected, Ade."

Then he turns and leaves.

Vauxhall, before she follows him, she comes over to me and leans down and puts her hand on my forehead and asks, "Is this what happens when you quit?"

She doesn't let me answer. She says, "You need to try. You need to change the future. I know you've tried it before and it went bad, but you can't do this. Not to Jimi. Not to yourself. Change the future, Ade. For me."

"Everything I'm doing is for you, Vauxhall."

She is crying when she kisses me. It is very tender like a flower petal.

And Vauxhall's only there a moment; her beautiful face is the moon just for a blink, so soft and so perfect. And then she's gone too.

By the time I get up off the sidewalk, my clothes are already starting to dry. On Colfax, there are only a few cars going by and most of them are cop cars or taxicabs. The winos have come out. The hookers as well. By the time I get up off the sidewalk, the sun is only a few hours away from breaking in.

Limping back to my car, my cell rings. The number's unlisted. I answer.

The voice on the other end is familiar, sickeningly so. "I was right, wasn't I?"

It's the obscene phone caller. The gravel-voiced old man.

"Yeah," I say. "Who are you?"

"Not one person. There are many of us."

I'm at my car. Pause before getting in. "What do you mean?"

"You can't change what you saw, Ade. You know that by now. Surely you know that much. Don't even try it."

"My mom set you up to this?"

Gravel voice laughs. "That's rich, Ade. Average life of a scryer, right?"

And he hangs up.

CHAPTER EIGHT

ONE

Dear Professor Susan Graham—

Thank you again for your replies to my letters. I realize they might come off as a bit nutty. I really appreciate your taking the time to help me.

To throw something new in the mix: How about alternate realities? Parallel universes?

See, I'm asking because there was a show on television last night, one of the educational cable channels, about how some physicists think that our world is all Swiss-cheesed through and through with alternate realities. The show mentioned something about infinite numbers of parallel universes where anything, and everything, I guess, happens. You agree with that? Also the show said there was no way to prove this idea. Like, ever.

I'm going back to the whole changing-the-future thing and I'm thinking, Hey, this parallel universe idea sounds like it could work just fine.

I mean, if you try and change the future here, who's to say it doesn't change in another, closely related universe? Or maybe the original vision wasn't of this universe in the first place? Or maybe I have no clue what I'm talking about.

What do you think?

Again, thanks so much for your time on this. I know that my physics teacher is already super excited about the idea and I'm sure I'll get an A. Just sure of it. And, who knows, but maybe someday I'll actually meet someone who can see the future and I'll have some advice? Kidding, of course.

Thank you,

Ade Patience

TWO

I'm standing in a parking garage.

My jeans are still a bit wet but nothing major. Nothing embarrassing.

I find a leaf, orange, in my hair.

When I left the house after a five-hour nap I told my mom I'd be out even later than usual. I told her that something important came up and it will probably change a lot about the way I do things, about the way I'm living my life. I said, "And by the way, I've stopped trying to see the future. I'm going clean for love."

My mom, she was kind of sleeping at the time. She yawned and mumbled something about me "taking good care" and "being a blessing" and then fell back into her pillow and let loose with a volley of lazy kisses. I know that in the morning, when it's sunk in, then she'll freak. The Revelation Book, she won't give it up easy.

I've been in this garage more times than I can count.

It's next to Paris on the Platte, this old café, and the garage is dark and gnarly and the walls of it are covered in a thick suit of soot like the place had been on fire for a few decades before the snows put it out. Not where I want to be waiting.

Especially since I'm on my knees behind an old Subaru.

Luckily, I'm not waiting long.

Belle shows up in her ride and steps out in a cloud of pot smoke. She's dressed sexily. The boots, the short skirt, the unbuttoned blouse. Her hair's all tasseled out. Teased and then sprayed still. Incredibly, she doesn't see me.

Why I'm in the garage, hunkered down behind a car, is 'cause I realized something last time I spoke with the old man. He used the word "scryer." I looked it up on my cell, it means a seer or like a fortune-teller.

Fact is: I find it very odd that both Belle and the old dude used the same random word. And why I'm in the garage is to follow Belle and make sure that when she took off at the end of the summer she didn't actually find more people with abilities like mine. If she did, I need to talk to them pronto.

Belle walks over to a door I never noticed before.

This door, it's on the back of one of the buildings that sit up right against the parking garage, only it doesn't look like a door to a warehouse or an office building. It looks like someone's front door with a little wavy glass window and a knocker on it. The knocker is a skull.

Oh, and there's a symbol painted on the door in white paint. It's like a crosshatch sort of thing and kind of looks like a hand if it were painted by a child or someone with very little time and education.

Belle takes the knocker, raps it twice, and then steps back.

Then she lights a smoke.

She's almost smoked the cigarette down to the filter when the door opens. A hand reaches out and summons her in. It's connected to an arm in a leather coat and the coat's wrapped around the skinny body of a guy. Front of the leather coat, in white paint, reads CHARLIE. Charlie slaps a tattooed hand down on Belle's shoulder. Smiles at her big with silver-capped teeth. Says, "Good to see you again."

They disappear into the lightlessness beyond the door and I run over before the door has time closing Just barely make it, wedge my foot in. And then I open the door real slow and follow them.

Charlie leads Belle down a dark corridor that looks like something on the tenth floor of the most boring hotel on Earth. "How long has it been? Weeks, right?"

I follow them down a flight of stairs by an empty kitchen and then to another flight of stairs under the kitchen where the subbasement and the boilers are. Then follow them left past a line of storage closets and the place is like a horror movie with just one lightbulb drifting down from the ceiling. The place is spray painted with cobwebs.

End of the corridor, after I've passed like fifty storage lockers and walked halfway across town, I lose sight of them near a big door that's rumbling the way low-riders with super bass do. This wooden door is like something you'd see at a fun park on a pirate's ship. Two doors that swing open wide open in the middle and they're shaking, jittering, in the frame from the bass doing double time on the other side of them.

I take a deep breath, let myself know that I won't die here, and pull the doors open wide in one big gesture. Inside, it's sick.

The walls, they're purple. The floors, they're purple too. Shag carpets. The ceilings, they're tiled with mirrors. It's like a discotheque imported from somewhere in the Baltic. The furniture is all leather. Black leather with yellow throw pillows. Only lights are thousands of Christmas lights wound up like bird's nests across the ceiling and over the walls. Video-game consoles line the back wall. Somewhere there's a DJ spinning. The music is raw, filthy electronics. On a circular couch in the middle of the room three people are sitting, two girls and a guy, and they're staring hard at me. Other side of the room, two girls, maybe my age, sit on a black leather couch. They're twins. Hands in their laps. From here they're like ice sculptures in matching white almost Middle Eastern–looking dresses.

Charlie gets the music turned off and the quiet is nearly as loud.

Belle smiles at me, motions for me to walk over, asks, "Following me again, huh?"

"Yeah, I was bored," I say, eyes still wide.

"Well, welcome to the Lair."

"What is this?" I ask.

"What you've been wondering about. What you always hoped existed."

"Like?"

"Like a world of people who can do what you can do. Who understand you."

I'm stunned. Rooted to the spot. This place, these people. It can't be real.

This looks like the present, though. It is not plastic. The scene is not overly shiny.

Leading me forward slowly, Belle tells me that there are thousands of people you will never meet trying to figure out what you're going to do next. She tells me they're trying to figure out what you'll say at lunch, what you'll eat at dinner, who you'll ask to prom, who you won't, what you'll name you first child, when you'll die and what you'll answer for number three b on the physics final. She says, "These people will use anything and everything they can think of to see the future. It'll be podomancy, which is reading the future by looking at lines on feet, casting lots, which is seeing the future in tossed dice or bones, empyromancy (from smoke), austromancy (by listening to the wind), icthyomancy (observing fish), or ophimancy (watching the behavior of snakes). They will drop molten lead into water and listen for the hiss. They will use precious gems. Stare at shadows. Run their fingers along the shoulder bones of sheep. Study cracks in pavement. Or if they live in Denver they'll just be the LoDo Diviners."

And with that, I arrive.

Charlie pulls a chair up, something padded and folding, and I have a seat across from the Diviners. The three people sitting on the couch, the one in the middle is a guy. Belle introduces me, the three on the couch don't move, don't even raise their eyebrows or mouth a hello, and then she says, "This is Gilberto Baumgartner, he's the leader of the pack."

"What's new, Ade?" Gilberto asks leaning forward to offer me a cigarette.

Gilberto's wearing corduroy pants and a Sonic Youth tee that looks about twenty years old. He's got a knit cap pulled low over his head, a graying soul patch, and thin fingers like pale spiders. Black glasses. And he's old enough to have a kid my age. Of course, he's the guy Belle was with at Rock Island.

I shake my head. Say, "No, thanks."

Smoking the way old people smoke, his hands cupped around his cigarette, Gilberto looks me over and then shrugs. "You think it was like a big deal, the girl in the lunchroom coming true?"

"To me it was. Is."

He leans forward again. Leather rustling like leaves. "It's freaking huge, man."

That gets my heart racing.

I can't even count the times I've daydreamed about this, about meeting these people, well, not necessarily these people but people like them. In my mind I saw them as super glamorous or wearing monk's robes or floating on little colorful clouds. For the second time tonight, I'm not convinced that what I'm seeing is real. Like right now real.

Belle standing behind me, hands on my shoulders, says, "Gilberto reads palms. He's one of the best in the world; people come from all over the world to see him. He's like the Ayatollah of Prognostication."

To Gilberto's left, on the couch, is a mousy woman with thick-framed glasses like legal secretaries wore in 1983. They are electric blue and match her eye shadow. She's wearing a frumpy housewife dress. Something even an Amish woman would feel overdressed in. She's old enough to be a college dropout.

Belle says, "Lynne Raver can touch you and know when you're going to die."

Lynn says, "It's a great party trick."

And then, fast, silently, she reaches out and touches my hand. Her ring finger, really just the tip of it, is on my wrist for maybe two blinks and then she retracts her hand back to her lap. She says, "In your sleep, in a nursing home. Must be nice to know."

Belle, lips by my ear, whispers, "She can't see her own death. Very frustrating."

To me, Lynne says, "Heavy stuff, Ade. Really heavy. Can't think of anything like it. Can't think of anyone seeing that far out, years like that."

Gilberto says, "Not even Grandpa Razor."

Lynne says, "Not even the Metal Sisters."

And that's when the third person on the couch, the woman sitting to the right of Gilberto, speaks up. She's dressed like a Euro café regular, black leather pants tighter than hipster skater kids', and a black-and-white-striped sweater. She's wearing a purple wig. She's chewing gum. She's old enough to have seen the Second World War break out. Her voice is all sharp and Germanic and she says, "We want you to show us the way."

Belle says, "This is Anka Welbert. She can remote view. When she's in a trance she can send her mind spinning out into the world, look in on people, see the sights. Be anywhere."

"Way to what?" I ask, turn and look at Belle.

Anka says, "The way to prosperity. The way out of town."

I have no idea what she's talking about and I stare dumbfounded.

"What about . . . them?" I ask, looking over at the twins.

Belle beams. "The Metal Sisters. Janice and Katrina Zinc."

The twin girls, they nod at the same time. The effect is creepy.

"What do you say, Ade?" Gilberto asks.

"I have no idea what . . . What are you talking about?"

Silence.

To this I add: "Are you people for real? Why have you been hid-ing?"

Anka laughs first. She says, "We were never hiding, Ade. You just never noticed us. Have you walked down Colfax recently? Have you seen the neon signs? The billboards? Called any 1-900 numbers? We've always been here. Surrounding you, you could say."

Lynne adds: "Funny what you don't see when you're not looking."

Gilberto interrupts. "The guy who's been calling you, his name is Grandpa Razor. That's not really his real name, but no one knows just what his real name actually is. Doesn't even matter. What mat-ters is that Grandpa Razor can see into the future the way you can. He doesn't need to knock himself out or anything like that, he just needs to eat something particularly nasty—"

"He's a gastromancer," Lynne says.

"Right," Gilberto continues. "He sees things after eating. The more obscure the food, the further out he sees. Only Grandpa doesn't have your skills, Ade. What he sees, it's fuzzy most of the time. He gets just snippets. Just like thumbing through a magazine and missing most of the story."

"You're the real deal, babe," Belle says.

I feel like hugging these people. In this den of shadows, for the first time I feel like I've found a real family.

THREE

I say, loud and grinning, "Can I like move in with you guys?"

Gilberto chuckles, says, "Belle told us about you a while ago.

We weren't convinced at first. She wasn't convinced either, but she kept on us. She's the reason you're here."

I look at Belle. She smiles, waves.

I turn around, stare Belle down, and ask, "Why didn't you tell me?"

She makes a face. Puts on a happy act. "Let's not talk about it now."

"What about you, Belle? Do you have powers too?"

Belle shrugs. "No, but I'm still hoping to develop some."

"How's that?"

"Gilberto says that certain combinations of, well, chemicals can spur the sudden development of . . . wait, how'd you say it, Gilberto?"

Gilberto says, "Opioid modification of genes to promote electrical abnormalities."

Shaking my head, I ask him, "You a scientist or something?"

"I just read."

Belle says, "Really I'm just getting started."

Sounds ridiculously dangerous and totally mad science, but I let it go.

To the Diviners: "So the guy who's been calling, the Grandpa dude, he saw me at the reservoir killing someone. He didn't see it that clear, but I saw it. I saw me killing someone and doing it soon. Maybe even days from now. Can you help me?"

"I think we can," Gilberto says. "Tell us what you saw."

I tell them everything about seeing Vauxhall years ago and how it went down in real life. I tell them how I quit to win Vauxhall's heart and how in the car accident I saw myself killing Jimi like a dog in the water. I say, "What I really need you all to tell me is how

I can change the future. What I need is for you to help me not kill Jimi."

Silence.

Belle squeezes my shoulders. She whispers, "I'm sorry."

Gilberto says, "Can't change the future." He says it like it's the law. "All of us figure it out in our own special way. It's like unspoken, I guess. We all try at one point or another to change what we've seen when we don't like it and we all have to learn on our own the pain of what it means to be able to let go. Frankly, it's not easy being us, and you get used to it."

I just keep on keeping on.

"I know that it seems impossible," I say. "I've tried to do it and things only got worse, you know. It was like things sped up. But I think that I just need to see it from another angle. Maybe if I can play around with the way I see the—"

Gilberto stops me. "Don't get caught up in the mechanics, Ade."

I say, "I just want to understand it. This is life or death."

Anka says, "Nothing matters but what comes next, Ade. Understanding how? Leave that to the historians. You get too caught up in the details and everything will just whiz by you."

I laugh out of anxiety. They don't laugh with me.

These aren't my people.

"You guys don't care that I'm going to kill someone?" I ask.

Belle says, softly, "Jimi's always been an asshole."

I stand up. Appalled. "I don't want to kill him," I say. "I'm going to change it."

Gilberto motions for me to sit. I don't. He cocks his head to the right, motions again. Still, I don't sit. He sighs, says, "You're going about this thing the wrong way. Getting all worked up over what is going to happen is like freaking out that the sun will rise in the morning. It will. It always does. Can't stop it. But what you can do . . ."

And Anka takes the wheel like it's some ventriloquist act. ". . . is change the way you see the future action. You have seen yourself in the future, correct? And have you ever seen yourself in prison?"

"No."

"And have you ever seen yourself talking with police about it?"

"No."

Gilberto claps. "You see you've already made the decision. Only you don't know it yet. Since you're not in prison in the future and I'm assuming you haven't had visions of visiting a gravesite every year, then I think it's safe to say that no one, well, no one but maybe us, knows that you kill Jimi. What I'm telling you, Ade, is that you should get over trying to stop it and move on to the next step: trying to forget it."

Silence for maybe ten heartbeats and then I say, point-blank, "No."

Anka looks to Gilberto. She cackles the way witches in cartoons do. "No?"

"I'm going to stop it," I say. "No wonder you're all hanging out under a parking garage. No wonder no one knows about this, this ridiculous scene you've got here. Fact is: You're all a bunch of pussies. But not me. You tell me that I'm something special, that my being able to see the future clearly, not in stops and starts and not in pieces, makes me somehow better than the usual, then I'm going to use that. I will not kill Jimi Ministry. That's why I'm not in prison in the future."

Lynne yawns. To no one in particular she says, "Another hero. That'll change."

Anka adds, "A comic book wannabe."

Gilberto shushes them, lights another smoke and, again, offers me one. Again I decline. He says, "I don't think you're an idiot, Ade. You've got balls. While I don't think it's going to make any difference, I'm going to recommend some people for you to meet with. Other Diviners. If anything, they'll help talk you out of this. When you've had enough, you come back here and see us and let us groom you for something better."

I choke. "Groom me? For what?"

Gilberto says, "Talent like yours is once in a lifetime—"

"I quit," I say. "Went clean, remember?"

"Yeah, you said that already," Gilberto says. "Look, let the Metal Sisters try their thing. If they can't help you, maybe Slow Bob can. Grandpa Razor's a last resort. Think of him as the puppet master. All of us, we live by Grandpa's rules. What he says is law."

I look over at the twins. Almost forgotten they were in the room.

The girls, they wave.

FOUR

Remember that one really old movie about a town filled with creepy children?

And at the end of the movie it turns out the kids have telekinetic abilities and they're like the offspring of UFOs? Yeah, well, the Metal Sisters are their older siblings.

I can't tell which one is which, but the one on my left, she pats the seat next to her.

I nod. Walk over, uncomfortable under her gaze.

She says, "I'm Katrina. I don't tell the future. Just read what you have. But if I try, I can really get in there. Get in deep. It doesn't always work flawlessly. It's sometimes all hazy. Sometimes people just aren't enough in tune to really get a good reading. But it means knowing everything. Intimately. All the moles and stray hairs. You want more details, you're going to have to open up to me. You game?"

The way she talks, it's totally at odds with the way she's dressed.

"Sure," I say. "But what's in it for you?"

Katrina makes this disappointed face. "How rude, Ade. Of course I'm just here to help you. You know, member of the community and all."

"Community, right."

She makes a thinking face. "Looking inside people's heads, there's a certain, you know, *high*."

I say, "I know."

She smiles. Pats her lap. "Come on over here. I'll be sweet."

I sit next to her. She puts her hands on my forehead. It begins like a massage and I close my eyes. Her nails in my hair. The sound of her soft breathing. The smell of spearmint.

All breathy, she says, "Think about how you got here. Rewind back to the vision."

Her hands on my head, I see it all unfold backward. Everything from school and Vauxhall and Paige and then I'm in the car with my mom and suddenly, in reverse, my head is leaving the steering wheel.

She says, "Oh, and I should mention that sometimes, depending on how I'm feeling, et cetera et cetera, I can erase your memory. Hasn't happened accidentally in a superlong time, so try not to stress too hard about it. Cool?"

I look over at Belle, the Diviners. All of them, in unison, as if this is some cheeseball sitcom moment, they give me a thumbs-up.

And then everything goes white.

FIVE

The feeling is sensitive.

Raw.

At first it's just the brush of Katrina's fingers through my hair. Like a cat's tongue. But then it hurts. Burns, even. This is when the white clears and I see Katrina smiling.

"How long?" I ask.

"Only a few minutes. But felt long, huh?"

I nod. Try to stand up, but I'm woozy like I'm plastered.

"Don't," Katrina says. She holds me down. Gently. "You're going to want to sit there for a few more minutes. Let things settle."

It's only when she says it that I realize I'm totally seasick. At least that's the feeling. Like trying to read in a car. I close my eyes. Pull myself together. Think happy thoughts. Steady thoughts.

"So?"

Katrina rubs my back. Her long nails clicking on every vertebra bump. She says, "Messed up. You're very angry. So much rage inside you. I tried to gather some details for you, stuff that you might not have noticed. You noticed the moon, right?"

"No."

"It was shaped like a C," Katrina says. "Waxing crescent. If it happens this month, that's in like next week."

"Okay. And if not?"

"Then next month, maybe three weeks from now. But, to be honest with you, I think it'll go down next week. Soon, huh? Last but not least, you saw the tattoos, right?"

"What about them?"

Katrina snorts, the same as her sister, and she says, "Silly, he's got a picture of your mom tattooed on his left forearm. It's freaking ridiculous you didn't notice it. Big and she's smiling. Kinda spooky, really."

"How about the masked guy? Any chance you saw him?"

Katrina rolls her eyes. She says, "You got yourself a parasite, Ade."

"A what?"

"Parasite. You know, like a tapeworm or something. Only this is the psychic kind. This guy, I've seen some like him before. They get into people's dreams. People's memories. Sometimes, like with you, it can be visions. He's feeding off it most likely. Getting kicks from it. You want to really change what you've seen, and I'm not saying you can but if you really, really, super really wanted to, I'd find that parasite of yours. Then again, eventually, he'll find you. Not easy to lose them once they've locked on."

When she says the word "locked" she makes a clicking sound with her tongue.

My stomach turns.

"Who do you think he is?"

Katrina shrugs. "Could be anyone. You need to see someone else about that problem. Grandpa Razor will know."

I ask Katrina if she thinks I can change it. I ask if she knows anyone who's ever been able to change the future. I say, "Even if I knew that one person did it once. That would mean a lot."

Katrina says, "I can't think of anyone."

"You think I'm stupid for trying?"

"You did try before. Didn't work so well that time, did it?"

"Don't think it's possible, do you?"

Licking her lips, she says, "Not really. Grandpa Razor frowns on anyone trying to break the rules. Besides, as I'm sure you already know, bad things happen when you try and take control. Trust in Grandpa, Ade. He wouldn't lie."

I'm getting very aggravated. I ask Katrina why she does this. Why she bothers.

She says, "Money, mostly. We're also famous. You seen the Web site? The photo spread? This is our life. Could be yours too, if you were willing to go with the flow. You know, not try to fuck up so much."

"Are you serious?"

"Of course."

I stand up, look back at them, point to Janice, the silent sister. "And what about you? Do you have any thoughts on this? Do you want to do a—"

Janice, she just shrugs.

I look over to the Diviners, and Gilberto stands up and walks over to me. He puts a hand on my shoulder and tells me that I really should consider just accepting the status quo. He tells me that even though deep in his heart he hates clichés and he hates corporate culture, he's convinced that being able to really live means learning to accept certain truths. "Basically, Ade," he says, "it means putting yourself in the driver's seat."

Him, I flick off. The rest of them, I ignore.

Charlie shows me the door, opening it and waving me out. Belle follows.

In the hallways leading to the parking structure, Belle tries to talk me into coming back. Just to talk for a bit longer. She says, "Promise we'll just talk casually. I so want you to be a part of this."

"I need a breather, Belle."

Belle blows me a kiss. Mouths, Sorry.

And I leave.

SIX

I take back roads.

Lose myself only a few blocks to the west of Paris.

My frustration boils over. The Sisters, the Diviners, no one wants to change the future. No one wants to even try. I tried to save Harold and still, he died. Jimi will die and no one but me wants to lift a finger. I smash my steering wheel repeatedly with my fists.

Then, still fuming, I pull over and slam on the breaks.

Also I roll down the window and chuck CDs onto the street. This is the new really pissed-off me getting crazy. Just needing to act out. Mostly I toss old CDs. Mostly beat-up, scratched-all-over CDs that work about half the time. Dinosaur Jr., Minor Threat, and some mix from Paige titled *Everyone About Everything* go sailing into the night.

And that's when I notice the smell in my car.

It's like heavy perfume.

I scan the rearview and see nothing.

"You've got to be kidding me," I say loud. Just in case.

"No." The voice comes from right behind my seat. A girl's voice. Brittle. I know the voice immediately. It's Janice Zinc, the lesser of the Metal Sisters.

I ask, "Janice?"

"Yeah."

"Any chance you'd crawl out from back there? Almost scared the living crap—"

She climbs up and settles down in the passenger seat. All slumped over into herself. Janice looks worn down. She pulls out a beat-up purse that's losing rhinestones by the second and from it she pulls out a cigarette. "You mind?" she asks.

I wave an okay and she lights up. Her white dress, it suddenly doesn't looks so nice. The ice sculpture's quickly melting away.

After two long drags she says, "Katrina didn't tell you everything. We're connected, you know? I can see what she can see."

"You said that."

"She's the best at the readings, knows how to navigate, but I'm there for the ride too. I see everything she sees. Know everything she knows."

Another drag and a deep cough and Janice informs me that she and her sister saw just about everything I've seen over the past few months. "Just because Katrina went in to see that drowning, it doesn't mean she didn't see more. When she's in your head, she can read it like a book. Just flip the pages back. When we're in your head, Ade, nothing's sacred."

She tells me that she knows about Vauxhall. She tells me that she feels bad about my home life. The slumped-over psychic next to me says, "You're much more messed up than anyone could even imagine."

"Why were you really in the backseat of my car?"

Janice rolls down her window and chucks the cigarette. "Your new girl."

"Tell me."

Janice smiles. "I know what you really think of me, Ade. I repulse you. You think I'm stupid. The dumb sister."

"I've never even met you before tonight! This is crazy, you've got me confu—"

"Don't bother, Ade," Janice interrupts. "Won't matter. Here's the thing: I'm a spiteful person and, honestly, I'd very much like to hurt you."

"I'm sorry, but seriously, I think you—"

"Won't matter, Ade. You were in Boulder just a few—"

"Yeah. I party. I . . . I was . . . What is this about?"

Janice puts a finger to my lips to shush me. Her nails sparkle. She says, "At Roger's party. You'd banged your head up something pretty bad earlier and when I saw you, you were all dazed. Drunk and all out of it like from the concussion. Didn't stop you from being incredibly sweet. I think you said something about having seen me before, about how you saw me in a vision years ago. Very poetic. Very sweet, Ade."

"Really, Janice, I don't think . . . It wasn't about you, it was . . ."

Looking at Janice, her sinking into the seat next to me, I can't recall a single image, not a moment, from the scene she's describing. No recollection of spending time with her.

She says, "We kissed a lot."

"Who?"

"You and me, silly."

"Nothing more, though, right?"

"Depends how you define more."

I groan and feel bad doing it, but it just escapes. "It's not you," I say. "Just that I don't remember any of this. I think I was confused and . . . Please, Janice, tell me about Vauxhall. Tell me what you know."

"Horrible," Janice coos. "You have no memory at all of it, do you? The things you told me, you would never believe how sweet they were."

"I'm sorry, Janice. Please. Tell me about Vauxhall."

Janice starts with, "I wouldn't be surprised if you've forgotten most of your life. I wonder just how much of what you think you see is real. These visions of the future, how do you even know they're yours? Just 'cause you see yourself, how do you know that's you? Amazing what the mind will come up with. Even more amazing what the mind can will itself to forget. Jimi Ministry was with you at that party, Ade. He talked to me. Asked me to look at something inside his head. Something, well, very bad for you and Vauxhall."

My heart tumbles. My mind is electric with anger. All the things I'm thinking are so ugly. So many of them brutal. The churning is breaking me apart.

"What is it, Janice?"

She laughs. "You sure you want this?"

I'm not, but I'm having trouble breathing.

Janice is like, "It's really sad stuff."

Bracing myself, I say, "I need to know."

"It will change everything."

"Tell me."

"You will never forget again."

I nod. I need to know this, but as soon as Janice starts speaking, I want to plug my ears. I need to know what she's going to tell me, but I don't want to hear it. Not from her and not like this.

Janice says, "You're here because Jimi wants you here. All of this, it's his little game. You're the pawn, Ade. He's been planning it, well, I can't even begin to imagine how long. And the thing is, you're just so messed up that he's made it work. Whatever I tell you it's already too late. Vauxhall is his. I've looked into his head. Jimi's been to Grandpa Razor, he's gotten the future. His future and, not surprisingly, you're not in it. Vauxhall and Jimi have a great little family. A nice home. Jimi one, Ade zero."

I'm biting my lower lip so hard it's ballooning out.

"Doesn't make any sense—"

Janice chuckles to herself. "That's just the thing, Ade. You have no idea what you've actually seen. You've forgotten us getting, well, cuddly, just a few weeks ago. Can you imagine the other stuff you've forgotten? Can you imagine the visions that maybe you've forgotten?"

"Everything I've seen I've remembered."

She laughs loud. "Not at all," Janice says. "Remember, I've been in there." And she taps my forehead with a cold finger. "The time you went to the ER, got hospitalized, surgery, you had a vision. You remember what you saw?"

I try. "Jimi's dad."

"And after?"

"Something really far out. Me looking in a mirror. And, I couldn't see—"

"You could see, though, Ade. You could see just fine. Only you forgot. Want me to show you what you saw?"

I'm in a daze, biting back my tongue. I nod.

Janice, stroking the back of my neck with her sharp nails, she says, "Your past catches up with you, Ade. All those concussions, all the damage, it has to go somewhere. To say you change is putting it lightly. The anger, the violence. You go a little nuts, frankly."

She touches my face, runs her fingers with both hands through my hair just the same as her sister did and my skin tingles. My eyes roll back. Janice's digging into my memory, cutting through the cloud of damage and mental scar tissue. It feels like she's swimming inside my skull.

The vision comes up quickly. Me again in front of the mirror. I'm focused in and older and I'm sitting in a wheelchair. The reason I had trouble seeing this, the reason it was so fuzzy, is easily explained by the look in my eyes. It's dull. It's the look of a fish in an aquarium. The dead-eye stare of an insect. This future, it's me as I've always worried I'd become. Me trapped in a failing brain. What's worse, I'm clearly in a hospital. The walls are white and the floors are white and the ceiling tiles in this place are white. The reek of ammonia is strong. At first I'm sure I'm just watching myself in this mirror, but it quickly becomes clear it's not actually a mirror, it's a window. Not watching myself, I'm staring through me to the parking lot below where a man and a woman are leaning against a car kissing. The man is an older Jimi. The woman, gorgeous and bright, is an older Vauxhall. I scream so slowly that it hurts my jaw.

Janice takes her fingers from my head. The vision evaporates and I'm back in the car with my ears buzzing, my fingers bloodless from tension.

And Janice says, "Jimi's under the impression that they do that, sit out in front of your special person's home and make out, on a monthly basis. It's cruel, but from what I hear Jimi's kind of a vindictive person, so—"

"Impossible," I interrupt. "What I see, it happens. Either Jimi dies or I change the future and I save him. But if I save him it won't end up like that. It can't end up like that."

"Can't win all the time, can we?"

I think I fly into a rage, but I'm not sure exactly how it happens or exactly what even takes place. I know that I kick my way out of the car. I don't open the door first. I don't roll down the window. I just kick and kick and kick until I somehow hit the lock and get out. In the street, I know that I swear up into the sky. What's last is that I kick my car and then I tell Janice she needs to leave.

She asks me to drop her off back at the Lair. "Not my fault," she says.

"You climbed in my car to ruin my life," I say. "You can walk."

She calls Katrina to pick her up and I leave her waiting on the side of the road. This little trail of rhinestones tinkling in the dark around her.

I drive to nowhere.

And as I move, the houses flashing past, the anger slowly subsides.

By the time I get to a park with picnic benches and a pond, I'm no longer churning. The rage has subsided. In its place, the sickening feeling of inevitability. I keep repeating to myself that old saying about how it's better to have loved and lost rather than never loved in the first place, and I realize how much I hate the expression.

But this part of me, its defeatist and I hate it. I refuse to give in to it. Refuse to listen to it anymore.

I'm not going to let Jimi drown.

I will not kill him.

I will be fine.

SEVEN

The morning sun is just starting to spray the sky orange.

I park across the street from the park and I go for a walk over to an empty drainage ditch and sit on top of one of the dirt mounds nearby and watch the sun come up. I watch the sun bleach the dirt and gravel and weeds inch by inch by inch. When it hits my feet I call Vauxhall.

She answers on the third ring, her voice all warped from sleep.

"Hey, Vaux. Sorry to call so early."

"Ade?"

"Yeah."

"What's going on? You okay?"

"I am."

I listen to Vaux breathe in the static. The houses across from me are now hit by the sunlight. Their windows not see-through any longer, just blankets of yellow.

"Vaux, what if you fall in love with someone?"

"What do you mean?"

I can hear her rubbing her eyes. I can see her propping herself up on her bed.

"I mean what if you love someone, you'd stop, then—"

I don't need to finish. Vaux, jumping in to fill any silence, says, "Yes."

"Really?"

"I don't . . . I haven't ever been in love, Ade. Not like what you mean."

"But if you were. If it was love like that, could you stop? Replace it with me."

Vaux is only a whisper on the other end. Just her breathing in electronic haze. The sun has fully risen and the shadows are so long. My shadow from the top of the dirt hill soars over the construction site to the houses so far away. My stretched-out head almost touching them.

"I think so," Vaux says.

She says, "For you, I will."

I sigh into the phone and all the way back to Denver I hear Vauxhall sigh as well.

"Are you happy?" I ask her.

"Very, very happy," she says. "What's funny is that for the longest time I thought I was so strong. Powerful the way people in control are. Me and these guys, I don't know what I really believed I was doing for them, but I felt like I was wanted. Like I was needed. Really needed. But, it wasn't power at all. It wasn't strength. I can see it now. Feel it now. You and me, for the first time in my life, this is real. And it feels so beautiful."

"I know. It does. It really does. Look, there are a few more things I need to do. But I can stop this, Vaux. I can make it so I don't kill Jimi, so the future doesn't happen. I'll come to you soon."

I think she blows me a kiss, but it's hard to hear, might just be static.

Just as I'm hanging up, Belle calls on the other line.

"Can you come pick me up? I'm not cool to drive."

"You're kidding, right?"

"Pretty please." And she even blows a kiss.

EIGHT

I make my way back over to Paris and find Belle sitting in the parking structure just outside the door to the Diviners' danceteria.

She's sitting cross-legged, smoking a cigarette, and blinking furiously.

I pull up, open the door, she hops in. Asks me to drop her off at a friend's place in Arvada.

I say, "And you can't drive because . . . ?"

"It's not obvious?"

It is. She's super messed up.

Being with Belle in my car again is oddly comforting.

Only, she's not the Belle I dated. Not anymore. Now she's part of some psychic underground. This girl, the drunk, the stoner, she's like me.

I've got all the windows down, the wind's rushing in, and Belle's hair's swirling around like a messy halo.

We've been talking about what just happened. Mostly I've been trying to get to what the Diviners want. I ask, "If they don't think I can change what I've already seen, then why would they want to meet with me? Have the Metal Sisters dig in my head?"

"To help you, of course."

"But they can't help me. They told me they can't help me."

"Well, they probably can't," Belle says. "But they'll throw you a few bones, send you in the right direction because they see something special in you. They think you're going to make them a ton of money."

I screw up my face. "That's just stupid."

"Seeing the future the way you do, Ade, that's a gift. Seeing the future so clean, so clearly, maybe you can see lottery ticket numbers. Maybe who wins the Super Bowl next year."

"But I can't control what I see, Belle. Why didn't you tell them that?"

"And ruin all the fun? Whole time we were together, I knew you were kind of disgusted by me. I thought about explaining it, but you wouldn't have listened. You were just too into your own thing to care. Me, I just liked you enough to hang around and I hoped you actually might be someone. Like really someone."

"Like Gilberto?"

She doesn't respond.

I apologize to her, but most of it is lost in the onrushing air.

Somewhere near Lakeside, Belle turns to me and says, "You wanting to change the future is sweet. I like that you've got that fight in you. But, if you really want to try this, really want to dig down into the heart of it, you're going to have to let me take you some places you're not going to want to go."

"Like where?"

"You remember that time I took you over to my friend Colin's place? You know, Colin with the one lazy eye? Wait, no, of course you don't . . ."

And I don't. I can't recall anyone with a lazy eye.

"Well, let's just say he and his buddies freaked you out."

"I can deal with freaky. If it'll help, I can deal with it."

She asks me if I ever worry about getting my memory back.

"Why?"

"You probably don't remember half the stuff you did last year. Doesn't that make you kind of crazy? What if you got someone pregnant or you were shooting up dope? That sort of black-out thing, whatever it is that's wrong, that would just make me so anxious I could barely stand it."

Being clean, despite whatever this nearly uncontrollable anger thing is, I'm looking at Belle differently. Not in some sexual way, it's more comfortable, lived-in.

Looking at Belle, I can only think of how much I want to be with Vauxhall.

On the Wadsworth exit ramp, Belle looks over at me, puts her hand on my thigh, squeezes, says, "This Vauxhall girl is totally not for you."

"No?"

"You're moving up, okay. Even though they acted all high and mighty, the Diviners are enthralled by you. This is a whole new world. You need someone who can understand that. Who speaks your language."

"Like you?"

"Sure."

"What's all this drug stuff? You seem to be doing even more, uh, dabbling than usual."

"Already I've had like two lucid experiences that Gilberto is convinced are the first stirrings, you know. The first suggestions of me developing powers."

"You're crazy, Belle."

"Why's it crazy to want to be special? To be amazing?"

"You're already amazing how you are. You don't need that Gilberto idiot giving you drugs to make you any more special. Besides, what I have, what they have, it's a curse, not a gift. You're going to end up—"

She cuts me off with a finger to my lips. Smiles.

Belle switches gears abruptly and tells me that lately she's been trying to touch as many things as she can. She tells me she took E a few weeks back, not her first time, and she really just wanted to cling to that touching sensation thing. She says, "Do you ever think about how instant the sense of touch is? I mean the only time you really ever feel something that way is when you're in direct contact with it. Scary how fleeting that is, isn't it?"

"I guess."

She squeezes my thigh again.

"Sometimes touching is so beautiful. You want that feeling to last forever. You want to just wrap yourself in that feeling and always be in contact with it. Thing is, as soon as you move your hand away, it's gone. As if it was never there."

Belle takes her hand away.

"Do you even remember what my hand felt like there? The weight of it? The warmth?"

I shake my head. Shift into third.

Belle says, "Our brains just don't store that info. It's pretty much only the other senses. Visual mostly. Sometimes smells. Also sounds. But sounds can be so tweaked with memory."

I ask Belle where she's going with this.

"It's all about what comes next, okay," Belle says. "Nothing else really matters, does it? Moving on is real life. Possibilities. Excitement. And I want to kiss you again."

"I knew that's where you were going."

"This Vauxhall girl," Belle says, "she's not your type."

"How's that?"

"She's an actress. A fake."

"Oh yeah?"

"Totally. The things I've heard about her, well, you've heard them too. It's almost like she's desperate. It makes me worry about you. You don't want this girl to break your heart, do you? Take advantage?"

"Like you're not?"

Belle snorts. "Okay. Funny. That's not what I'm doing at all."

Looking straight ahead, my eyes narrowed down to nothing, I say, "Belle, I love Vauxhall. Nothing, not a single thing, will change that."

I turn off Wadsworth and take many turns onto many side streets before we wind up in a residential area where there are twigs for trees and the grass is yellow having only just been planted.

Belle says, "In Polynesia there's this ritual where a young kid, a teenager, as part of his becoming a man, has to keep his hand on the first woman he sees. Has to keep it there for as long as possible. And then, when either the woman is just too sick of the guy standing there or the guy just gives up, he needs to go back to the village shaman and describe exactly how the woman's skin felt. Describe it in detail. Later, after a few more rituals, he's blindfolded and taken to a hut where there's like five women. He's supposed to touch just the shoulder of each of the women and tell the shaman which one was the one he has his hand on for two days or whatever. If he can do it, he's passed the test. If not, he's still a boy. Most teenage guys don't pass. Takes them years."

I say, "Interesting."

Belle smiles and says, "It's not true but it should be."

She directs me to a sketchy neighborhood where the houses are all on top of the factories and the train tracks and the empty looking warehouses. It's this no man's land where the lawns have rotting cars on them and the streets are all dinged and dented like meteors fall here all the time. We pass one house after another. She directs me left and then right and then right again.

And that's when I see it.

Right there, on the rusted-iron garage door of some gnarly looking concrete bunker building is the spray-painted hand symbol I saw on the door to the LoDo Diviners' lair. Same symbol on Janice's T-shirt. Right there. I hit the brakes and I hit them hard. Belle almost gets her front teeth lodged in the dash.

"What the hell, Ade?!" she shouts at me.

I just point over at the weird bunker building. At the hand.

"So?" Belle plays cool.

"Uh-huh," I say. "Nice try. Who lives there?"

"What?"

"Who lives there?"

"I don't know," Belle says, shaking her head too hard.

"Well, we're going to find out."

NINE

What it's called is breaking and entering.

I don't knock on the door.

I don't yell out hello when I walk in, Belle in tow.

What this is called is getting some answers the only way I can.

Good thing kicking down the front door actually works.

We walk into this place and the first thing I'm struck by is the fact that it's like totally festooned with wires. So festooned we have to duck under cables and cords and wires like the place was a tech jungle.

There are so many computer monitors on that everything in the room flickers like it's underwater. Fans whir. Something not a cricket beeps. Something not a bird chirps.

And there's this dude sitting in the middle of this mess.

He's in a reclining leather office chair surrounded by computers. On his lap, two laptops side by side. One for each skinny thigh. He's gaunt, his head shaved clean, and he has his bare feet in a tray of what looks like dirt. There are empty cans of demolished energy drinks catching the green light under his chair.

Belle, in my ear, she whispers, "Slow Bob."

And I see why they call him Slow Bob almost immediately.

This guy, he'd lose a race against my coma dad.

We're standing there long enough, in full view, that you'd worry the guy was dead. The way he turns to look at us, it's like he's moving backward. And when he speaks, he stops and starts like a busted-up cassette tape. His voice, it's the blandest thing I've ever heard.

"Gilberto told me you might stop by," Slow Bob says. "Funny, that."

"So you know me already too, huh?" I ask.

All slow, Slow Bob says, "I've heard a fair deal."

"Who doesn't know about me?" Mostly I ask Belle that.

Belle says, "You weren't ready, Ade. I've told you."

I just let that go. "So, what's this guy do?"

Slow Bob motions to the computers around him, says, "With these I can get everything I need. So long as I've got an inch of skin in some earth, I can read anywhere. And that means that I can see what goes down in the ground. Geomancy, I can read a place like you read the future."

I look down at the tray of dirt his feet are buried in; it's clear plastic but cracking and there's dirt spilling out. I'm pretty sure that through the yellowed plastic I can see worms, but they might be roots.

"Where you want to go?" Slow Bob asks.

"Cherry Creek Reservoir, the north end, east side. Beach area," I say.

"Big beach." Slow Bob yawns. "Can you narrow it down more?"

"Right across from the tennis courts."

"Cool."

He types away at one of the laptops, fingers like bird beaks, and then leans back in his chair and says, "Okay, this look like the place?"

I walk over, lean in, and look at the screen. It's an aerial shot of the beach. "Looks like the place," I say. "Right there in the water is where it goes down."

Slow Bob says, "Someone needs to grab me a drink from the fridge over there." He points behind us. Belle volunteers to get the drink but has a hell of a time finding the refrigerator. Slow Bob shouts directions, only he does it so slowly Belle looks at me and gives a silent scream of frustration. When she does find the fridge, she slams the door shut hard. Computers rumble and belch. Slow Bob yells about that too. Belle comes back shaking the can vigorously.

He puts it on the floor by his feet and then tells me to give me his hand.

I do, his skin is cold, and he bites me.

Hard enough to draw blood. I pull my hand back fast, look down at the wound. Belle, she's looking around for something to drop on Slow Bob's head. I tell her I'm okay and Slow Bob says, "Part of the process. Just need a teensy bit."

He spits into the dirt at his feet and then leans back in his chair and closes his eyes. He says, "This will probably take a few minutes. Just sit back and relax."

A full sitcom later we're still standing there.

I've been watching the bite mark on my hand, looking for swelling, redness, pus, or any signs that it's as horribly infected as I'm afraid it is.

Belle says, "It looks fine, stop stressing."

I dream about hand-sanitizing gels.

I whisper to Belle that I'm ready to jet, that this isn't working.

That's when Slow Bob comes alive again.

Even though the approach of his voice is distant, sluggish, it still spooks us.

"Geomancy's totally different these days," Slow Bob says. "I don't know a geomancer who's had to go to an actual location in the past five years. What with the GPS and the mapping software, most of us are doing just fine like this. Sure, there are some show-offs like Stanley Pulse who feel the need to go trucking around with a rod, but that's all sport. This is the future of our art. Besides, if I were out there checking out every landfill for Indian Burial Grounds and digging my nose into snowbanks for lost hikers, I wouldn't be here developing software and making a killing on my GeoMagic Toolkit CDs." Slow Bob points to a stack of disks sitting in a crooked pile on a monitor.

He opens his eyes, swivels his chair a bit to face me, without moving his embedded feet. He points, says, "That beach is a terrible, terrible place."

I ask him what he means.

"Murder's what I mean," Slow Bob says. "That beach's seen its fair share of blood before. What you're going to do to your buddy, it ain't the first time, is all I'm saying. The place has a funk to it. The way truck-stop restrooms do. Locker rooms. This beach has a bad aura. Most people, probably running around in the sand, sun-bathing, fishing, whatever, they don't even sense it. Cursed, is what it is."

"Can you see what happened?" I ask.

Slow Bob coughs. "That'll cost you fifty."

Belle shakes her head, digs into her purse, pulls out two twenties and a ten. She hands it over, says, "Better be worth it."

" 'Course it will."

This scrawny, pale man reaches down, grabs his energy drink, pops it open, and ignores the spill of fizz before downing a mouthful that gets most of his shirt wet. He wipes his chin with the back of his hand and then, to me, Slow Bob says, "Maybe ten years ago, maybe not that long, there was a kid swimming in the reservoir. It was winter. Kid was swimming hard. He was freezing. This kid's mom was yelling at him from the beach, right there where you will do your thing. No one else nearby, just these two out in the freeze of it."

"Jimi," I say. I think back to how Vauxhall told me the story. How it was the thing that really stuck in my mind, it might have been one of many abusive things Jimi's mom did, but it was one that haunted Jimi. One that haunted Vauxhall.

"This kid, little guy, skinny like me," Slow Bob says, "he just can't take it anymore. The bitch on the beach, screaming at him, smacking at him when he gets out of the water all red like a lobster from the cold. This shaking boy, he decides right then and there that he won't take it anymore. Whatever this woman had done to him it had been bad enough that the kid cracked. He grabbed a rock. His mom was screaming, top of her lungs, calling him horrible names, embarrassing names, and he hit her. Just plunked the rock down on top of her head."

We are all silent. Slow Bob closes his eyes. There is much motion under the lids.

He says, quieter, even slower, "What happened next was kind of funny. Funny not like in the ha-ha way but in the uncanny way. You know the word 'uncanny'? That's what this was like. The mom, she just stood there with this crazy, confused look on her face. The rock hit her head and her shouting stopped and then, just a trickle of blood. Tiny trickle. Stopped yelling, looked up at her kid with this look of just total shock and confusion, and then she keeled over. Time she hit the snow she was dead as the rock that hit her. The kid, he was a calculating type, he pushed, dug into the snow with his already numb fingers, grabbed some more rocks, stuffed them in his mom's yellow parka, and pushed her out under the ice."

I look to Belle. Her eyes are probably as wide as mine.

"Killed his mom," I say softly.

Slow Bob opens his eyes, turns back to the flickering screens in front of him, says, "That woman sank like she had been made of rock all the time. And to add to the surprising nature of this little story, she was never found. Probably getting her bones gnawed on by catfish right this moment."

"What about the kid?" I ask. "What happened to him next?"

Slow Bob shrugs. "He left the beach. Rest, I don't see."

Learning that Jimi is a murderer, honestly, it doesn't faze me. I'm not surprised either. If anything, I was expecting it. Not this exactly, not him having sunk his mom in the reservoir, but knowing my feelings were justified feels right. It's satisfying. First thought is: Jimi's a danger. Vauxhall needs to stay away from him. And the follow-up: How come she didn't know this earlier? Or did she?

"Anything else?" Slow Bob growls.

"Yeah," I say. "There's another thing. A guy in a mask. He's following me around in my visions. Past and future. It's like he can—"

"Time travel?" Slow Bob asks.

"Yeah."

Bob laughs. "Sure. But he can't do that. Impossible. Nah, he's just getting into your head. Into other people's heads. Anything you've seen, it turns to memory instantly. Almost even before you've seen it. And then it gets filed away. He's able to get into there, this guy. What you need to do is stop thinking so linearly."

"But how can I figure out who he is? Why he's there?"

Slow Bob says, "Dunno that. Why he's there is easy. Most likely it's a thrill thing. That's the most common reason. Then again, could be he wants to tell you something. Could be he's desperate. How do I know?"

"All right," I say. "Last question. Do you think I can change what will happen?"

Slow Bob looks over to Belle. The look on his face, it's pretty much what you'd expect. It's the old is-this-guy-a-nut-job-or-what? look. Then he turns back to me and says, "Can you change the orbit of the moon? Rhetorical question. Grandpa Razor's the best of us. He set down the rules for a reason. You don't try and break them. Not for anything."

"That's what I thought," I say, all dismissive. "But either I do or I don't. Can't have two futures, right?" I don't give him time to answer. "Look, Slow Bob, I need to see Grandpa Razor."

Belle shakes her head. She mouths, Not a good idea.

Slow Bob rolls his eyes. "Can't," he says.

"For sure I can," I say. "I'm betting you could find anyone."

"Again," Belle says. "Probably not a good idea. He's a last resort."

"I'm sure he's already expecting me," I say to both of them.

Slow Bob says, "I've only ever met Grandpa Razor twice. Last time was years ago. I suspect he's slowed down a bit, but for a long time he was the scariest thing around. Back in the early eighties, and this is just to give you an example of what kind of cat he is, people were talking about him eating someone. Said he'd had the best visions he'd ever seen. Ate some guy, an old junkie, over the course of five months. Ate every bit too. Started with the knuckles was how it went. Ended with the ears."

"Bullshit," Belle says.

"You don't get out much, Bob. Besides, we're not interested in boogie man stories," I say. "Grandpa Razor's been calling me, I know he's just waiting for me to stop by. You tell me where he is and if I get eaten, no skin off your back. You warned me, right? For this thing to end, for me, I have to see him and I have to know what he knows."

Slow Bob smiles slowly.

"He's in the Esquire Hotel, penthouse. Good luck."

TEN

"The best thing you ever did," Belle says, "is quit."

We're in the foyer at the Esquire Hotel and already a handful of junkies have walked up to us to beg for change. This place, it's the last place you want to be at night. During the day, from what I've heard, it's even worse. The carpets were rust colored once and possibly plush, now they're gray and they've got holes in them the size of sewer covers. In the corners, under the decaying furniture, up the stairs, are chewed-up sunflower seeds, cigarette butts, beer bottles, crack vials, condoms, and rafts of different colored hair. The lights flicker. Even the sun seems to flicker the way it comes through the thick shades. The graffiti of the hand, the divination symbol, it's all over this place. In fact: I saw the hand sign spray-painted on two buildings on our way down here.

"How's that?" I ask as we head to the elevators.

I'm ignoring the junkies. I'm ignoring the prostitutes. I'm pretending I'm somewhere else. Belle, oddly enough, does not seem uncomfortable.

Belle says, "I can see it in you. You're changed. Used to be you had this air about you; people who were willing, who could read it, saw you as someone easy to take advantage of. You being knocked out, strung out, all the time, it was in your eyes. Have you ever seen someone with a concussion? A really serious concussion?"

"Only myself," I say.

"You looked that way all the time, Ade. Now, not so much. Now you look new."

We get to the elevator and the first thing we notice is the buttons are missing. Belle takes the initiative and pulls a bobby pin out and sticks it in the metal hole where the button used to be. There is a spark and we hear the elevator groan to life.

This place, it's lurked just off the highway since before I was born. We'd come downtown, me and Mom, and walk the Platte in the summers and look over the highway where the Esquire was looming, an albino hawk. I heard stories about it the first time in middle school. Kids who wanted to talk tough told stories about decapitated heads found in the Dumpsters there. They whispered about ghost lights on the eight floor. About the screaming woman who jumped from the roof thinking she was leaping into the sea.

When the elevator comes, the door jerks open. Inside, the reek of piss.

On the back wall is a faded framed poster from maybe 1982. It has a picture of the Esquire gleaming in sunlight. There are

futuristic planes flying overhead. The poster reads: VISIT THE FU-
TURE OF LUXURY, TODAY!

We get inside and hit the button for the tenth floor.

"Going up!" A gutter punk jumps inside just before the doors
close. He pushes the button that used to be labeled five. This guy
has white-boy dreads and stinks of cloves and B.O. Looking at us,
he scratches at something behind his right ear and looks like he
goes to say something but doesn't. He mouth opens and then he
closes it, licks his chapped lips. He turns around.

"How many in Denver?" I ask Belle.

"Hard to say, there's no census or anything."

"The hand sign. That spray-painted thing."

"Yeah."

"I'm seeing it everywhere now."

Belle nods. "You're awake now, babe."

"But I'm not using my abilities? I'm not knocking myself out?"

Belle says, "Kind of ironic, right?"

The elevator moves like it's being operated by Slow Bob, crawling up floor by creaking floor. We don't talk until the gutter punk
gets out. He waves good-bye, his eyes all bugged out. Belle gives
him a weak smile.

When the elevator gets moving again, Belle tells me that she
has the feeling that something big will happen. She tells me that
with me being clean and all, she can just feel the change buzzing in the air. She says, "How good you look, it makes me feel like
I should totally get into swimming or running or something. You
know, just clean house."

"It does feel good," I say. "But I miss, you know, knowing."

"Even if nothing ever happens in terms of me evolving to the next level, it's nice to not know what's going on when you don't know what's going on. Does that make any sense? If it does work, well, how cool will that be?"

"You should quit, Belle. Clean house. You're already brilliant."

Belle bats her eyes, says, "You were never this sweet before. I'm not sure how I like it."

We get to the tenth floor and the elevator doors screech open. The hallway outside is dark, it's musty. There are greasy stains like shadows on the walls and only one door, a gold-plated one, at the end of the hall to the right.

Belle goes first, says, "What I'm trying to tell you is that I think if anyone can do what you're trying to do, and I've never tried it, you can do it, Ade. Just feels right to me. What I'm telling you is that the Ade Patience of before couldn't do this, wouldn't do this. The new Ade, well, I think he can."

We knock on the metal door and wait.

A voice, the same gnarly one I'd heard on the phone, says, "Enter."

We do.

The room we go into consists of pretty much just one large banquet table. There are enough chairs around it for a whole school busload of people. At the end of this table, where there windows are overlooking the stadium and the highway, is an enormous old man in a sickly green-checkered suit. Grandpa invites us to sit at the opposite end of the table.

We do.

In front of him there's this plate with what looks like cheese.

"Go ahead. Take a look," Grandpa says.

I get up and step forward and peer into the bowl. It looks like a sunk-in cake. The kind you're supposed to throw away. The kind that didn't come out right. Before Belle can look, Grandpa Razor pulls the bowl back in front of him.

"This is casu modde, my dears. It's a most extraordinary cheese. Pecorino cheese, a hard sheep milk cheese from Italy. The cheese itself has a strong, salty flavor. You see it mostly on pastas. But this one is . . . extraordinary."

It's only then that I smell the cheese and feel something in my stomach turn over. The way an engine turns over. And it makes me gag. It's an entirely muscular feeling. Something I have no control over. It's instinctual. My body letting me know that the bowl sitting in front of Grandpa Razor, the bowl he's about to partake of, is completely taboo. Against nature.

"This cheese is illegal. You can only get it on the black market in Italy. Finding it here, middle of the country, unheard of. What they do is take the cheese and leave it outside to ferment. We're not talking about aging. We're talking decomposition. As it's being prepared the cheese skipper, the person preparing it, introduces the *Piophila casei*. A fly. Said female fly lays eggs all over the rotting cheese and soon, it's heaving in maggots."

I hear Belle gag.

Grandpa continues smiling. "The grubs eat the cheese and as they do they produce an acid the starts to break down the fats inside the cheese. It gets gooey quick. Seeps out. Thousands of these little white worms working over time. Producing a spectacular dish."

I recoil. My guts churn.

Grandpa notices and sighs. "I'm not even done. You eat this cheese while the maggots are still in it. Still alive. These suckers are crazy, too. They can jump. Right up out of the cheese. You need to cover it while you eat it so the buggers don't leap up into your eyes. Your nose. I've heard the maggots can also pass through your stomach unharmed. Get into your gut and start eating you from the inside out. Nasty beasties indeed. There are also allergic reactions contend with. This is, after all, toxic cheese."

Then Grandpa Razor says, "You're probably not going to want to see this."

Before I can turn around he digs his fingers into the cheese and then places what he's removed on a piece of thin bread. *"Salut,"* he says. Then he pops the bread in his mouth. Belle gags again. She spins around and stomps over to the corner. I can hear her coughing.

Grandpa Razor, his lips greasy, tells me to have a seat. Points to a chair. "Talk," he says.

I start: "You saw me at the reservoir, before I had the vision. You saw me killing Jimi, only you didn't tell me everything. How can I change it?"

Grandpa Razor cracks his neck. The bulky flesh like a whale turning over. The sound of the crack when it comes is like a backfire. I jump.

He says, "I don't remember exactly when I heard about you. I think Belle must've told Gilberto and he must've told me. This was way before the stunt in the lunchroom. Way before you'd proved yourself. No. I heard about you when you tried to stop your friend from dying."

"Harold."

"Right, car accident, if I'm correct. I don't know who you told about it, but I heard. I heard how you raced out there, the hero, trying to change what you couldn't. To say the least, it intrigued me. Learn by fire, so the saying goes. And you did learn. But then, this?"

The new anger, I can feel it stirring. I say, "I guess I learn slow."

Grandpa laughs. He says, "Let me have a look-see."

Runs his hands through his hair and then grabs another chunk of gooey cheese. It comes curling out between his fingers. This he shoves into his mouth. Most of it dripping into his beard. He chews slowly. Looks like he's sweeping the stuff around in his cheeks. Savoring its taste. And then he closes his eyes and his eyeballs move around under the thin veil of skin. His mouth hangs open and his body jerks but just for a second. As if he fell asleep and then caught himself. He swallows hard and then speaks like he's channeling something dead. His voice comes out the way a voice comes out of a ventriloquist's dummy. Grandpa says, "You kill him. In the sand, his feet kicking. Drowned. The look on your face is cold, smug satisfaction."

"When?"

"Days. Week at the most. But there's more, Ade. Other visions. Your future, it's getting bleak, isn't it? It's growing darker and more unstable. You trying to change it, you trying to affect the things you've seen, has upset the whole balance. Keep it up and you won't even have a future, my friend."

"Ah, Grandpa, interesting you should mention the future. Didn't you read Jimi's?"

This obese man, he smiles hard. He says, "I see you're already getting how complicated this all is. I've got to tell you that this thing, like most things really, is very puzzling. Not puzzling confusing but puzzling like a puzzle. You can't think you've got it all figured out if you've only gotten your hands on a few pieces."

"Janice says all this is Jimi. That he's—"

Grandpa shakes his head. The way he moves makes it that much easier for me to believe we evolved from monkeys. "Janice says so many things."

"But there can't be two futures, Gramps. Everything I see happens. Everything."

"Me too."

"No."

"I've been at this a long, long time, Ade. That's why I wrote down the Rules. Codified them, so to speak. You've seen a future where you kill Jimi. Jimi's, well, I've seen a future for Jimi where he lives just fine. Also, and Janice did mention this to me, you've seen yourself being, I guess, harassed by Jimi later. Much later. How can that be?"

"Exactly."

Razor says, "Someone's lying. That or you don't actually see what you think you do. Kind of confusing, right? I think you'd be better off getting a few more pieces for that puzzle."

"How 'bout I ask Jimi's dad? The masked wrestler."

Grandpa Razor's eyes get heavy, his face falls back. He says, "If this were a movie, right now would be the big dramatic pause. The soundtrack would go silent, maybe there would be a big heartbeat sound, thud, thud, thud, all measured like that, and I would tell you something life-altering. It's the climax. Sure, everything rising to this one revelatory moment. But, alas, this is an anticlimax, Ade."

I want to punch this sad old man in the face.

He notices. Smiles. Says, "I agree that Jimi's dad's a big, big piece of the puzzle. You come here and let me show you. I can bust it wide open for you, explain it all, but you need to understand that information can be a treacherous thing. What I tell you, you can't unlearn. What I show you, you can't unsee. Sound good?"

And I say, without hesitation, "How?"

"You knock yourself out. Knock yourself out really, really good. And don't focus. Let the future come to you. Find Poppa Ministry in it and confront him. Come back here in two days, bring your shrink, and I'll guide you."

ELEVEN

Belle and I drive in silence.

At least until we hit Colorado Boulevard.

"This is the kind of thing I was hinting at earlier," Belle says. "You have just graduated to the next level, Ade. So how's it feel?"

"I never really imagined there would be some sort of community. Always knew, Borgo always told me, that there were others, it's just that I never thought so many would be here. Around me, ignoring me."

"They weren't ignoring you, Ade."

"No? That's what it feels like. What's the point, anyway?"

"Point of what?"

"Of this underground deal. Of hiding like mice in the walls. And them blindly following what that fat animal back there says. Honestly, if you all got spines and stood up to Grandpa and his rules I'd bet you could do almost anything."

Belle looks upset. She pops another cigarette into her mouth and searches around in her purse for a lighter. She does this haughtily. I reach in, find the lighter for her, flick it to life. She leans into the flame and I watch the flicker of it in her eyes. She is very pretty right now.

Taking a long drag and then releasing it, Belle says, "What this is really about is how you're not accepting who you are. I can't tell if it's that you think you're better than the rest of us or you just don't want to take your place. Right? You just don't want to take responsibility."

"Probably more the former."

She looks at me, makes a face. "Why is that, Ade? How could you possibly be better than the rest of us, Mister No Memory?"

I look away, out over the factories making clouds for Globeville, and say, "It's the hiding thing. At first I thought it was cool. You know, when we talked to Gilberto and Lynne and that other chick it was like being in a secret club. It was being allowed to pull back the curtain and being welcomed into a special place. That part, the belonging part, felt good for a little bit. But then, after the rest of them, the further down the rabbit hole we went, I just started seeing them all for what they really are."

"And what is that?"

"Like everyone else. Cowards, losers, children—"

Belle coughs loudly, it's her choking on smoke, and gives me this disgusted look. "How can you say that? We're trying to help you. We're offering you insight for the first time in your life. These people care about you. I care about you."

I say, "Yeah, you do. I know you do. But this whole thing, it's just a charade. Sure, the Metal Sisters can poke around in people's heads and Slow Bob can look at a map and get some vibes from it, maybe have a quick glance into the past, and Grandpa Razor, well, maybe he can kind of do what I can do, but at the end of the day, they're hiding because they're as scared of the future as anyone else. They have powers, you know, like superheroes, but really they can't actually do anything. They choose not to do anything. You take away all the razzle-dazzle and it's nothing but flair like at any chain restaurant."

"And you, you think what you do is so much better? I can't believe I'm even having this conversation. You want to know the real reason we didn't even let you in? The real reason why you didn't know about us until now?"

I shrug.

This just pisses Belle off even more. She says, almost shouting now, "We wouldn't let you in because I told them not to trust you. I told them that you were gifted but so damaged, so beyond hope of repair, that it would just be better to pretend you didn't exist. Only it was harder to do than I thought. I felt sorry for you. I still do. Ade, you need to think beyond yourself for a few minutes and think about the opportunities out there. For you, mostly."

"Maybe the old me, the messed-up me, wasn't ready for all this, and it's probably true that I was beyond repair for a while, but not now, not anymore. But the only opportunity that I see here is the one to show all of you that you're wrong. Enough with the navel gazing, you're like a bunch of prima donnas who don't like getting their hands dirty."

To Belle I say, teeth grinding like a dog's, "I will deny the past, Belle. I will change the future. And it will end the way I say it ends."

CHAPTER NINE

ONE

Dr. David Gore—

Fuck you.

—Ade Patience

TWO

What I do first is go to Vauxhall's house.

This is after I've dropped Belle off and after she told me that she forgave me for being so rude to her. This is after she told me that she knew I was just trying to process it all and probably just need a good night's sleep. This is, of course, after she said, "You just call me when you're ready to get back into it. Just think of me as your mentor!"

At Vauxhall's all the lights are off. She is asleep. It is nearly one in the morning.

I have no idea how it got so late, but I need to see her right now. I walk over to her window and tap on it lightly. She doesn't respond, so I tap harder. And I call out, kind of whisper yelling, "Vaux! Wake up, Vaux!"

There is a rustling behind the blinds. A soft light comes on.

Her face, all puffy with sleep, appears at the window, like a gorgeous spook show. When she sees me she grins and pulls the window up and open. Then she leans out, my Juliette, and asks, "Do you know what time it is?"

"This is important," I say. "It's crazy the stuff I've found out."

"And what stuff would that be?" She is so cute the way she asks it.

"Jimi. This whole thing is him, him setting it up, and it's ugly, Vaux."

She puts on a sad face. It's not acting.

I switch gears. "Come with me for a drive," I say.

"Now?"

"Yeah. Right now. Jump into some clothes. Come on."

Vauxhall shrugs, disappears back inside. I back away and watch a lone red car navigate slowly through a distant intersection. A dog barks. Leaves fall. Weather. Then Vauxhall reappears, jumps out of her bedroom window in jeans and a dark hooded sweater.

THREE

We drive to Stapleton Airport.

The streets are empty.

There's this side road where the apartments edge the runways. I park there, right at the end of the street, with the hood of the car up against a chain-metal fence. We lie on the hood of the car. It's hot but feels good.

"We need to talk more about Jimi," I say. "I need to tell you what I learned about him. It isn't good, Vaux. What he's done is—"

Vaux shushes me with her index finger, soft on my lips. "Later," she says. "Please? Just for a few minutes."

"Okay."

I calm down. A little.

Lying there, we're looking up at the sky and counting stars. Vaux points out a blinking light. One so distant it fades in and out of existence with every blink.

"Satellite," she says.

Still watching the sky, she says, "My dad worked on satellites. Engineer. Did mechanical stuff for recon satellites like the Corona, later ones. My dad, I told you he killed himself, right?"

I say, "No. At Oscar's party, you just mentioned he'd died."

Vaux says, "He got laid off from his job, some bullshit company reorganization. Couldn't get work after that. He just kind of collapsed into himself. You really would have liked him, Ade, before, when he was working and happy. He had such a great sense of humor. Self-deprecating. My dad came from a religious home, Grandpa was a rabbi, but we didn't keep Shabbat or keep kosher or anything."

Looking at Vaux, at her looking up, I tell her I'm sorry, that I wish I could have met him. I tell her that he must have been an amazing person. I say, "Judging by you, an incredible person."

She says, "A funny story, he once put a prayer into one of the satellites. Tiny, on this sheet of thin silver metal. Took him a few weeks to etch it. Prayer was the *Mi sheberakh*, for healing, for relief of suffering. Dad told me, after it launched and we were looking at the sky once, that he wanted something good, even a little something good, up there in the cold night. Those satellites, he said, were reckless. Just our hubris. He wanted to add some real weight to them."

I look over at Vaux and want to kiss her. Soothe her the same as a prayer.

Without turning to me, Vaux says, "I got my smile from my dad."

A few seconds later we're surrounded by the unmistakable rumble of an airplane. I mention to Vaux that she should brace herself. The growl of the jet's engines gets louder and louder. She takes my hand. Squeezes harder and harder as the noise of the plane comes closer and closer.

Squeezing until it's on top of us.

And really, it almost is. The plane passes maybe a few hundred feet over us. For a few seconds, there on the hood of my car, we're bathed in the red and white blinking lights of the plane as it glides overhead. Our hair blown wild by the rush of it. The car shaking. And then it's over. The plane lands half a mile away.

Vaux says nothing but she smiles.

"Cool, huh?"

"You bring all your girls here?"

"Only the ones I think I'll get lucky with."

"Ha."

"You must have some spot you take the boys? Your little nest?"

"I was never that practical. You bring that Belle girl here?"

"Belle?"

Vaux makes a face. "Yeah."

"No. We weren't like, you know."

"Serious?"

"Right."

Vaux says, "Okay." Then asks, "So what did you discover out there?"

"There's this whole world of people like us, Vaux. All of them with different abilities. All of them addicted and all of them lame. A world of losers who spend their days reading crystal balls and looking for lottery numbers. None of them is—"

"Did they help you?" Vaux interrupts. "Did they show you how to stop it?"

"Maybe. I'm getting closer."

"Do you feel good about it?"

"Yeah. Underneath the bullshit, I think so. But Jimi, he's known about these people too. He's been to see them, asking them questions, getting his future—"

"Looking for his dad," Vauxhall says. "That's what this is about."

"No, Vauxhall. It's bigger than that. Did you know he killed his mother?"

Vaux's mouth falls, her eyes spin wide. "What?"

"You never saw it?"

Vauxhall's eyes start to water. Her lips tremble.

"I don't know how come you never saw it. You saw everything leading up to it. The reservoir, where he swam in the snow and the ice. That day, he killed his mom. Pushed her out under the ice, weighed down with stones."

Vauxhall swallows a few times, sniffs, wipes her eyes, says, "There were things always blocked out, you know? Times when scenes, memories, would just end suddenly like the film ran out. And other times when the memories were just so choppy. At first I didn't think much about it, but . . ."

"I'm sorry," I say.

"I don't know who he is, do I?"

I shake my head. "I'm not sure you do."

She moves close to me. Nestles up to me. Her face on my chest. Then she kisses me. I wipe her eyes and I kiss them. I kiss her face. Her neck. She kisses me back.

Then Vaux starts to say something, but the car rattles and her voice is drowned out by the throb of another plane engine.

In the flash of airplane lights, we kiss more and I move my hands along the lengths of her legs. My hands three places at once. The whole surface of them trying to take in the whole surface of her. I want to feel every inch and move up to her chest. These breasts that have enslaved her, the curves that make her a prisoner of stares, I have them in my hands and I want to sense every inch. I want to know every bump. Trace every vein. But we're clothed. There are planes passing overhead. There are people watching us from their apartments. People in the sky.

We stop, both together breathless.

Vaux's like, "Can we go somewhere else?"

On the way to somewhere else we stop at Safeway. For condoms.

Honestly, I don't know what's wrong with me. The part of me that needs for Vauxhall to go cold turkey, the part of me that wants nothing more than to help her go clean, that part is gone. It's frightening how I know that doing what we're planning on doing will only make me her accomplice and yet I don't care.

I've overruled myself.

In fact: I've got the devil in me.

We go to Sundial Park and I spread out a blanket from the trunk of my car under one of the fir trees at the far-west end. It's late enough that the houses across the street are dark. No one on the road either. The cool air feels fresh and great on my skin. The moon is just a sliver, but it gives us the half-light we want. Just enough to make out shapes. We fold the blanket in half. Then we lie next to each other, both of us still as the park. We don't talk and I run my fingers across Vaux's face. Find her eyes. The faint brush of lashes. Her lips. Swelling. Warm. We undress each other. It's not frenzied.

We kiss and then I ask Vauxhall if this is really what we should be doing. Even as I say it I know, deep down, that I don't believe it. We need this. I need this.

"Why not?"

"The Buzz," I say. My throat is parched.

"You don't want to be with me?"

"I do. Want it more than anything."

"What if I promise not to enjoy the high? Ade, I can do this. I'm only with you. It won't be like that, like how you're imagining it. Please."

I can't speak. My voice is gone.

Vauxhall giggles. "How about this is the last time?"

I think I growl. Something terrible inside me needing out.

Vauxhall laughs. "We'll get married right after, okay?"

And I pull her to me.

There is no clawing and hissing the way you see people do it in movies. I am slow and convinced. We trace outlines, our fingers gliding and entwining when they meet the way planets spin around each other. I put my mouth on her. Vaux leans into my mouth. And then everything else, the supernova parts, happen magically. Our bodies take over and our minds shut off. I'm in the back of myself, watching myself explore. Watching myself relaxed and possessed at the very same time. Myself sweating and cooling off. Myself slow motion the way I am underwater.

What happens next is hard to explain. What it is is science fiction. It's impossible mathematics. It can only be love.

My mind spins out above my body, above the roof of the house, and it goes up into the night between the stars and jumps through the clouds until the sides of everything come curling around me. The tunnel forms. It is a filigree of light and shadow and I move to the middle of it. The middle of everything.

The tunnel doesn't end, but I take a detour out.

And what I see is not the future. I see Jimi.

Jimi talking to Grandpa Razor and they're sitting at a White Spot diner on Colfax sharing a plate of pancakes and talking amiably. I can't hear really what they're saying, but it's a heated conversation. Some snippets sneak through. Jimi, wearing sunglasses and a beanie, is forking pancake into his face and asking, "But does he really need to die?" And Grandpa Razor, his beard all slathered in syrup, saying, "Of course, that's essential. You've done so well this far. Don't let everything fall apart. Keep it hidden, keep it safe." Things go quiet again, the dialogue getting all fuzzy, until Jimi stands up and storms out. Grandpa Razor, that fat man, just sits there laughing to himself.

And the vision ends.

Back in the tunnel. The walls collapse in. The stars zip back into place.

Then it's just me breathing heavy in Vauxhall's arms. My muscles are slick and electric. I sigh so hard that my body racks.

Vaux asks, her voice barely a whisper, "Did you see what I saw?"

"What?" My throat is so dry, it's cracking my voice. "What did you see?"

"Jimi. Jimi and some guy with a beard."

I'm surprised enough that most of my skin jumps.

"I saw the same thing," I say. "Them eating and talking."

"Oh, my God," Vauxhall says. "This is so crazy. What just happened?"

I fall back on the blanket and let all the air out of my lungs and push it up at the sky and the stars and the moon hiding somewhere on the far side of the universe. Vaux lies down beside me and covers herself with my shirt. She says, "The high, it's like . . ."

And I feel it too.

It's not the numbing, scattershot thrill of the Buzz. This is something new, something entirely different. This high feels, if anything, organic. It feels like it was made for me. Like stepping into a perfectly tailored suit. I can see my skin glowing. Vauxhall's too.

She says, "Maybe we cancelled each other out? Me seeing the past, you seeing the future. The two of us together, maybe what happened was we both saw the present. You know, it like evened things out. Just minutes ago, Jimi and that guy were eating and we just kind of eavesdropped in on them."

And it kind of makes sense. Yin and yang.

"But why Jimi? I've never seen anything but myself."

Vauxhall says, "I don't know. I've seen so much of Jimi's past. Maybe I kind of directed it. You know, moved the frame over. Kind of a beautiful thing, don't you think?" And when she gives me a kiss, there's a spark like when you get static buildup from walking crazy in socks on a carpet.

I go back over the vision in my head. "What was Jimi saying?"

"I only heard part of it," Vauxhall says. "They were arguing."

I sit up and tell Vauxhall that I know the guy Jimi was eating pancakes with. I tell her that he's at the heart of this whole thing and that he knows how to find Poppa Ministry. I say, "Jimi being with Grandpa Razor, that's not a good thing at all. I think it's a setup is what it is. They're planning something."

"You think this will happen every time, we, you know?"

"God, I hope not," I say.

Silence follows. Both of us chewing it over.

Then Vauxhall says, sitting up, "Tell me everything about the weekend."

I do. I tell her about Belle and the Diviners and how we went to the park and met up with the Metal Sisters. I leave out the Janice stuff, but I tell her about Slow Bob and Grandpa Razor. "With all the names and everything," I say, "it sounds like something from a cartoon, but these people, I've seen them, Vaux. They know what they're doing. I just don't want to walk in there blind."

Vauxhall says, "Then you don't."

I tell her I have an idea. I tell her it's one that I hate but the only I think will work. But knowing what we know, I say, "It's probably not safe. It's certainly not safe."

And after I explain my idea, Vauxhall says, "I'm only doing this for you."

"Tell me it's a terrible idea. What about what he did?"

"But it'll work."

"No. I know. But still, he's—"

"I'm not a wuss, Ade. I've known him long enough."

She kisses me so hard I fall over. On top of me, her elbows digging into my chest, she says, "Only for you, and only this once. I love you."

FOUR

I'm at the Tattered Cover bookstore, trying to drink a coffee, trying to read through a copy of *Juxtapoz,* but mostly just driving everyone else in the place crazy.

It's because I'm shaking.

The place only just opened ten minutes ago.

My feet are kicking. My fingers tapping. I keep cracking my knuckles. I keep sighing a little too loudly. It's like I'm sitting on the bench ready for my turn at bat and I'm always the next one, I'm stuck in this jittery limbo. Also I keep checking my cell.

Vauxhall is with Jimi.

She's at his place. Doing things.

My hand shaking as it stirs my cup of mint mocha for the eightieth time, I'm reminding myself why I set this up. I'm convincing myself, this for the ninetieth time, that Vauxhall going over there is worth it. That this needs to happen.

Fact is: I've whored my girlfriend out.

The love of my life, I've sent her over to Jimi's so she can jump his bones and read his memory. I've sent her over there so she can dig into his head and find out what he knows about Grandpa Razor.

My stomach, it's like someone else's fist is in there going nuts.

The reason I keep checking my cell is because Vauxhall told me it'd only be an hour. Just one hour and she can get the information and get out of Jimi's house. Hopefully, get out of Jimi's life.

It's only been twenty minutes.

I'm sweating like it's raining on me.

My heart, it's doing things it shouldn't be able to.

And worst of all, sitting here pouring more sugar into my already too sweet coffee, my anger is starting to surge again. My ears getting hot. My skin almost blistering. But then my cell rings and the anger, the stress, it's almost instantly relieved.

Almost.

It's Paige. I answer, voice strained, and she says, "I thought fall break was all about sleeping in. What the hell are you doing sipping coffee and reading, wait, is that a graffiti art magazine?"

I'm confused only for a flash before Paige sits down across from me and winks. She makes a big dramatic show of flipping her cell off and then says, "I think you need to catch me up."

"What are you doing here?"

Paige says, "You know what's really funny? I like to come here second Monday of the month, bright and early before Mrs. Schmidt's class, and just flip through a few magazines and sip some coffee. Mostly I read the politics, though."

"You don't ever come here, Paige."

She claps. "You're right. I had a doctor's appointment and was taking the scenic route, you know, Colfax, home and saw your car parked out front. What exactly are you doing here and why haven't you called me about anything?"

I tell Paige first and foremost that it's been a crazy ride. I tell her, in no particular order, that Vauxhall and I had sex, that I've been hanging out with Belle, meeting a whole tribe of people with crazy abilities like mine, that I'm going to confront Jimi's dad, and that there's a really good chance something gnarly will go down. I say, "And it's going to happen soon. Really, something super gnarly is about to happen in the next thirty minutes."

"Like what?" Paige asks, looking around the store. She's panicked. I've seen it before. She looks the same way she did when her parents walked in on us smoking pot the first time. Her face is registering that level of high-grade nervous tension.

"Like I think I might explode. That's the other thing I didn't mention. Me, I've kind of started changing. You know how a guy slowly realizes he's becoming a werewolf. Yeah. Like that."

Paige leans in, softly she asks, "You're turning into a werewolf?"

"Pretty much," I say. "I've got this anger management problem that's just come up out of nowhere. Before, when I had the vision of me killing Jimi—"

"Wait? What?"

"I didn't tell you that?"

"Uh, no." Paige cocks her head to one side and looks at me with one eye the way a parrot would. "I think I'd remember you telling me about killing someone."

"I haven't, though. That's the thing. I'm trying to stop myself."

Paige grabs my mocha and takes a long, hearty swig of it. Then she wipes her upper lip with the little napkin my drink was sitting on and says, "Okay, you're going to have to explain all that stuff at a later date. You know, like a time when I'm more awake and didn't just have a really awkward conversation with the pediatrician I've seen since I was five about why I don't have a boyfriend at the moment. But for right now, tell me again what you're doing sitting here looking all stressed out?"

"I sent Vauxhall over to Jimi's house so she'll have sex with him and read his memories."

"What? No you didn't. Tell me you didn't."

I nod. "She went like twenty three minutes ago." Then I check my watch, "Actually, twenty-six minutes ago."

Paige grabs my face, both her hands biting into my cheeks, and she stares me down and says, "That is one of the worst things I think you've ever said. You need to leave. You need to find her. This is the most retarded thing you've done yet."

I say, through smushed-up lips, "You're right. I should leave."

"I'll keep your drink," Paige says, letting me go. "Call me."

And I go running out, knocking over chairs, knocking down tables.

FIVE

Jimi's house is maybe seven minutes away by car.

I make it in three.

I'm pretty sure I was going fifty-three on Colfax and weaving like a drunk. I do know that I went through six red lights. I'm worried I might have caused one accident, but it looked like a fender bender and both of the cars were SUVs, so I'm not that concerned.

Maybe this is just the new me, but it was kind of, sort of, fun.

Thing is, I'm here walking up to Jimi's front door, my head pounding with my pulse, and I'm running through all the different scenarios, all the different positions I might find these two in. Inside my head I'm kicking myself for letting this go down. For setting this up. Me the prognostication pimp.

I don't pound on the door, it's open.

I barge in and don't see Jimi but I do see Vauxhall lying on the couch. She's there like she was tossed aside. All laid out like a car accident. Hair in her face.

My chest lurches seeing her.

It's like seeing my own face hit with a sledgehammer.

I run to Vauxhall. Grab her up off the couch and push the hair away. She's okay. Makeup is smudged and her eyes are watery, but she's okay. When she sees me, like really sees me, she smiles. Such a sweet smile. Her voice broken down, she says, "Nothing happened."

I just hold her to me tight. Collapse her to me.

She says, over my shoulder, "I tried. It was horrible."

My throat all lumped up, I say, "You're okay now."

She says, and I can feel my shoulder getting wet from her tears, "I tried and we kissed, he kissed me hard like he knew what might happen, and then I just got pulled into his past. It was like I lived it too. All the . . . all the horrible things, Ade."

And Vaux picks her head up, takes my head in her hands and, through smeared eyes, says, her voice jumping, "How can people be so cruel? What sort of world is this?"

I tell her I don't know. I tell her that whatever she saw happened a long time ago and that she's okay now, that Jimi's okay now. I say, "I'm so sorry I put you through that."

Vauxhall kisses me.

"Where is Jimi?"

I look around the house, my eyes darting. I want so badly to kick Jimi's ass right now. I want so badly to just smash him into a thousand tiny specks. Just mash him down into the ground, where he'll never touch Vauxhall again. Where he'll never even see her again. My temples are pounding with adrenaline.

"He left," she says.

"Where?"

"I don't know." Then she says, "Nothing happened."

"What do you mean nothing happened?"

Vaux, through these tear garden eyes, says, "After you and I were together. You know, after what happened last night, it all changed. Have you had a concussion yet today?"

"No," I say. "How come no one remembers I quit?"

Vauxhall says, "The two of us coming together was like what happens when an unmovable object meets an irresistible force. Both get changed, though not on the outside. I didn't need to sleep with Jimi to see his memories. No high."

"What?"

"No high. No Buzz. Whole time I was there I was thinking about you. Needing you. And as soon as I was leaving, as soon as I said good-bye, I felt so free. I felt so unburdened, so light. Like what you feel after a massage. It was just being totally relaxed." Then her face changes, her expression dips, and Vauxhall says, "Don't go back to Grandpa Razor. You don't need to go to him, you can change things without him."

"What did you see?"

"The two of them are plotting. Grandpa Razor told Jimi at the diner that he would unravel what they've been working on for years if he wasn't careful. He said it was a process. He said that Jimi couldn't go soft now, that despite what happens next he couldn't try and stop it."

"Why was Jimi so mad?"

Vauxhall tells me that whatever this thing is, Jimi isn't as into it now. She tells me that Jimi is getting cold feet and that he doesn't want it nearly as badly as he used to. She says, "He wasn't being his usual asshole self. He was worried about you."

"Did you find out what they're planning? Couldn't you read back further, see that in his memory? Get the rest of it?"

Vaux shakes her head. "It was like he knew why I was there. Like he was blocking the rest of it. Almost, it was like he was letting me see just enough."

"I have to see Grandpa Razor. I have to go."

"But it's a trap, Ade. They want to hurt you."

"I'll be fine."

For the first time ever I notice a twitch in my left cheek. It's a flutter like a flap on your heart makes. Something just under my skin waving. I put my hand up to stop it and press down on it, but it vibrates under my fingers, trapped there. I turn to Vauxhall and ask her if she can see it. She says, "Yeah. Kind of cute."

We kiss and fall back into each other on the couch.

Me on top of her, me kissing her ears and the nape of her neck and the place where the two wishbones come together on her chest, she giggles and then, sitting up, pulling me up with her, says, "I forgot something."

I sit back. Try to stop the twitch again.

"It's crazy," Vauxhall says, "but I think Jimi has your mom tattooed on his left arm. And I think he has, yeah, he totally does, he has a dragonfly as well."

Pushing at the tremble in my cheek, I say, "I just hope this stops soon."

CHAPTER TEN

ONE

Dear Dad—

No one ever gets letters anymore, so I'm kind of proud of the fact that I don't really use e-mail. That I actually take the time to write out letters to people.

Lately, it's been experts. Everyone from scientists to black magicians. What I've been asking them is this: Why can I do what I do? And sometimes: What can I do to change the future? You'd be amazed at the responses I've gotten. But what you wouldn't be amazed by is the fact that most of the people I write to take me at face value. Most of them are more than happy to talk to me even if they think I'm totally bonkers.

I want to tell you a story: I read about this guy who lived something like eighty years ago. He was German or maybe Austrian and he was a farmer. A really simple dude. He was also mentally ill and tried to assault a girl. That got him put in jail and then, eventually, he was put in an asylum. This simple farmer guy, he starts writing in prison. It's collages and hand-made paper, and he's writing these long stories about another world. He's writing these stories about people in this other world and he just never stops. Writing, writing, writing. And then drawing. All these little illustrations cramming every corner of the pages. Not a single inch that's not filled in with tiny pictures of birds and people and buildings. The stories that he writes about this other world, they're very basic. Just descriptions of the place, of the habits of the people, of the religion, the army, the navy. And the interesting thing is that the more he writes, the more this guy, the farmer, becomes part of the story. At first he's like the king of this world, but soon he becomes the pope and after something like thirty years of being locked up in the asylum, just writing and drawing in his notebooks, this guy, he becomes the God of his imaginary world. When the man dies and they clean out his tiny room, this one tiny room where he spent most of his life, they find just stacks and stacks of these journals. This whole history of another world so detailed there are even reams of tax information. What's amazing, what I want you to get from this, is that even though this poor bastard was locked up in one room his whole life, had only one view of the world, he was able to escape to a place where he had complete control. This guy with nothing became a God.

What this guy did was not limit himself.

What this guy did was to say fuck it to the boundaries and embrace the one thing he really owned: himself.

That dude died as happy as anyone. As content as anyone.

I don't really know why I want to tell you that story, but that guy reminds me of you sometimes. Not that you're schizoid, just that you're *trapped in a room with one view. You need a way out, but can't see the door that's right there inside you.*

Love,
Ade

TWO

As expected, Dr. Borgo is not at all down.

Grandpa Razor's got it set up like this: A bedsheet's laid out over most of the massive table at the center of his sleazy penthouse apartment and there is an IV-drip thing standing, waiting. There are syringes and there are little glass bottles labeled with things like FLUNITRAZEPAM and ZOLPIDEM.

Fact is: This place looks like a mad scientist's laboratory.

Dr. Borgo is really not happy about any of it.

"None of this is kosher, Ade," he says, picking up one of the little glass bottles and turning it over in the light. He shakes his head. "None of it."

Getting Borgo to come here wasn't easy.

I stopped by his office unannounced and kind of barged in on one of his sessions. He was sitting in his leather chair, legs crossed, looking very professional like a psychiatrist in a movie, and talking to a redheaded fat woman about how bad her marriage was. When I busted in, Borgo jumped up and waved a finger at me to leave. I said, "Sorry, Doc, but we need to talk now."

He excused himself and pushed me into his other office, the little one just off his bigger one. First thing I told him was how I'd gone clean. I told him that I felt like I'd just woken up in a new body and I thanked him. And then I said, "But . . ."

He knew it was coming. Sighed hard.

I said, "I need your help something awful."

Long story short, he cleared his afternoon and here we are. Still, he's not at all psyched. And when he sees Grandpa Razor shuffling in like an old Sasquatch, he really makes it clear this in not a good idea. All raspy in my ear, Dr. Borgo's like, "This is not the place to be doing something like this. This is totally unhygienic and unsafe."

"Besides," he says, "there is no evidence whatsoever this will work."

Grandpa Razor overhears, moves his head side to side like a robot, and then says, "It might not work, you're right. I've done this three times and there was one time where the lady didn't wake up for a week. She got something out of it, but it wasn't like I'd planned. Not really."

Dr. Borgo gives me this look that suggests we leave immediately.

I tell Borgo to just relax a little. I tell him that, and this is just yet another reminder, I have never seen myself in a coma in the future, so the odds are that even if this doesn't work it won't have any serious, lasting effects. I say, "Everything I know points to nothing really bad happening here. Future looks hunky-dory, Doc."

But Grandpa Razor clears his junky throat. He looks at me, tilts his head disapprovingly. He says, "Janice seems to think that what she and Katrina saw of your future, well, what you saw of your future, is getting not so good. Sure, no coma. But they said the future isn't nearly as bright as you're suggesting. I think we can both agree that being in a wheelchair, being a lifetime member of the neurotic club, has a few drawbacks."

I want to smash this fat guy's face, but hold back.

Instead, I say, "Tell me how this is going to work."

Grandpa Razor takes a seat at the head of the table; the chair groans. "You are going to go sleepy and I will be right here, my hands"—and he wave them in the air—"at your temples. I will be eating, this. . . ." He pulls a tin of what looks like canned fish from out of his left pant pocket. "This is something Icelandic, it's specially prepared shark meat, and I'll be enjoying it, chewing it very slowly, while you do your thing. Think of this as a human electrical grid. I will boost your abilities, allow you to interact directly with a future. Not sure whose or which one yet."

"And Jimi's dad?"

"He, being the psychic troublemaker he is, will, of course, be instantly attracted. You just hanging out in some quasi-liminal space and him just . . . Look, the details of the procedure don't really matter, right? What matters is you getting in there and trying to figure out whatever it is you're trying to figure out."

"Changing the future."

Grandpa laughs. Really, it's more of a burp. He says, "Sure, of course."

Then he pats at the table with a pudgy paw, says, "Hop on up."

I do.

It's now, of course, that Borgo gets really vocal. His hands up, head shaking, he says, nearly shouting, "This isn't going to work. No. No. No. Not like this, Ade." And then, turning to me, leaning down, getting close, he says, "Ade, these medications, this setup, it's not going to get you where you want. I mean, you need a concussion. Just putting you into some drug-induced coma isn't going to do it. That makes sense, right?"

Grandpa Razor laughs all hearty. "Oh, that won't be a problem."

He holds up a billy club. "I'm actually pretty good at this," Razor says. "Just a quick flick of the wrist and we can knock you down plenty fast and, well, kind of gently."

I lie down on the table and Dr. Borgo stands over me. He puts in the IV line. He loads up the meds, measuring the doses extra carefully. The needles go in, the needles come out. Almost immediately I feel drowsy. Doubt it works that instantly, but it might. And then Borgo backs up, anxious to the end, and Grandpa Razor appears hovering over me, his face a bearded blimp.

" 'Night," Grandpa says.

And then he whacks me in the temple with his billy club.

THREE

Again with the beach.

Back at Cherry Creek Reservoir.

Looking at the sand, it being night and the place desolate, I tell myself that I'll never willingly come back here again. I tell myself that not even for a million dollars will I have my feet in this sand another time. Out loud, to the bugs and the lamps hovering over the tennis courts and the sickly lap of water, I say, "I'm thinking this place could really use a massive parking lot."

And from behind me comes a response. "Wouldn't help," the voice says.

Per usual I'm not at all shocked to see Jimi's dad in his Mexican wrestling mask. He's standing behind me, hands in the pockets of his white suit pants, and his mask is gold. He says, "What happened here, it's going to keep happening. Asphalt or not."

Poppa Ministry's close. If I slip off my shoe and throw it at him, at this distance, I'd probably get him right in the face. That's good to know.

I say, "So lay it on me. What do you want?"

Poppa says, "I want to help you."

"And why couldn't you help me before? You know, when we were on the beach. The other beach, I mean. The future one."

"You weren't ready. Your mind wasn't."

"And how's that?"

"You needed to be clean. Totally clean. I want you to understand, Ade. To see through all the fog, to make sense of this."

"One of *those* conversations, huh?"

"Yeah."

"And you're not a parasite? Some sort of psychic junkie that's like—"

"Not at all, Ade."

And Poppa Ministry takes off his mask. There's a zipper in the back and the sound of it is long and loud. Like a train getting nearer. I brace myself for anything. At this point, I'm expecting him to be melted like a monster or to be a woman. I'm expecting anything but what I actually see.

Poppa Ministry, the masked man, he's my dad.

Even though I'm not really in the here or the now, even though my body's lying on a cold table in Grandpa Razor's filthy basement, I can feel myself physically start wobbling. My knees are broken, not holding me up. My eyes, they just suddenly start watering like I need to sneeze. Only I don't. Only my heart is overwhelmed.

My dad, it's him from twenty years ago.

I've seen photos of him like this. With his big head of thick dark hair and his thin eyes and his nose, my nose. In the photos he's smiling and he's looking beyond the camera, he's pointing up at the sky, he's noticing something at his feet, but here on the beach, my young father is looking straight ahead at me. He is not broken. He is not sleeping. He is not dead.

Neither of us move.

The mask sparkles in the sand.

I can't speak, so he speaks for me.

"I'm sorry to do this to you, Ade. To surprise you this way. I wanted to tell you the very first time, but the connection . . . It wouldn't have worked. I had to . . ." And he pauses; somewhere dark a duck sounds. "You're in big danger, son. You know what happened on this beach, what Jimi did to his mother. If you kill him, if you come here and let the future play out, it will only make him stronger."

I summon words. I say, "That sounds awfully fairy tale, Dad."

He laughs his laugh, the one I grew up with, and says, "I knew this was going to be difficult to explain. I should start by telling you that I'm not who you think I am, that I'm not—"

And I interrupt him, "You can save me the evil-genius speech, Dad. How are you even here? How are you not in a coma right now? How are you, like, almost my age?"

He sits down in the sand, smiles up at me. "I figured out I had an ability when I was just a kid. When I tried really hard and really concentrated, I could send myself out of my body. I could project myself into other people's heads. See what they could see. Into their dreams and, well, if they had visions of the future or the past or whatever, I could send myself there too."

"Why didn't you ever tell me?"

"I stopped long before you were born. To be honest, it was simple: You really don't ever want to be in another person's head. It's not like stepping into a movie. Doing it, you get twisted by the emotion. Bent out of shape and heavy, like you just stepped out of a flat surface into a three-D one. The pain was, is, incredible, but the high . . ."

I nod slowly, me being the understanding father here. "I know the high."

"I got pretty ugly. Your mom, she helped me so much, but I needed . . . I was desperate to get that back." He lets all his air out through his nose and says, "It's easy to make yourself believe that what's in a bottle or a can will make you whole again. It's not too hard to believe in an easy way out."

I haven't talked to my dad like this, well, never actually like this, but we haven't talked this long and this in-depth since I was old enough to put myself to bed. Honestly, I don't have time for small talk. Something major's going down.

I tell my dad that I'm sorry he's in a coma. I tell him that I'm sorry that for the past really long time I've been treating him like he's basically dead. I say, "Really though, what you did was very, very shitty."

"I know," he says. "I'm weak. I was a stupid drunk. Will you forgive me?"

"I'm sure I will. Eventually."

"Will you visit me?"

"Of course. I have been. I've been telling you everything. You never heard?"

"No," he says sheepishly.

"Not a thing?"

He shakes his head. I can't tell if he's lying. He asks, "Can I give you a hug?"

And he stands up, sand sliding down his suit, and I walk over and we hug. He cries. Right there, this ghost version of him, this escape pod version of him, just cries and cries in fits and starts like a bad engine. When he's done he pulls away and cleans his nose with his sleeve. Says, "Thanks."

Me, not losing it, I ask, "You need to tell me how to stop it. How to change what I've seen."

"I don't know. But I can tell you what you're up against."

"Okay. And what am I up against?"

"I was unfaithful to your mother. Before your mom got pregnant with you, I had an affair. The woman was bad news. She was sick and she was mean. I have no idea why it happened, but it did."

I have nothing to say. My dad reads the anger on my face.

The way I'm turning red, the way my fingers bite into my palms, it's a rage that's new to even me. I only know that I don't want to be the pillow my stupid dad cries into right now. I only know that I'd rather see his teeth go flying out of his head.

He says, "You're mad, I can understand that. But it gets worse."

I bite my lower lip.

Dad says, "This woman, the one I was having an affair with, she got pregnant. She had a son that she didn't want. I took off, went back to your mother. She never knew about the affair. We had you and I never looked back. It was over."

A headache swims up the back of my neck, sinks its fangs into my brain.

Dad says, "The woman died. She drowned. Right here in this reservoir."

The headache intensifies. It screams at me with a megaphone. Tells me to kick, to kill, to bite, to fight. The headache raging in my skull wants me to scream uncontrollably and crush down my father with my feet. What he's telling me only happens in bad movies. It's the end, really.

Dad says, very quietly, "Jimi is your half brother."

And that's when I clock him.

It just happens. My fist connects with his jaw between heartbeats. The blood pushes out, I knock my dad to the ground, the blood pulls back in. I stand over him with my eyes fast turning red. My skin is shaking around me. The whole beach feels like it's vibrating on the same wavelength as my fury.

FOUR

My father, this young version of him, is lying at my feet.

The punch didn't do much but knock him flat.

It feels good having done it, but still I've got this stress wrapped tight around my heart as if it's bound up with coils of ragged rope.

What he's told me, it's impossible.

It's the worst thing, the very worst thing, he could have said.

Sitting up, wiping at his chin the way boxers do, Dad says, "It's terrible, I know. I should have told you sooner. Should have seen it coming. But I'm warning you now just the same as I've been warning him through your friend, the girl. If you kill Jimi, it will be a stain, a mark, on your soul for the rest of your life. It won't come clean, Ade."

Shouting, spitting, I yell, "That doesn't help me! Tell me something that helps me!"

Dad pulls himself up onto his knees. His arms hanging down like he's just a puppet put down there, he looks to me and says, "I believe in you. You need to trust your instincts, trust that you can do this even though everything tells you you can't. Don't think about the future. Don't think about the past. Think about right now. About here. You're already come so far, Ade. Just push further. Push yourself fully awake."

I close my eyes; try to make the anger fade.

The thoughts stampeding in my mind are hideous. Jimi being my brother makes me want to vomit, to pull myself in half. It makes no sense and yet it makes all the sense in the world. Even though he's not really, really my brother, not one I've ever known or one I ever cared about, my killing him looks even worse now. It's biblical is what it is.

Jimi is the villain. He's the corrupter.

I wish, my ears burning, that my dad had never told me this.

"Why?!" I shout at him, kick sand at him. "Why are you telling me this?!"

My dad says, "Because I love you. Both of you."

"But you betrayed us. Both of us."

Dad says, "And I'm asking you to forgive me."

"I can't stop what will happen. No one can."

Dad says, "You can try. You have to try. You can save Jimi."

"Not from me."

Dad says, "From himself. Don't let him make you do this."

I want to tear the stars out of the sky, to bury them in my dad's eyes. I want to rip up the beach and pull Jimi's mother's bones out of the water and beat the world with them. This anger pulses and thrashes away inside me like a lizard. Standing here, in never-never land, I know I need to calm myself down. I know that if I don't pull back now, I'll lose control.

I think about Grandpa Razor, about Dr. Borgo, standing over me watching my eyes run crazy under the lids. I think about them shuffling their feet in anticipation. But mostly, I think about my poor mother and about Vauxhall. I remind myself of why I stopped the concussions. Why I decided to go clean.

And I feel the anger slip.

I step back from my dad, turn to the water, and I put my hands on my head and press down hard to press the pain away.

And little by little I can sense the fury trickling out.

Little by little it gets smaller.

Clipped away just like that orange monster Bugs Bunny shaved down to shoes.

It's hard pushing my hate away, but it works. I take long, deep breaths, slow it down, and I'm able to cool it. I count a few stars, focus on the spaces between them, and then look back at my dad and ask him if this is going to be a regular thing.

"Should I ever expect to see you again?" I ask.

Dad shrugs. He stands up and puts a hand on my shoulder. This move, the one he's doing here in the moonlight, it's as old and established as anything else dads do. It's nice. He says, "I certainly hope so."

"How come you never did it until now? You've been in a coma long enough."

"I've tried. For years I've tried. At first the door was just locked, like you hadn't discovered your abilities. And then, I could just see from the outside. Like looking in at a diorama. The addiction kept me out. I don't know why. It was like there wasn't room for me in your mind."

"What's it like in there, Dad? Asleep like that."

"It's like nothing. It's like a waiting room."

"I hope you do visit again. I like this."

"Me too. Just, no punches next time, 'kay?"

I agree.

We walk down the beach to where there's a lawn chair I didn't notice before. Dad sits down in it and takes a cold glass of water from out of nowhere and sips it, the ice chiming. Then he crosses his arms and looks over at me and says, "You turned out wonderful."

Then, standing up with a huff, the chair and glass vanishing behind him like they were smoke, my father says, "You can't trust Grandpa Razor."

"How do you know that?"

"I met him, once, long time ago. Back when I was doing my thing, there was a group of them. We used to, well, when I was with this woman, Jimi's mother, there was a wild scene going on in Denver. It was the late eighties and people were funny then. There was this punk rocker kind of guy, Bob, I think his name was—"

"Slow Bob?"

"Right, so you've met him too? Well, he kind of put together this group of people with similar talents. It wasn't anything but a feel-good club, an opportunity to talk and drink and get our respective highs in a private place. Things, of course, got bad fast. Excess always leads to, well, regression. Deep down, people really are just animals. Grandpa Razor, he was the worst animal of all. What I'm saying is, be very careful around him. Be strong."

And with that I'm pulled out of the vision the way a stuntman on a bungee cord is, just snapped back up into the sky and into the night and back behind my eyelids.

FIVE

Before I even open my eyes I know something is wrong.

I can hear it.

The room is silent the way a cat is silent right before it jumps on an insect. I open my left eye first, just a crack, just enough to see through the haze of my eyelashes that the lights are still on and there's no one standing over me. Then I open the right eye. Again, just a crack. I move it around, open it just a tad wider, and see a shadow to my right, in the corner. A cat ready to pounce.

I roll to my left and I do it fast.

I fall off the futon onto the floor and then stand up quick, both eyes wide open.

Grandpa Razor's the cat; he's standing on the opposite side of the bed with a syringe filled with red liquid. He looks surprised, but it's hard to know 'cause his eyes are so heavy-lidded.

I back away from him, my fists up like I'm a boxer.

"What's the deal, Gramps?" I ask, pushing back my fear.

He says, "Seriously? You weren't supposed to wake up so soon."

I notice a pile just under the table; it's Dr. Borgo. He's lying there pretty jacked but he's breathing. Has a big lump on his head. Pointing at my shrink, I say, "You sure get around with that billy club. I hope that right now he can see the future and I really hope he's enjoying a nice screening of me kicking the shit out of you three minutes from now."

Grandpa Razor doesn't laugh like I expect him to.

If anything he looks more determined and jabs his syringe around.

"You knew, didn't you?" I ask, summoning up my new angry mode. Trying out my new angry voice. It sounds very effective.

This gets Grandpa Razor talking. He stops moving at me with the needle and he says, "You have no idea what you've gotten into, Ade. Wasting your gift, throwing it all away to try and . . ." He shakes his head in frustration. "You need to accept what the gift brings. There should be no debate about it. And if—"

I cut the slob off. "If you believe this rules business, then you couldn't stop me. Doping me up here or OD'ing me wouldn't do anything, right? If destiny is destiny, then why the hell are you trying to inject me with that?"

"This isn't what you think it is," Grandpa Razor says. "Regardless of what you saw, what Jimi's father told you, you still don't know what's really happening. You're still just as clueless, and what Janice told you, it'll happen, and I'll be there just cheering them on—"

He stops right there.

He stops because my rage boils over and I kick him full in the jaw. He goes back fast and he falls down hard, crushing a chair. There are teeth on the table and I see blood, but it doesn't stop me. I jump on top of Grandpa Razor and just start whaling. After a while my knuckles hurt and they look ugly and I take a breather, but then I just go back to it.

At least until Dr. Borgo stops me.

I'm about to bring both my hands down together, my fingers all intertwined, down on Grandpa Razor's mess of a face, when Borgo grabs my hands and tells me to stop. He tells me that if I don't, I'll kill this guy. He says, "Already, he won't look the same for a few months at least."

I stop. I fall back on the floor, my legs crossed, and look down at my hands.

They're shaking from my rage. They are all ballooned up and red. My hands, they look like the hands of a boxer's after a night of cheap rounds and hard faces. I look up at Borgo and say, "You don't look very good, Doc."

Borgo's lump on his head is bigger than I thought at first. A classic egg.

Borgo says, "It'll heal."

"You see anything?" I ask.

My shrink tries to laugh but he says it hurts his ribs. He says, "If I didn't stop you, what do you think you would have done to him?"

"Pounded him into a deep retardation."

"Where do you think that's coming from, Ade? You were never this way before."

I shake my head, look at my hands again. "That's because I think I'm someone else now, Doc."

SIX

The two girls in my life, both of them are sitting on Paige's bed, staring at me.

One of them, Paige, has her mouth dropped open. I've seen this look from her before, it's the same expression she had when she saw Vanessa Pallor, who she was sure was a lesbo and had a major crush on, making out with Carlos "Mad Bull" Lopez.

The other, Vaux, is closing her eyes and, I think, holding back tears.

I've just finished telling them that this guy I've been battling, the same guy Vaux's been sleeping with, is my kin. I've just described, in almost excruciating detail, how I tried to turn Grandpa Razor into a pile of something he'd probably eat. And I said, "Basically, it comes down to something entirely biblical here. It comes down to brother versus brother and even though I'm still going into this with a plan of stopping it, of changing it, only now I think I might actually for real have the capacity of doing it. I mean, I didn't before, but now I could totally see myself killing him."

It's been pretty much silent since then.

Paige's never liked anything too quiet for too long and so she's the first one to talk. She says, "That's not good."

Vauxhall starts to talk but stops herself. She looks way vulnerable.

"I was thinking at first that this is kind of the way the Incredible Hulk was, you know? The smart guy, the weak guy, Bruce Banner, trying to stop himself from raging into this monster of destruction. But it's not really the same because it's still me. It's just like me amplified. And really, what I'm most worried about is that I won't go back. If I kill Jimi, then this is it. This is me forever. The future Janice showed me, it's pretty much for sure."

Paige asks, "What do you think's happened to you? This change?"

I take a deep breath, hold it in a while. "I don't know, but it's something severe. And what's funny is that I'm not sure which I like better, you know? Me being messed up and concussed and high and not remembering most of my life, or the clean me who has some serious anger issues and is dealing with this familial insanity? Honestly, ignorance truly is bliss, I think."

Another spell of silence and then Vauxhall asks, "Have you tried to see?"

"See what?"

"The future. Have you tried knocking yourself out after we were together?"

"No. What are you thinking?"

Vauxhall looks to Paige, gives a half-smile. I'm not sure Paige knows, but now she has a pretty good idea something went down. Vauxhall says, "I think that maybe your abilities changed. Mine did, they got heightened, so maybe yours did too. You think it's worth trying?"

"Maybe. But I don't know if I want to try now. I don't want to see something that will just crush me. I think it's best to stay right here, in the now," I say.

Vauxhall asks, "What's next then?"

"It's about time I went home," I say.

CHAPTER ELEVEN

ONE

Dr. Borgo—

Funny getting a letter from me, right?

How old-school is this? Anyway, I'll keep it short and sweet. First off, I want to thank you for helping me out with the whole Grandpa Razor scene. Really, it wasn't you helping me out so much as you saving me from killing the guy. Sometimes, when I'm thinking back on it, I worry it wasn't the best idea to have stopped me, but then I come to my senses and realize I'm just being pessimistic. And that's the reason I'm writing.

What the hell is going on with me?

Seriously, it's like I've got that multiple personality disorder thing that always pops up as the killer's motivation in those bad cable movies. Actually, I don't think I do, but whatever it is that's going on with me, it's disturbing. Not so much disturbing to me as it is to everyone else around me. My friends, they're kind of freaked out by it. My girlfriend, the person I've been in love with for like ever, she seems scared of me. How terrible is that?

So I was just writing you for those two reasons. 1. Thanks. 2. Can you help me explain this? I don't think I'll be able to stop by the office anytime soon. And I don't think it's something you'll need to run blood tests or whatever over. Frankly, if the future that I've seen happens, then I'm sure you'll be seeing tons of me when I'm in the Alzheimer's Wing.

Cheerio!

Ade

P.S. Chances are pretty good you'll get this letter after everything goes down on the beach. Just wanted to let you know that I appreciate all your help over the past few years. Means a lot to me. Late.

TWO

I don't bother with the side entrance tonight.

There are two freaks on the porch, a young dude I've seen before and a woman with a baby asleep in a sling on her chest. When they see me they do these excited little jumps and even clap their hands.

The young guy wants me to tell him when he's going to get married.

The woman, she wants to know the same thing.

I sit down on the porch and they sit next to me looking with the most eager eyes the same way they'd sit listening to a guru. These people have never actually met me. Never heard me speak. They have no idea what sort of week I've had and what I'm gearing up to do when I step inside my house.

Honestly, I feel bad about what I say to them. First I clarify that I've gone clean and there won't be any more visions. "Besides," I add, "I only ever saw *my* future. Not anyone else's. Also I should mention that the last time I did something, it didn't look good. You might want to forget about the future being anything but grim." And then I get into detail. Some of it, I'm embarrassed to say, I make up.

The young guy, he lopes off the lawn head hung low and shaking.

The woman, she's just trying to keep her baby from screaming.

I get inside to find Mom waiting up for me.

I haven't seen her in a few days, but we fall quickly into old habits the way trained monkeys might. When I walk in she does not get off the couch to hug me. She just smiles and opens the Revelation Book and clicks her pen open. Also she's sipping tea and watching PBS.

I sit down on the other end of the couch and she shuts the television off and says, "Thank God you're back." Then, opening the Revelation Book, she asks, "Where do we start?"

"With nothing," I say.

She starts writing. Says, "Okay, and in the nothing?"

"No. Really. Nothing. No visions. Like I told you."

"No visions?" She looks me over. Sees my skin unbroken. My bruises yellow if there at all and nothing wrapped around my head. No busted lip. No stitches. She asks, "What are you doing, Ade?"

"I'm not knocking myself out anymore, Mom. I'm done. It's been a while now."

"Did Baby Jesus tell you to stop?"

"No."

"Why? I don't . . ." She's shaking her head robotically.

I tell her that I don't talk to Jesus. I tell her that I never have talked to Jesus and that Jesus never has and never will figure into the visions. I say, "All the things we've seen, all the things we've traced out, all the stuff about my future self, it doesn't get good for me because of Christ. It gets good because I stop."

Mom closes the Revelation Book and sighs.

I say, "I'm in charge of my own life, Mom. What if right here and right now is all that matters? What if everything else, everything you want to read in that book, what if it's all just dreaming? Just wishful thinking?"

Mom moves over to my side of the couch and starts massaging my shoulders. Says, "You remember when we went to Cave of the Winds in the Springs? You were only ten or maybe nine at the time and the whole drive down you were carrying on something crazy. Anyway, we're in these caves and you're just having this fit. The tour guide is ready to leave us behind. She's looking at us and frowning and ready to just kick you down into some bottomless shaft. The whole tour you're getting on everyone's nerves. Just driving everyone crazy and I can't seem to do a thing about it. I'm embarrassed as all hell. I'm trying to calm you and trying to look like a decent parent, like an effective parent, but it's going nowhere. I'm temped to turn back when we enter one particular part of the cave system and we're looking up at all the stalagmites and stalactites—I can never remember which is which—and you suddenly stop com-

plaining. You go silent. We had to stay in that room for five minutes longer than most tours stay. Everyone on the tour was fine with
it because you were finally being quiet. You sat down on that cold
stone floor so deep beneath the ground and just stared up at these
rock formations. It was like it was the most beautiful thing you'd
ever seen. As though you were staring into the celestial heavens.
Staring straight into the face of God himself. Sweet Jesus, that's
when I knew. Right then."

"Knew what, Mom?"

Mom says, "I knew that you were a miracle. To be honest with
you, I saw you in that cave and immediately realized that there was
something more going on in your head than just the usual kid
stuff. And you weren't marveling at the strange developments of
nature either. You were seeing beyond what all of us see. The
world's a curtain, Ade, and you were seeing right through it. Right
though to the other side. To the strings and the hands that hold
them. You saw the geometry of the Maker's design. We see the simple
wings, but you see the souls headed to Hell. You see the needle.
What the rest of us only guess at. What scientists can only dream
about."

Mom's talking dragonflies again.

She says, "Come in the kitchen with me."

I look around the corner, up the stairs, and to the kitchen where
the lights are on and two women, both Mom's age and type, are
sitting at the table drinking tea and looking back at me. They're
smiling, faces wide and warm. Also there's a laptop and a projector
sitting on the table.

In the family room, now with my back to the kitchen, I ask
Mom who these women are.

She says, "Part of our flock. You've met them before."

"When?"

"Many times." And she touches my head. "It's okay if you don't remember."

"Why are they here? It's the middle of the night, Mom."

"Waiting for you, Ade."

I'm tired and trudge into the kitchen, head down, ready to just bulldoze through and maybe give these women a wave. That doesn't work. As soon as my feet cross into the light of the kitchen, they're up off their chairs and wringing their hands and patting my back and pushing me (so gently) to the head of the table. There's even a cup of tea waiting there for me.

I sit and one of the women, a chubby one with a mess of curly hair, says, "You need to put your faith in the Lord. If he beckons, you answer the call, don't you?" And Mom says, "Jesus *is* love, Ade."

Of course, this all sounds very familiar. I saw this when Jimi hit me with the baseball bat and the vision was dull. Well, here it is again only in real time. The déjà vu built right into the very fabric of my life.

I actually look forward to seeing where this leads.

"What are you guys talking about?" I ask.

"Love. Duty," Chubby says.

The other woman—she's got straight brown hair and a long-time-smoker's face—says, "Being in love is the best thing ever. Wonderful. Have you seen this girl in the visions? Has the Lord directed you to her?"

Mom tries to answer, but Chubby shushes her.

I say, "I did seen her in a vision."

Eyebrows up, Smoker says, "How far out?"

"I saw her two years ago. She's here now."

Smoker smiles. Chubby sips her tea. Mom crosses her arms and looks at me sad. Her eyes flickering closed and open and closed and open. Not blinking but signing something unconsciously.

I say, "I've loved her for years."

Chubby, hands in prayer pose, says, "Wonderful, but . . ."

Smoker says, "Amazing, but . . ."

Mom says, "Your future, it's already written itself. For you to get to where you want to go, baby, you need to trust in the Lord and do his bidding. Past few weeks, at the church, we've been working it out. These ladies have been there right along with me, sleeves rolled up and getting in the trenches. As it's written, Proverbs 10:4, 'He becometh poor that dealeth with a slack hand; but the hand of the diligent maketh rich.' You're the wealth, Ade."

"Mom, I'm super tired, just want—"

"Aren't you interested in what we found out?"

"Found out?"

Chubby fake-claps her hands. Smoker says, "Something wonderful."

I look to Mom. She grins, says, "We weren't looking as deep as we needed to. We weren't seeing all the connections. You know, watching you put all those cards, all the string, up around your room, that project you and your friend were working on, it gave me an idea. Take a look at this."

Mom turns the projector on and nods for Chubby to dim the lights.

THREE

And she starts a slide show.

Pictures of me up first. Me when I was ten with freckles and my hair like straw. I'm running. Wearing a train conductor's hat. And there's me at the zoo riding the bull sculptures. And there's me in a swimming pool. And then me only a few years ago with a black eye I don't remember having. Next slide is a painting of Jesus. He with a crowd of followers. He in his robes, looking the ancient Israelite but all the people around Him dressed in modern clothes. A chef, a businessman, a surgeon, a woman with a child on her hip and a wooden spoon in her hand.

Mom says, "All the signs were there from the get-go."

Next slide is a time line. It starts now and goes out for years. Right near the middle, maybe when I'm forty, there's a big red cross and under it, written in Comic Sans, is the word "Rapture." The next slide, it's a Photoshopped cloud in the shape of a hand. A big exclamation point next to it.

Smoker says, "We found it. You saw the hand of God in a cloud. Pointing east to Jerusalem. The sign everyone's been waiting for."

Mom says, "There all along."

I start getting up from the table. I tell the women, my mom, that I'm just really tired and I appreciate them sharing this. I tell them that I'd love to spend a little more time on it tomorrow. I say, "Nice presentation. Must have taken some time."

Chubby stands and raises her hands, "It's not over, Ade."

Mom says, "Please, Ade. Five minutes."

I sit back down with a groan. The slides continue. More pictures of me intermixed with passages Mom's typed in from the Revelation Book. There are charts and even diagrams. My future laid out in black and white, with a terrible font. I'm really not paying much attention but nod when they look at me. Smile when it seems like I should.

Everything they've got, the whole presentation, is based on all the stuff I made up. All the stuff I pretended I saw in my visions. See, my mom's organized it all chronologically and, looking it over, she thinks there's a pattern. This slide show, it basically says the Rapture's due any minute now.

All of this from my lies.

From the cloud I said looked like a hand. From the dude I saw pulled on the breach who was drunk, the dude I added the Jesus just off the cross pose to. The mourning dove I added to the tree in the college vision. And older stuff like the chrysanthemum seen in a mall store and the eyes of a child that were pale fire.

She goes all the way back, years and years of my fibs all lined up and trotted out like they're real signs, like this is the road map to Heaven. What's odd about it though, and what I seem to have forgotten in all my making stuff up, is that the further out she goes, way out to when I'm middle-aged, the visions get darker.

Where she's got it marked as the Rapture, there are the words "cloudy" and "darkening" and "nightmare." And what's uncanny about it is I can only think of the visions I've had showing me a future that's indistinct, murky. I think back to the visions that seemed threatening, the ones that made me frightened. The storm at the beach. I see what Janice showed me and I honest to God shiver right there.

Smoker notices, she rubs my shoulder, says, "It'll all be okay."

And suddenly I'm actually paying attention to my mom's slide show and I'm waiting with bated breath for her to show me what comes next, what happens after the Rapture. When she flicks on the slide of the mental institution I almost fall out of my chair.

"What the hell is that?" I ask, half shouting.

My mom looks at me worried. She says, "It's from the vision you had after you crashed your car on Ninth Avenue. It was only this past summer. July, I think."

"I don't remember," I stutter. "What did I say?"

Mom looks to Chubby. Chubby looks to Mom. Chubby shrugs.

Flipping through the Revelation Book, Mom says, "It was some-where right over here, just by . . . Right, okay, here it is. You said that you saw yourself living in this place. That you were crippled or something but that you weren't too worried about it because some-how, down deep, really, you knew it was only an illusion. You said there was an angel there, an angel told you."

"What angel?"

Reading right out of the Revelation Book, Mom says, "A man in a mask told you." Then mom looks up and grins, closes the Revelation Book and folds her hands over it. "The Lord certainly works in such funny ways."

There it is, this whole thing already known. The past right here.

If anything, realizing I've seen it before and forgotten, it makes me sick to my stomach. It makes me want to run screaming out of the house and smash my head against something hard. I want the Buzz so badly. So incredibly badly.

When the presentation is over and Chubby puts the lights back on, I lean back in my chair and struggle over whether to burst their bubbles. The way I'm feeling, I think I have to.

Smoker asks what I think. If I'm convinced.

Chubby says, "This is why you can't stop. Jesus will provide you with another love. This girl, she could be sent here for another reason. To distract you. Satan's certainly been known to do such things."

I wait for a moment of silence. A few breaths in and out.

And then I say, "Mom, I make up most of the stuff that I see. All those little details that you guys have based this whole presentation on, I made all those up. I didn't see that dude in the Christ pose. His arms weren't out. He was squished. And the chrysanthemums? Never once saw one. The sun. The clouds. All of that stuff I made up so you'd be happy with me. So you'd make me dinner. Take care of me. Talk my teachers down."

Smoker looks to Chubby.

Chubby looks to Mom and Mom just shakes her head.

"You know, you do look tired. You've had a long week. Why don't you go ahead and get some sleep. I'm sorry we bothered you with this tonight . . . it—"

"Made up, Mom," I say, standing. "All of it to make you happy. To give you the world you really truly wanted. And for a long time, well, for the whole time, I was fine with it too. I was happy to do it. But not anymore, Mom. My head is clear now. The only future we need to care about, to really think about, is tomorrow. Maybe next week. I'm not going to throw away my life just to make sure I get into the next one."

Chubby screws her face up.

Smoker nervously picks at the back of her neck.

Mom asks, "Well, what made you so worried about the slide of the mental hospital? You were visited by an angel, you told me so yourself. Please don't try and backpedal away from it, Ade. I'm here to help you."

I feel sorry for my mother, but I say, "Lies, Mom. I'm a good actor."

Mom is breathing quickly. Nostrils flaring. Mom's in sympathy mode. Only it's not the kind of sympathy you associate for someone who's sick. For someone with something terminal or wasting. This, this is the kind of sympathy reserved for people who work really long hours. People who sacrifice themselves for their beliefs. Priests. Kamikaze pilots. The way she looks at me when she's with it is the way you look at an icon. At a saint. Her eyes are deeper than they've got any right to be. Crying without tears. She says, "After all we've done for you? You say these things in front of my friends? The only people who really care for you, Ade? The people who—"

But I don't hear the rest because I'm in my room with the door locked.

And then the slamming begins. It's Mom's fists hammering my door. Hammering it so hard that I can hear the wood cracking, I can see the hinges shaking loose. There're plumes of dust hovering near the lamp by my bed. Mom is shouting all sorts of things. Mostly she's painting a picture for me of what Hell looks like and how unfortunate it would be for me, for someone so gifted as me, for someone who'll always be that brown-eyed kid on J.C.'s lap, to wind up stoking the flames with the rest of the sinners. Mom says this, but then, after a pause, she backs down. She tells me that she didn't really mean it. She tells me that she loves me and appreciates me. She says, her voice muffled by the door and by her ravaged from screaming throat, "All can be forgiven. Let's talk."

I don't open the door.

I lie back on my bed with my arms folded up under my head and I try and sort everything out in my mind. I try and pull the threads together. Try and figure out how there can suddenly be two futures. How I can see myself healthy and happy in one and crippled and tormented in the other. I close my eyes tight and beg my dad to visit. I want to see his young self, his masked self, standing in the corner of my room. I want him to explain it all to me again. Which way is which? Does killing Jimi lead to the happy life? Does not killing him? My head hurts. I massage my eyes, pressing down hard on the giving spheres of them.

After a long time of silence, I hear Mom in her room sobbing. I can hear her praying and I know she's on her knees with her eyes closed and her head bowed.

I'm sure she's speaking in tongues.

I'm sure she's biting the insides of her cheeks until they're bruised and swollen.

The two of us, we're both confused in different ways.

The two of us, we're both hypnotized by something neither of us understands.

FOUR

When the sun is highlighting the horizon, I climb out my window and drive over to Vauxhall's place.

Just like in all the teen movies, I throw pebbles at her window in the backyard and duck down into a bush when the light in her mother's room comes on. I'm throwing rocks for fifteen minutes before I toss a real big one that I worry is going to shatter the window, but only makes a super-loud thud. Vauxhall, in a tank top and Umbros, comes to the window and looks out at me and shakes her head. She opens up and says, "You're a very bad boy. It's way too early for breakfast."

"I know," I say. "I can't sleep."

Learning out her window, her cleavage as pale as the moon, she says, "Watch TV like a normal insomniac or something."

"I don't like TV."

"Play on the computer. Download a movie."

"I want to see you."

Vauxhall says, "Naughty."

She invites me in and her room smells like sandalwood and vanilla. She curls up on her bed on a mound of beaded and tasseled pillows and I sit on the floor, legs crossed, just staring at her. As my eyes adjust to the darkness, she blows me a kiss and, head on her hands, says, "You were like a superstar tonight."

"Thanks," I say. "I felt really alive."

"So, superstar, you ever dream about flying?"

"I used to," I say. "But now it's mostly swimming."

Vauxhall thinks about that for a beat and then reaches into her nightstand and pulls out her video camera. I can hear it whir to life and then a green light comes on and suddenly the room is bright with neon lime.

I say, "I was wondering when that would reappear."

Vaux's like, "Tell me about the swimming dreams."

The camera hums. It is soothing.

I say, "It's swim practice. I just feel alive in the water. Must be because they keep it at like eighty-two degrees at Celebrity's and it's like swimming in a womb or something. These dreams, they're mostly about me swimming in this shallow sea, like the Great Barrier Reef. You know, really super-clear blue water. Lots of fish too. Colorful fish. Some so big that when they swim beneath me it's like the whole bottom of the sea is moving."

As I talk my eyes adjust to the light from the camera. And soon I can see Vauxhall's legs and chest and her feet and the top of her head, a beautiful green ghost.

Vaux asks, "In the dream, are you alone?"

"Yeah. Almost always. But in a very peaceful way."

She asks, "Are you naked?"

"I don't know."

She says, "In all the dream books it talks about swimming meaning sex. Particularly if it's in warm water. Supposed to be like your subconscious yearnings. Your desires. Do you feel like that means anything?"

"No."

The voice behind the green light asks, "Why?"

"I don't buy all that dream interpretation bullshit. Dreams are just what happens when I turn my mind off and let the screen saver play. Mine, it's one of those tropical screen savers. Helps that I'm relaxed."

"Want to know what I dream about?"

I nod and can only imagine that my eyes are reflecting in the green glow the way dogs' or tigers' do in those nature shows. The feral me sitting on the floor, ready to pounce.

Vaux says, "Lights."

She says, "I keep dreaming about stars that are really high above me that drop lower and lower and then become the lights around the edge of a stage. I'm in the middle, standing there in all sorts of outfits, and the lights are creating the space I'm in. Outside of it, I know there's an audience and I know I'm supposed to act, but I'm purposely not doing it. I'm purposely restraining myself from giving them the show they want. There's this tension."

I say, "You could read a lot into that."

I can't see her, but I imagine she raises her eyebrows.

Uncrossing my legs and leaning back on my hands, I say, "It's like the universe has just come into focus. Like all the pieces are snapped together and everything's quiet."

Vauxhall turns the camera off.

She whispers, "Come here. I want to feel beautiful with you."

I climb up onto her bed, the weight of me making it groan, and then I put my mouth on hers and my hands on hers and we just sink into each other and let our bodies do what they want.

Afterward, Vauxhall's body shivers while she plays with the sparse hair on my chest and says, "It was really strange. Well, I didn't see into the present like last time. Did you?"

"No," I say, my voice crackling. "That's odd, right?"

"I saw your past," Vauxhall says. "But still no high."

"Good," I say, smiling, "Sorry."

"Ade, your past. Your childhood. Everything before meeting me was like static."

I take a deep breath and just let it sit inside me. I can make out the edges of the furniture in the room and the slope of her shoulders and the dune of blankets that her hips make. I realize I wasn't really hearing what she was saying.

"What about my past?" I ask.

Vauxhall says, "It's gone."

CHAPTER TWELVE

ONE

Dear Mom—

Why I put this behind the crucifix on the back porch is because I knew you'd find it when you were gathering stuff for your Sunday Midnight Bible Class. You've never told me why you take this particular crucifix, but I figure we'll have time to discuss it later.

First of all, sorry about the other night.

I've been going through a lot of changes recently and I'm guessing that most of them, probably 90 percent, can be chalked up to your average teen anxieties, but there's a decent 10 percent that's totally unaccountable.

I remember you telling me about how dragonflies change from nymphs. How when they're young, they're these underwater monsters with crazy snap-out jaws. Those nymphs, you said, are insatiable. They terrorize ponds and creeks. But then, for whatever biological reason, those monsters climb up out of the water and transform into dragonflies. Their skin cracks open and the wings pop out and then they fly off into the sunlight as some of the most beautiful things on Earth.

Lately, it seems like I've been doing something similar. Only it's in the reverse. I'm a dragonfly that used to be all caught up in the clouds and the sky and whatever was blooming in the next valley and the next lawn but decided for whatever reason to climb back into the skin of nymph and go terrorize the depths again.

What's really weird is that I'm content with it. It feels natural to me.

Is that a bad thing?

I'm not so sure. Sometimes, and I think this was another thing you said when you were telling me about dragonfly nymphs, the worst things that happen, the worst urges we have, are really just blessings in deep cover. I'm thinking, right now, that's probably true.

Anyway, in case you were wondering, here's what I'm doing: I'll spend the morning with my girlfriend, probably have breakfast at Pete's on Colfax, and we'll go for one of those holding-hands walks in the park. Lunch will be with Paige, and then we're going to the Mantlo football game. I know, what? Well, it just felt right to do something totally out of the ordinary on such a strangely momentous day. After the game it's to the reservoir, actually the beach at the north end, and I will see if I can't stop what I saw when we had that car accident a few weeks back. That's it. If I'm not in bed in the morning, chances are good I'm in jail. So look for me there.

I wanted to end this letter with a quote I found that I thought you'd appreciate. Love you, Mom. "Take therefore no thought for the *morrow; for the morrow shall take thought for the things of itself." And that's from Matthew 6:34.*

Ade

TWO

The football game happens, but Vaux and I notice maybe 10 percent of it.

Mantlo wins, apparently.

Vauxhall spends the game just people-watching and she's convinced by halftime that there is no better place to people-watch. The mall has nothing on the football game. Here, the whole of the human race is represented. The good. The bad. The weird. The ugly. All of Mantlo's various tribes and subcultures are on display.

Me, I try and remember my growing up. But oddly enough, I can't seem to nail down anything clearly. Not school. Not my dad. Not even a single birthday party. I chalk it up to nervousness. I tell Vauxhall that maybe the first time we were together did something funky. I tell her that maybe memories and such got scrambled. I say, "I'm not worried."

Vauxhall is quiet. There's just the feedback of the crowd. She kisses me lightly and says, "If you're not worried, I'm not worried."

I say, "I'm not worried."

And really, I'm not.

After the game we go to a party at Oscar's. Again.

It's funny being back, passing the bathroom where I concussed myself, walking past the stairs where Vauxhall led Ryan Mar and seeing the bedroom door, open now, and imagining what took place behind it only a month back. Vauxhall thinks it's funny too, and when she sees me looking around, my eyes unfocused, she takes my head and turns it to her and kisses me and says, "Let's not think about anything but right now."

"That sounds great."

The Vauxhall of now, she's everything I imagined she would be. Back when I was just a freshman and scribbling down notes about her I saw her the way she is here, so light on her feet and so much the center of everything. The way the lights play around her movements, the way the ground just swells to her feet, it's as if I'm in one of her dreams. As if all of us, this whole world, is merely a figment of her stunning imagination.

We find a seat in the backyard on the deck and talk to random people but mostly to each other. I'm very conscious of the time, checking my phone constantly, and watching the moon slide up and over the trees. Vaux pats my knee. She squeezes my hand. It's like I'm waiting for a flight or I'm about to go into surgery, this level of reassurance is almost stifling.

"Everything's going to be fine." Vaux says.

She says, "Jimi's probably at home sleeping safe and sound."

"And me?"

"Just be cool, right?"

I find myself starting to panic a bit, my heart jumping irregularly, but then I'm distracted by what's going on over at the side of the pool. What distracts me is Paige.

She's wearing a sundress and sitting by the pool with her feet in it. And she's laughing and making goo-goo eyes at the girl next to her. This girl with short blond hair and eyelashes as long as her arms and boobs that sit upright. I wave from my perch under the tree and Paige yells for me to come over. She says, "Bring Vaux."

We go.

"This is Celeste. Sophomore at DU. Majoring in art." Paige is grinning ear to ear.

Celeste extends her hand. It looks like she's wearing fifteen rings.

We shake hands and Vauxhall introduces herself and we sit and talk for a few minutes. Vaux and Celeste have this detailed discussion about how brilliant some French sci-fi cartoonist really is while Paige and I whisper to each other about how amazing it is that we got these two hot chicks. This could go on all night, Vaux and Celeste immediate best friends and bonding over obscurity and Paige and I snickering like ten-year-old boys, but I need to piss and head inside to find an empty bathroom.

The one I knocked myself out in last time, it's being used by more than one person. So I head upstairs to where I suspect the master bedroom and hopefully master bath will be.

I haven't been drinking but I'm hopped up enough on adrenaline that I don't bother knocking on the door at the end of the hallway and just bust in. Bad idea. Garrett Shepard, the guy whose teeth I knocked out, is in there date-raping a girl. She's passed out, hair in her face and makeup smeared, and limbs limp, dress pulled up and legs spread. Garrett, eyes almost busting loose from his head, stands and walks over to me and puts a hand on my shoulder and the veins in his forehead are throbbing as he says, "She's just had too much to drink."

His shirt off and his boxers at his knees, Garrett says, "There's a toilet downstairs. You go ahead and knock yourself out down there. Let us have some privacy?"

I look over Garrett's shoulder. I recognize this girl. I think her name is Rose and she was in my history class freshman year. She has red hair and a soft laugh and knows a lot about Scandinavia.

I ask, "What's going on in here, Garrett?"

He shakes his head frantic, pushes me toward the door.

Still looking at Rose lying there, I say, "You're a sick fucker, Garrett."

I push him out of my way and he starts up burbling behind me, his voice higher, panicked. He says, "No. No. No. She's fine. She led me up here. Wanted it and been asking for months. Months now. Just had a bit too much to drink."

He closes the door and the room gets dark just as I'm leaning down next to Rose and wiping the hair out her face. Grinding my teeth, my fists opening and closing and opening and closing like heartbeats, breathing shallow, I say, "You're not getting away with this. This is . . . this is inexcusable."

And that's when he hits me.

The way it feels, I'm guessing it's either a vase or a lamp. It doesn't shatter the way props do in the movies. If anything, it bounces up off the back of my head. It's not the hardest hit I've ever taken. Honestly, I stand there thinking Garrett is totally weak.

But my eyes don't shut off.

There is no vision. Only the darkness of the room and the wet feeling at the back of my head and there is no Buzz, just rage. Uncontrollable rage. I'm not sure how it happens, but just like in the car after Janice told me about the vision, after she tried to break my heart, I go nuts and my arms and legs move on their own. My hands move before I can even will them into motion.

Fact is: I don't even feel my knuckles on Garrett's nose.

Fact is: I barely feel them on his metal teeth.

This isn't me being a rock star. This is me being an animal.

When my body's settled back into its frame, Garrett is lying on the floor beside the bed moaning or crying or both and someone's opening the door to the room and light is slipping back in, steadily climbing the length of the bed, and that's when I pass out, my focus just spiraling into infinity.

This time, I'm back in the future.

The vision I have, it's way off the charts. My mom's setup, her year-by-year accounting of the next me, doesn't even come close to reaching the age I'm at. My eyes open to sun and then zoom out to city. I'm standing at a window, looking out over a city I've only seen in movies. A city like Tokyo or Hong Kong. Even though it's day, the streets below me are burning with neon. Cars are honking. The city buzzing like a hive of wasps.

I am old.

Really really old.

I can just feel the strain of it on my spine. My hands are shaking. Nothing major, just tremors like you feel when you have your hands on the wheel and the car's going over seventy. I can see a ghost of myself in the window. My bald head. My thick glasses. And behind me, sitting in a white leather chair, is a woman. She's old like me. Her hair gray and pulled up, and her legs crossed. She looks like Vauxhall now, only she's also wearing glasses. She's regal and beautiful and I want so desperately to kiss her.

Vision ends.

Wake up and I'm on a couch downstairs. First thing I hear is someone talking about me being up to my old tricks. There's someone saying, "At least he took a few weeks off. What a loser." I'm lying across Paige and Celeste and Vauxhall. My head in Vaux's lap. She's stroking me and doesn't ask anything. What's amazing, other than looking up at Vaux who's looking down at me, is that there is no Buzz rampaging beautifully through my body. There is no high. Just a kind of warmth. A peace, like all my cells are aligned. Like a full-body cosmology.

I say, voice trembling, "It's amazing."

Vauxhall asks, so quiet, "What?"

"Us in the future," I say. "What happens next."

I can feel Vaux's body breathing in deep and I tell her that it's time. I tell her that we need to go to the reservoir now. I say, "Wait's over. Time to break the rules and see if I'm right."

"You're not in any condition—"

"If I can walk, then I'm fine. I've had worse hits than that."

"Still, I'll drive."

On our way out to the car, Paige lets me know that Garrett is locked in an upstairs bathroom and that Rose is still passed out but okay. "The cops are on their way. They're gonna want to speak to you." She says, "By the way, you're incredible."

I can hear the cat scream of the sirens.

Before closing the door, Paige leans in and kisses me on the cheek. She says, "I know it's not like you're trying to save the future president or the guy who will cure cancer, but I really hope you don't kill Jimi. And if you do, I'll go on the lam with you."

THREE

And then, I'm there.

Vaux parks and lets me out and the moon is hanging in the sky just like I imagine it's supposed to be. She asks me why I want to go alone. Why she can't come.

I say, "You weren't in the vision."

"But I'm here right now."

"Please, Vaux. I don't know what to tell you. Just let me do this on my own. I mean, this might be totally obsessive-compulsive of me, but what if the reason you're here now, but not in the original vision, is because the minute you step out of the car you're hit by a stray bullet. Or an asteroid. Or something. I mean, that's a bit—"

"Ridiculous. You said this is about breaking the rules. Why're you freaking out?"

"Just want to take it one step at a time. If it doesn't work—"

"You're being silly."

"Look, please, just let me do this my way."

"Fine." And she pecks me on the cheek and turns up the radio.

"Don't leave me like that."

"Okay." Vaux turns the radio off and tells me that she trusts me and that she knows this will work. She tells me that she can feel energy in the air tonight. She says, "Being with you is the best thing that's ever happened to me. Come back soon."

That's better.

I walk to the beach, slip off my shoes, and then wade into the water. I'm standing there and the sky is just crazily spitting out stars above me. The night is warm and the crickets are going apeshit in the elm trees.

The sand, it's not sandy the way tropical beaches are but rocky with these little perfectly oval brown stones mixed in with what looks like the kind of gravel you find on playgrounds. And under that, my toes find mud. Thick, black mud.

Facing out, over the water, there is just the twinkling of distant cars crossing over the dam and beyond them the hulking outline of the mountains, all crouched like hounds. And behind me, only the sodium glare of the tennis court. The emptiness of the beach.

I'm in the water long enough to have memorized the timing of the crickets' response to the cicadas' drilling noises when Jimi shows up.

How I know he's in the shadows is funny.

I feel it.

I say, calmly, "I'm ready."

The night answers back in Jimi's distinctive voice, "Good."

And then he walks down to the beach. He is wearing what I knew he would, what I saw he would. It's funny seeing this vision happen. I've replayed it so many times in the back of my head that to have it happening now, coming real, it's almost prosaic. "Bland" is a better word for it. That and just looking at Jimi, seeing the snappy grin spreading out across his face, the anger is starting to bum rush my veins. My face is getting hot.

Jimi gets closer, looks me over, then he puts on this very self-satisfied look.

He says, "You're very, very mad. Mad enough to kill me, right?"

"I'm not going to kill you," I say.

"But you're angry. Ferociously mad," Jimi says. "Have a look at this."

And he pulls his sleeves back and shows me his arms and the tattoos covering them. I look; it's dark but I can make out faces, swirls of color, motion.

Jimi says, "Look closer."

He takes a cell out of his back pocket and flips it open and positions it so the light cascades down his right forearm.

I step closer, see better.

Jimi's arm, the whole tattoo sleeve, is images from my life. There is my mom teaching me how to ride a bike on the driveway. There is my bedroom set up just the way I had it when I was in second grade. There's me in the surf on our trip to San Diego to see Aunt Miriam. And in a swirl of crimson and orange is my father's car accident. He even has the license plate number down perfect. Jimi shifts the light and on his left arm I see more. There is my first dog, Grover. There is my favorite Transformers toy. There's me and my father watching fireworks from the roof of the parking structure at the Cherry Creek Mall. And I even see myself lying in my crib, a pacifier in my mouth, swaddled in the green blanket Grandma Josephine knit for me.

Jimi says, "It's all there, in my skin."

"Why?" I ask.

A car sounds on the dam road behind us, its honk reverberating out across the reservoir in time with the lapping of tiny waves. The night is so very still in response.

Jimi, my brother, says, "That anger in you, I used to have it too. It drove me almost crazy, how short a fuse I had. Used to blow up at the slightest thing. And I saw everyone, almost every single person, as an enemy. All of them fake, all of them lying to me. You know that feeling, bro?"

I nod. "This whole time, you knew?"

"No," Jimi says. "Only the past year or so. I tracked down Dad last summer. Figured it all out and then decided to get to know you. Everything I told you was true, Ade. You have a great life because you didn't have to go through the hell that I did. What you never counted your lucky stars for was a great childhood. Just came natural to you, right? Never had to think much about it. Not me."

"You killed your mother."

Jimi pauses. Stares me down. Says, "I saved myself."

"This same water, you drowned her."

Jimi nods slowly. The night turns so slowly around us. And it's as biblical as anything, what's happening. I half-expect a spotlight from the moon to flick on.

"Not anymore," Jimi says. "Now, that's your baggage. You see, Ade, we switched childhoods. What's on my arms, it's my history now. And you, you've got mine. That's why the anger boiling in you. With my past, it's hard not to feel nearly out of control all the time. We both have abilities, bro. You can see into the future, and me, well, my power's a bit less well defined. What I do is sneak into your home, talk with your mom, wear your clothes, and basically act like you. And if I throw a little pain into the mix, you know, a few tattoos here and there, I can absorb your past. Just soak it up like ink. Voilà, your history becomes mine and I can think back on a happy childhood. The brother who didn't deserve it forfeits it."

Really, I can't think straight. "What?" I ask.

Jimi puts his hand on my shoulder, the first time we've touched sharing a father, and he says, "Close your eyes and think back, look back to when you were a kid and see."

I'm hesitant, but do it. I close my eyes tight and hold them shut while I ransack my brain looking for childhood memories. They are there—me at the beach, me playing with the dog, me at my dad's bedside—but the images I see are faint. They are ghosts of memories and I can't get into them, I can't feel the emotions associated with them. Laid on top of these memories, like a sick film, are new ones.

On top, there are bad ones.

These new memories, they're things Vauxhall told me about Jimi. I see myself being whacked on the hands with a wooden ruler, my fingers numb and the knuckles cracking. I see a woman that's not my mother calling me her useless child and locking me in the garage in the middle of winter. I see myself alone at home, having been there for days, eating cat food I'm so hungry. This is my new past, my new where-I-came-from. This is why I'm so angry, so abrasive.

Jimi says, "The whole thing, it was never about Vauxhall. It wasn't a love triangle. It was just me getting my due. It was just me reclaiming my own history. Something admirable in that, right? Dad tried to warn you, didn't work. He tried to warn me, to stop me via Vauxhall, but it was all garbled. That's what happens when you're a screwup. Besides, I consider Grandpa Razor to be more of a father to me. He took me under his wing and when I met you, when I found you and the plan started to come together, well, he was there to guide me."

Jimi squeezes my shoulder, the muscles in his arm, my family, tensing, and he says, "When you talked with Dad over at Grandpa's place, Razor was trying to stick you with some of my blood. Not sure where he got the idea that it would work, probably online, but basically that a syringe was going to make this process faster. He was helping me get what I deserved sooner. Really, this world is mine now, Ade. You got my past and now you got my future too."

And of course that makes sense.

All the visions, all the menace so far out. The reason I'm seeing the edges all frayed and darkness creeping in is because I'm seeing some strange combination of mine and Jimi's future.

Jimi says, "I've imagined that future. You should see what I imagine now."

I'm ready to kill him.

It happens almost instantaneously, I jump forward, my body arcing like lightning, and I push him down into the water, my hands around his throat. What it feels like, what it looks like, is exactly like the first time I lived it. Call it déjà vu. Call it instant replay.

Jimi's face is under the water. His arms are thrashing. His legs kicking. But I'm bearing down hard. My arms out straight, locked. My fingers, they're white from blood loss. Jimi's face, it's white too. His eyes are so bugged out.

There is surprisingly little noise. Just the kick of him in the sand.

And I close my eyes.

I know already how this ends.

I know already how Jimi's body goes slack.

I know already how Jimi's past pushes me to do this.

I know his eyes are bugged out because for whatever reason, he never really believed I'd do this. He was laughing so hard. He was so sure of himself.

And with his throat getting smaller and smaller in my hands.

And with my hands getting number and number around his neck.

I see the vision of me and Vaux, the two of us ancient, overlooking a city, and there is a release.

FOUR

His arms don't go slack, mine do.

I open my eyes and see, in slow motion, with the moonlight breaking all over the surface of the water, Jimi's face, eyes wide open, break the surface.

I fall back, not even feeling the water.

The future has changed, it's settled down onto a certain track. I'm just not sure which track it'll be. Right now, I know why there have been so many futures. The futures of me crippled. The ones with me and Vauxhall old. They're all intertwined because Jimi and I are intertwined now. What happens next, no one can see. Now, nothing is certain but uncertainty.

Jimi retches. He sways, standing there with half the reservoir coming out of his lungs. He puts his hands on his knees and looks up at me, his eyes red with burst blood vessels. Right now, it's like looking at myself in a mirror after a concussion.

We're brothers in damage.

Jimi, he wipes his mouth and sighs, says, "The transfer . . . So freaking close, you don't even . . . You can't even get . . . If you'd killed me, I would be where you're sitting right now. You've fucked this whole thing up, Ade. Unbelievable. Me, I'm supposed to be you."

"But you'll never be, Jimi. Never. There was enough," I tell him, my voice coming out in gasps, "there was enough of my past still left. You lose."

Jimi coughs. Swaying uneasily, he says, "There's no going back now, Ade. I might be alive, but you and I, we're wrapped up in this thing now. Like half-completed people. I'm looking forward to seeing how you work with what I gave you. The new you, I'm excited to see you struggle."

I grab Jimi, my hands wrapped around the back of his head, my face right there in his, and I say, "No, I'm not going to struggle with this, Jimi. I'll work it out. I'll get over it. I've got a good shrink and good friends. And you, I can't imagine you'll be the same asshole with my childhood behind you. Storm's over, brother. Time to pick up the pieces."

And I let him go.

And I leave him standing there in the water, his head hanging, spitting out dark water into the shaky reflection of the sky.

FIVE

I don't go home.

Vauxhall takes me to Village Inn in Cherry Creek and buys me a slice of pie and gets me two cups of coffee. Still shivering, I sit there and eat the pie quietly while Vauxhall stirs her coffee and watches me. Every now and then she reaches across the table, squeezes my hand.

I'm having trouble focusing, her face blending in with the emptiness of the lights.

Vauxhall tells me that this moment is like something from a movie. She tells me that there will be people talking about this forever, that the whole scene will be different now. She says, "Maybe, us teamed up, we can even change the past."

I'm dreading that future and praying that I can change the rest of it too.

Vaux asks, "What do you want to do next?"

I don't have a response, but that's when the divination community shows up.

All of them. The Diviners, Grandpa Razor, the Metal Sisters. And every two-bit psychic with a shingle downtown. Every ghost hunter and palm reader. At least sixty people come filing into the restaurant near three thirty in the morning, all of them nodding and clapping as they form a circle around our table. Vauxhall, like she doesn't even notice them, keeps her eyes on me.

They lift me up out of my seat and parade me around the restaurant, some of them shouting things like "Hail to the King!" and "Welcome to the New Age!" Katrina and Janice, smaller and younger than ever, stand before me, their eyes lowered. They apologize. Ask forgiveness. Paige and Celeste appear. Clyde and Ambrosia too. And then my mom shows up with the All Souls congregation and they've got a crown, this gold, sparkling crown. And they lay it on my head. And my dad shows up too, he's the last one in, and he's got the letter I sent him. He sits down, watches the crowd surge around me, and mouths, Thank you.

And then Vauxhall shakes me awake.

We're still in Village Inn, the place empty besides us.

Vauxhall asks, "You okay to talk?"

I nod and wipe my eyes.

"How did you do it?"

I say, "It was like when it was seen, once it was seen, the future got stuck. That's just how it's always been. Grandpa Razor, the Metal Sisters, none of them could change it. Once you see it, the future is made."

"But you did change it, Ade."

"See, that's the trick. *I* didn't really change the future. I got changed."

"—"

"Jimi changing me, that changed the future."

Vauxhall gets up, sits next to me. Kisses me.

I say, "It's what none of them got. You can't force yourself on the world, get your hands wet with time and space. That's fighting uphill, trying to move a mountain with a spoon. You turn the equation around and that's when anything is possible."

Vauxhall says, "Sounds like my parents talking."

I laugh and it hurts. "Maybe the hippies were onto something."

"You think I'll change too?"

"I do."

"Tell me how?"

"Well, the obvious way, for starters. Parties won't be the same, people won't be worried about me busting my head on their sinks or toilets or starting fights. And I don't think you'll be running away from Mantlo. You're not going to be chasing the high anymore. No more intimate mysteries. Instead, something stable. More rewarding. Let's hope."

"I love you," Vauxhall says.

I blow her a kiss.

Fall asleep.

CHAPTER THIRTEEN

ONE

Heinz—

I appreciated your card and I've been meaning to write you for a few months now, but things have been nuts. Summer already, school almost out, and, to tell you the truth, I'm a changed person.

It might come as a surprise, maybe you'll be bummed, but I haven't had a vision in over six months. You know how they say that when you stop smoking, your body almost immediately starts to recover. How after just fifteen minutes your lungs are cleaning out the gunk and loading up on new cells. How after just a few weeks you're breathing like a nonsmoker. Me, with my brain, it's the same way. The docs might not agree (they're all "damage is done, dude"), but I honestly feel better than I have in years. Straight up.

That doesn't leave me with a lot of insight regarding your recent situation. Sorry to say, but I'm not too surprised nothing happened with

the whole chicken pentagram deal. (Isn't that way too old-school any-
way? That's like your grandfather's Satanism.)

Oh, and I've given up trying to figure out how it works. I've got a
few ideas, and oddly enough my girlfriend actually knows, but I just
don't really care as much now that I'm not using it. The why, it's over-
rated.

Late,

Ade

TWO

My first official competitive swim meet and it's a big one.

Mantlo v. George Washington.

Bitter rivals.

Dark outside, the windows of Celebrity are all fogged up and
the fans are turning in the rafters something furious. The place is
so quiet, everyone so focused on the meet that the sound of the fake
waterfalls spilling their guts onto fake rocks is deafening. It's us
against George Washington and Coach has me swimming in the
first lane, the outside one, where the slowpokes loiter. There are no
carrots here, no fine Beverly Morrison asses to follow.

I'm on the block and tensed to jump, my muscles all pulled to
their limits.

On the chairs across the pool, Vauxhall and Paige and my
mom are sitting with their hands in their laps, necks stretched
out, none of them talking now, but when we first got to the meet
my mom was going on and on about Vaux's documentary. I think

she just liked seeing me in it. The film debuted at a student film festival in Boulder and what's funny is that Vaux dubbed over all my lines, all my brilliant lines. Like the reverse of some comedy flick, she dubbed in Chinese from a kung fu movie. Funny, really. But right now, they're not thinking movies, just thinking about me. I'm watching Vauxhall and her eyes, the way she's holding herself. Sitting there she looks comfortable. She looks tamed in some way.

And then the gun goes off and every cell in my body jumps.

I don't feel the water going into it. Suddenly it's just there all around me. There's the whoosh as I push and pull, the bubbles of legs kicking out in front of me. The beckoning of the black cross painted twenty-five meters away. Then I'm at the wall and I'm turning and I don't see anyone else. The pool, it's empty beside me.

I feel no strain. My breathing is so tightly controlled.

Everything in me sings in time, perfectly tuned. How good this feels, I know already why in the future I'll be jumping off of buildings and surfing. It's the adrenaline rush. It's just the replacement of the Buzz.

A minute.

Two minutes.

The race is over and I come up for air and hear the roar of the crowd, only it sounds like thousands of people. Taking off my fogged-up goggles, I look around to see that I'm second to last. Lane two, that guy's out of the pool toweling off already. He's shaking hands. Fact is: This has been the best swim of my life and I'm in fifth place.

Vaux waves. Paige waves. Mom smiles.

Two nights ago I saw my dad in a dream. He wasn't young the

way he was in my future visions when he was wearing the mask. No, he looked like the same guy parked in the hospital bed only moving around, only talking. The setting was a park bench near a lake. It was fall and the leaves were spinning down. We've met there like seven times over the past few months and had pretty good conversations.

This last time I told my dad more about my mom, how she's gotten a bit better and put the Revelation Book away. I told him that she's still super Churchified but now she doesn't look at me the same way. "It's not like she's disappointed," I said. "Just like she's moved on. It's like, and this is kind of strange, she's even more confident in what she believes. Doesn't have to look for it anymore. Also it's nice that the freaks have cleared off our porch."

My dad, the old him, said, "That's good. That's very good."

"Sorry I haven't stopped by to visit you in a long time."

He smiled. "I haven't noticed."

I told him more about Vaux and me. Told him that I'm thinking of going to college and that my grades are actually better than Ds now. I said, "I'm thinking of majoring in psychology or something. Though maybe physics."

"That's excellent. How's Jimi?"

"Good. He transferred schools. Last time I saw him he was in a play downtown. Funny how it's changed him; the cockiness is still there, but he's actually not as good an actor anymore. Forgetful too. How crazy would it be if somehow getting my childhood he got my memory with it? I heard he's getting his tattoos removed."

Dad, and this was right before the dream dissipated, said, "I'm proud of you."

Today, at the swim meet, I pull myself out of the pool, the water beading and melting off, and walk over to where everyone's sitting. Some of my teammates, they pat me on the back. One of them says, "Good try, dude." Vauxhall kisses my cheek and hands me a towel.

What no one else realizes here, what most of them will never know, is that I'm operating on a whole other level now. The Buzz is gone, I'm getting high from life just like the rest of the losers around me. And I'm loving that. But what I'm really loving is what none of the people here, well, almost none of the people here, can see.

Vaux sees it. She knows it too.

We are so brilliantly awesome right now.

The two of us, me and Vaux, after blowing kisses to Paige and my mom, are on our way to my car after Mantlo's won the swim match. Celebrity's has cleared out, the lot is pretty much empty save my car, and it's getting dark. We're speaking loudly as we walk. Vaux is making some cracks about my stroke and then talking trash about one of George's swimmers, a dude with man tits who probably has an adrenal problem. I'm laughing not because it's that funny but because it's so inappropriate.

We're almost to the car when he appears.

Not the man-tits guy but another George Washington swimmer. This guy is beefy and blond and he is wearing his letterman jacket. He's holding a beer and smoking a cigarette. This guy, he's standing between us and my car.

Doesn't look like he's gonna budge, either.

This is going to get exciting.

What happened over the last six months is that both Vaux and I have had our energies changed. Our bodies have healed, the highs have been replaced with what I imagine most mountain climbers feel, a kind of ultra-human zing. The sick energy of the Buzz is gone and now it's just this beaming love, it's this clean feeling. Incredible really.

And sure, in me, the rage is still swirling, but all the memories associated with it have been erased. The Metal Sisters did some trick and even though it felt like a psychic lobotomy the nastiness is gone. I might have Jimi's childhood, but I can't recall a single second of it. Clean and clear. The Diviners, of course, were still trying to talk me into helping them. Grandpa Razor, they've told me, is a changed person. Also I've seen the Diviners' sigil, that clumsy spray-painted hand, nearly everywhere I look.

Tonight, in the parking lot, I call out to this moron blocking our way. "Hey," I say. "Need something?"

I am not stressed. If anything, I'm kind of giddy inside. Vaux is too. It's the way she's squeezing my hand.

"Yeah," this guys says. "I heard your girl there, that she might be . . ."

"You heard what?" Vauxhall asks.

This guy sips his beer and laughs. "You know, looking for some."

"Some what?" I ask.

This asshole's eyes narrow down, his face puckers, he says, "Look, dickwad, I think it'd be best if you just stepped back and let me have a conversation with your bitch here."

And he steps forward, trying to spook me. Vauxhall touches his hand, just lightly, almost like she's pushing this dude backward, only she isn't. The touch is sudden and then she turns to me and smiles, says, "Ask him about his dog."

I look to the dude. "Tell me about your dog."

"What the fuck are you talking about, son?"

Vauxhall says, "Ask him to tell you about how he lost his dog.

About how he's really broken up about it and worried his mother might find out about how he used to kick the dog."

Still looking at the dude, I say, "That true? Did you kick your dog?"

The guy is confused. Stumbles forward. "What?"

And I let him hit me. He's sloppy and just barely connects. I don't move, not even a hair, and his loose fist smacks up against the side of my head. Ear stings a bit, is probably red, but it's what I wanted. After he hits me, I say to Vaux, "About six feet to the left and in front of the driver's side door. Quick. And I'm guessing a broken nose."

"Ouch," Vauxhall says, cringing.

What happened over the past few months is that my ability changed, just the same as Vauxhall's did. And then the both of us, we got even more powerful. It's like the ability knob got turned up to eleven. The longer we've been together, just having our souls near each other or something, the more boosted our abilities have gotten. Vaux, now she can just touch someone and see everything in their past, not just the dark stuff, not just the hidden shit. And me, I can do the same only in reverse. Someone touches me, even the slightest contact or in this case not so slight, and I can see a person's whole future. Every inch.

Even better, for both of us, it happens fast and it happens clean.

Best I can compare it to: like downloading something. I click and it's here, in my head. Vauxhall clicks and it's there, ready to be used.

Standing in the parking lot outside Celebrity's tonight, this drunken ass swimmer throws down his beer can and it goes skittering across the asphalt. Then he stomps out his cigarette and puts his fists up like he's in a boxing movie.

Vauxhall says, "Dog's name was Rusty. Super original, right?"

The dude shouts, "Shut up! Come on."

He motions for me to fight. I say, "Just move over a few feet. You're not in position." And he actually moves. When he's there, I tell him to stop. Then, his fists still pumping in the air between us, I tell him that it would really be a good idea for him not to try and fight me. I say, "This is just going to end up embarrassing for you."

The dude yells an expletive.

Vauxhall says, to me, "You warned him."

"I did, didn't I?"

That's when the guy makes his move, he throws a punch at me and I move right out of the way. He stumbles forward and that's exactly the time I knee him in the nose. His nose splits and the blood scribbles all over the asphalt. He falls on his ass right where I expected him to, about six feet to the left of the passenger-side door of my car.

As we're leaving, I say to Vauxhall, "You should totally bust out that Negative Woman costume again. The two of us, you in the past, me in the future, we're going to be the next Doom Patrol."

Vauxhall, her face dials up a mischievous grin. "We defeating evil?"

"Definitely," I say.

"We helping orphans?"

"Of course."

And we kiss like the soon-to-be superheroes we are.

What Vauxhall sees, she doesn't mention.

And what I see I don't let her know either.